WYVERN'S LAIR

DESERT CURSED SERIES, BOOK 5

SHANNON MAYER

HiJinks

Wyvern's Lair
Desert Cursed Series, Book 5
Shannon Mayer

Copyight
Wyvern's Lair
Desert Cursed Series, #5

Copyright © 2019 by Shannon Mayer

All rights reserved.

No part of this book may be reproduced in any form or by any electronic or mechanical means, including information storage and retrieval systems, without written permission from the author, except for the use of brief quotations in a book review.

Photography by With Magic Photography

Models: Bayley Russel and Parker

Cover art by Ravven

❀ Created with Vellum

ACKNOWLEDGMENTS

Thank you to my supervisor, Oka, for always making sure I am in my office for as many hours a day as possible. To Cougar for reminding me that the bond between a girl and her horse is worth waiting for.

"By the pricking of my thumbs, something wicked this way comes.
What a shithead. I'm going to puke acid all over his stupid face."
Lila

ZAMIRA

The mauve clouds filter the dying, yet brilliant, rays of orange falling from the fiery ball lowering to its nightly death. The nearly purple glow afoot reflects in the sand beneath my paws —ethereal and full of magic, as if with each step, I would find myself transported to another plane of existence.

No time for poetry, idiot.

The world picked back up, reality all but spitting in my face. I dug in hard, my back feet kicking up tiny pebbles in a spray that littered out behind me, my muscles firing with all I had as I took a hard right turn in a last ditch attempt to catch what was supposed to be dinner. Teeth gritted, I made a desperate lunge, front claws extended to hook the hind end of the desert jackrabbit that currently moved like lightning in a bottle.

Come on, come on! I stretched to my full length, reaching for all I was worth.

The tips of my claws brushed across the thin hide and *just* raked his scrawny little dust-colored butt with a distinct sound—like a zipper sliding down—that made me think I had him. But just that fast, the thought was gone along with him, as if instead of pricking him with my claws, I'd hit a button that had given the little bugger the extra burst of speed I never saw coming. He was there one second and the next, not.

I slid to a stop at the base of a sand dune as the rabbit shot across the open spaces between bush and hills, flicking his tail at me as if waving goodbye. Me? I just stood there breathing hard, my sides heaving and my whole body aching terribly as though I'd been beaten repeatedly. I licked my too-dry lips. I'd not had enough water, obviously—it was an issue out here in the desert even to those of us who knew better.

Desert born, I might have been, but that didn't mean I couldn't screw up. And the last day or so, my head and heart had not been in the game, which didn't help. I was distracted, heartbroken, and just fucking tired.

I knew it. Lila knew it. Even Ford seemed to have known it. My companions walked around me as if I would shatter—which only irritated me more. Hence, my offer to get food, to give them a break from me more than anything.

Maks would get it. Hell, if Maks were here, I wouldn't be so damn irritable.

"Fuck," I muttered, spitting out a mouthful of sand, and shook my head to knock the sand from it. Though it was my turn to catch dinner for the three of us, I'd been at it for a couple hours with nothing to show for my pitiful efforts. I rolled my shoulders and flicked the tips of my ears, listening for something else that might show itself. Ideally not a super-speedy rabbit.

Something slower and fat. Something even I could catch at the rate I was going. I looked around for a clue and settled on working on a better vantage point to get my bearings.

Putting one paw in front of the other, I made the long slow climb to the top of the dune, hoping it would be what I needed. Being a shifter was supposed to be awesome and powerful and all the things that I most certainly was not. Born into a pride of lion shifters, I should have been the queen of the desert.

My luck—or my mother's luck, seeing as she passed it to me—was not particularly good. Thick black fur covered my whopping six-pound house cat frame instead of the golden lion that I could have been, or even the elusive black jungle cat that I'd had a taste of only a few days prior. I sighed as I climbed, the sand slipping out from under me with each step, the weariness that ate at me a sure sign I was near the end of my rope. Too much had happened to my body and my heart.

I snorted to myself partway up and shook my head again at my own stupidity. The fatigue had nothing really to do with my body. I had been trained to run, fight, work, on nothing but an empty belly, exhaustion, and sheer stubbornness for years. This particular fatigue I was dealing with came straight from a broken heart, and I knew it.

I'd made myself say goodbye to the one man who was meant to be at my side. Maks had called me his mate, and then had willingly sent himself into a deep sleep—disappearing, for lack of a better word—so our love couldn't be used against me by Marsum and the Jinn masters who now resided within Maks's body.

A low hiss snarled out of me at the thought of just what they were making his body do—or worse, *who* they were making him do. Marsum wanted a child, an heir to the throne, and no doubt if he couldn't have me and the bloodline I represented, he'd take someone else. Just to have a backup kid.

"What a dick," I muttered. No one to hear me, but I felt a little better anyway, just saying it out loud.

The reality was I knew without a shadow of a doubt that with Marsum now in control of Maks's body, he would do anything he could to hurt me, if for nothing else because I'd turned him down. Though to be fair, the last time I'd seen said body, it had been in the clutches of an oversized desert falcon winging to the west away from us. Which was good that he was far from me, where I didn't have to see his pretty blue eyes staring at me with a Jinn master's soul coming through instead of his own.

So yeah, it was good that Marsum and Maks were far away from me, far away from where they could hurt me.

Wasn't it?

A very large part of me whispered it wasn't the way my story was meant to go. Maks was meant to be with me. Not trapped, not taken away.

I frowned and pinched my eyes shut tightly as I took the last few steps to the top of the dune and sat my furry ass down with another sigh. I was at the top of one of the highest dunes and my view was nothing short of spectacular, despite my emotional upheaval. I found myself staring at the beauty of the land instead of looking for dinner. For just those few moments, I let myself sink into the present, ignoring the past and not thinking about the future and what it might hold.

The smell of water in the distance, the cry of a hunting bird with no doubt better luck than me at finding dinner, the residual heat in the sand under-neath me. This was where I had been raised, and there was a comfort and familiarity to it even though it had its dangers. Things like sand wraiths, gorcs, Jinn, and ophidians. You know, the usual plethora of deadly creatures.

My breathing took a long time to normalize and a pang in my chest made me put a paw to it as if that would stop the pain. Was this true heart pain, or some leftover bruise from all the fighting? I suspected the former.

I'd said goodbye to Maks, and even toasted him as I'd poured out a drink of țuică to make it official, a proper send-off. A proper goodbye.

But even with that, I couldn't stop thinking about him; something I truly needed to do if I was going to move on. I found myself glancing back in the direction where my camp with Lila and Ford was set up. Three miles away, and even at this distance, there was a tiny wisp of smoke, the smallest glimmer of a fire. I narrowed my eyes and could just make out something flitting through the air around that smoke.

Lila, I was sure of it even at this distance, even though I couldn't really see her.

A tiny dragon almost the exact size of my house cat form, Lila was as much an outcast for her size and shape as I was. Only, her family had tried to kill her because she was so small and considered not even worth keeping alive.

Corvalis, the leader of the dragons, who also happened to be her father, was legendary in his violence. He was still out there possibly looking for her. To exact revenge for the thumping she'd given him in front of the other dragons. For a short time, the curse on her had been lifted and she'd been the dragon she'd always been meant to be—huge, powerful, and more than enough of a match for her asshole father.

I looked past Lila's flickering shape in the smoke but couldn't see Ford. He'd be there at the campfire, too, waiting for me to come back with dinner. My throat tightened with the thought of Ford and what he offered me.

With what I was trying and failing to make work with him already. What my uncle Shem wanted me to try to make happen with him. What Lila wanted for me with him. What Ford wanted with me.

To have a new mate, a new love, and to forget Maks ever had been in my life. Two days in to trying to move on, and I knew the answer to me and Ford.

"I can't," I whispered to myself, then bit down on the words.

That was the real reason I was out here alone without even Lila for company. She'd been pushing me hard to make it official with Ford for the last two days. To make him my mate and put Maks behind me once and for all. Not because she didn't love Maks, but because he was gone.

No one but me had any belief that Maks was still there, that there was still a chance.

Lila had decided she was going to help get us together by pushing Ford on me. And by pushing, I mean stealing our clothes and hiding them right before bed. Trying to get us drunk on a bottle of whiskey she found god knew where by slipping it into the stew. Flat out telling us she was leaving for one hour, so please get to it because she was ready for some cubs to play with.

The look on Ford's face with that last line had been nothing short of hilarious, and even now, it made me smile to recall the horror in his dark gold eyes. No one—not him and surely not me—was looking for cubs, not with the Emperor, Ishtar, and Marsum on the loose. Well, Marsum and Ishtar anyway. The Emperor was still technically bound in his prison as far as I knew.

Goddess, help us keep it that way.

I shook my head. Lila meant well, and no doubt she thought if I slept with Ford, I'd finally truly let go of Maks. But I wasn't there yet, three days was hardly long enough to turn my heart off. I didn't know when I would be there. No, that wasn't entirely true —I didn't believe I'd ever get there.

The good part? Ford took all the pushing from Lila in stride. He wanted me as his mate, but he wasn't pushing me.

He was easy on the eyes, and a big powerful lion shifter that my father would have loved for me to have as a mate.

Ford held me at night when I was cold.

He gave me the room I needed during the day.

And he listened to me as the alpha I was and didn't try to make his ego a part of the package.

I should have been falling over happy as a camel in an oasis that he was into me, that he cared for me enough to wait for me to figure my shit out. A sharp stab went through my head, right behind my eyes, cutting my train of thought off in a damn hurry. I let my lids flutter closed as I breathed through the pulse of pain that beat at me.

I was sure it had nothing to do with my heart, or my emotional state. I really needed to drink more water before I went out on a hunt. I knew better.

The pain receded and my thoughts drifted back to Ford. If I were being honest with myself, and Ford had been the one I met first instead of Maks, I *would* be happy with him. I would think myself lucky to not be with a cheating sheep humper like my ex-husband, Steve.

But I hadn't met him first.

I'd met and fallen for Maks, and that love was not something I was having an easy time walking away from.

Maybe you don't have to. Maybe you shouldn't.

My thoughts, or something from outside of me?

A soft exhale slid out of me and I opened my eyes. There was no one around, but those words just kept slipping through me. Maybe I didn't have to say goodbye to him. But which him?

"The course of true love never did run smooth." Shakespeare's words tumbled out of me and seemed to hover in the air. Talking to myself was probably a sign I was going crazy. Even so, nine little words took away the anxiety riding me hard the last few days. I'd been unable to sleep, barely ate, and hadn't been drinking enough water as my heart wouldn't let go of him. *Let him go.*

"I have to let him go." The words were whispered, and I breathed out the last of my fears, the last of my worries about this particular issue.

Because I didn't mean to let go of Maks.

I had to let Ford go. There was no fairness in keeping him on the hook when I wasn't sure that even years from now, I could love him the way he deserved. When I wasn't sure I could *ever* let Maks go, no matter how far he was taken from me. Ford deserved to be loved. He was a good man, and some woman was going to be happy with him.

Part of me screamed I was a fool, that Ford would never hurt me, that he would be loyal and give me beautiful strong cubs that would face this world far better than any other mate. He would never care that my heart was still tied to his adopted brother.

The other part of me continued to ride a wave of calm. The anxiety and stress I'd been dodging since I'd told myself I had to let Maks go slid away like untangling my hands from weights I had no idea I'd grabbed hold of.

The course of true love never did run smooth. Why did I think it would? Certainly not with my luck.

I would wait for him. A smile tripped across my lips, spreading wide as I embraced Shakespeare's words. As I let myself trust my heart, truly trust it even if I didn't know what the future held.

No matter how long, no matter if he never came back to me, I would wait. There was no other way for my heart and soul to accept this part of my life. I sat up a little straighter and drew in a breath that filled my lungs as I nodded to myself. My father had been alone a long time after my mother had died, and he'd been an amazing alpha to our pride. I would follow in his footsteps and whatever happened, happened. I would not force myself into the arms of another man when the one I loved was trapped.

When the one I loved was not truly lost. I knew my friends would think me crazy, but I couldn't help but believe that there was a way to bring him back.

The sun dipped as my thoughts settled, my decision made and my heart lighter for it.

Of course, with that one good thing to come of my hunt, I needed to move and find some food for the three of us. And maybe find the courage to tell Ford the hard truth.

Gah, I didn't want to hurt him.

Around me, a gust of wind rushed across the

sand, through my fur, and tickled at my nose. I turned my head slowly, trying to track where the breeze had come from. An icy cold edge to it had me on my feet and the fur along my spine and tail puffing up. The wind smelled like the cold north, like the land of ice and snow and magic that had tried to kill me repeatedly.

"Seriously?" The word slipped out a moment before a noise turned me around to look behind me, which was wrong. Not behind.

Above.

The whoosh of feathered wings snapped my head up as a dragon-sized white raven dropped from the sky.

"Son of a camel's rotten hump!" I bolted forward, slipping and tumbling down the dune as the bird's talons skimmed the sand where I'd sat only a split second before.

Gravity helped me out, tugging my feet down the steep hill, pulling me faster and faster until I could barely keep my balance, rolling the last few feet but still managing to land upright at the end. I hit the bottom of the dune and shot across the open land-scape, heading away from the campsite where Lila and Ford were.

I had my flail with me—like my clothing it became a part of the chain around my neck, though it seemed to also give me extra strength and damage done by my claws and teeth—and I'd used the weapon before against the White Raven. Sure, the last time I'd seen the Raven and her mistress our meeting had gone okay, but I'd been warned not to trust them again, and I was no fool.

"Fuck off!" I yelled as I scooted across the sand, suddenly the hunted instead of the hunter.

As I passed the desert rabbit I'd been hunting earlier hunched under a tiny bush, watching me run for my life, the irony was not lost on me. Stupid fucking rabbit.

The oversized talons reached for me again, cutting through the air like knife blades, whistling as they came for me. I flattened my belly to the ground at the last second, breathed out and that last exhale kept me from being snatched. I spun and headed for a narrow section of dunes that wouldn't allow for the big bird to swing in and scoop me up. The sides were steep and narrow enough for an escape. I hoped.

"I thought we were friends!" I yelled, and the Raven just cawed loudly, shattering the air.

I turned on the speed as best I could, wishing once again that I had a more robust frame, one with longer legs and enough power within me that I could tackle what life threw in my path.

My thoughts scattered as the sound of a dive-bombing bird tugged at my ears. I dared a glance back, and that was my mistake.

As I turned my head, my feet caught in a dip in the ground, and that fucking exhaustion dogging me made me sloppy. I flipped over myself, literally head over ass, and that was that. Talons closed around me and tore me away from the ground. Trapped, I was trapped and there was no way out of this.

With my legs pinned to my sides there was nothing I could do. Well, there was one thing I could do.

"What the hell is going on? I thought Maggi was on my side?" I snarled the words as I wriggled to get a leg free. Just one front leg loose and I could shift and grab my flail. Maybe.

"I do not ask her opinion or why she does what she does, Wall Breaker. My job is to only do as I'm told. That is the calling of a slave." Her words were bitter and sharp and followed up with a clack of her razor-sharp beak.

I grimaced.

"I'm sorry you are her slave, honestly, I am—"

"Yet, you did nothing to free me." She clacked her beak at me again and I sighed.

"I can't save everyone, you oversized bird brain. I can't even save myself, if you've noticed." To emphasize my point, I tried again—futilely—to free myself. Her talons tightened over me and I grimaced as my bones ground against one another before she relaxed again.

My words produced a laughing caw from her, surprising me. "True, you are the least likely to survive the coming storms, yet here we are, asking

14

you to navigate what is in the cards for our world. Ridiculous, really."

I didn't like the sound of that, but I slowed my struggles. I was too tired to fight if I didn't have to. "So, she wants to talk again? That's it?"

"I think she wants to play fairy godmother," the Raven said as she circled down from the higher air currents. I looked to where we were headed, taking in the odd scene. Below us lay a tiny oasis that had been turned into an icy patch of winter in the middle of the desert.

Maggi—or the Ice Witch as most knew her—was a weather mage as best as I could tell. She'd held one of the stones that increased the power and magic of the user and had gone mad with it. Cray-cray mad. I'd fought her, taken her stone, and that removal of the blue sapphire allowed her to regain some of her lost sanity and humanity. Sort of.

Like most mages, she had her own idea of how things should be done.

This was the second time she'd snagged me from my journey and taken me to where she was to "talk" with me. The White Raven slowed her descent and landed with a single foot, flinging me away from her across the snow. The cold air was bracing and welcome after the heat of the desert, and I breathed it in as I tumbled through it. With a final roll, I came to my feet, shifting forms as I did, clothes intact.

For me, shifting was like walking through a doorway. Human on one side, cat on the other. It used to take me time to shift, but now I was quick, faster than any of the bigger shifters, with no pain unless I tried to shift multiple times back and forth in a row. And those bigger shifters always ended up naked as the day they were born, having their asses slapped.

So, maybe there were some benefits to being a smaller shifter.

The snow crunched under my boots as I did a slow turn, my hands out at my sides but ready to grab a weapon. The palm trees hung heavy with icicles, and the small watering hole was a solid sheen of ice, much to the consternation of several desert animals that crept toward their normal watering hole. A small herd of gazelles pawed at the ice. Their lean bodies didn't have the strength to even put a dent in the edges of the ice.

"Maggi?" I called the Ice Witch's name. "You here or just throwing around a snow fit for shits and giggles?"

Behind me the White Raven took a few steps back so she stood on sand instead of snow, her talons digging into the heated grains. I tried to put a reason to why she would step back. Was there truly that bad of blood between her and her master? Or did she just dislike cold feet? Either was possible, the latter the more likely answer. At least, that's what I told myself.

Muscles aching, head throbbing with a growing headache and my tongue dry from all the running in the sand, I made myself take a few steps deeper into the frozen oasis, a hand going to the tip of the flail. Just in case. "Maggi? You here or should I just leave?"

"I am here," she answered softly. I did another slow turn to find her sitting within a clump of frozen smaller palms that acted like a small throne, appearing as if she'd been there the whole time, but I'd looked there, and she hadn't been.

Her eyes were dull and no longer the vibrant icy blue they had been the last time I'd seen her, her skin gray and ashen. No longer did she look like a witch in her prime, but a hag in her final days.

"You look like shit," I said. The Raven cawed, that sharp laughter hard on the ears. I grimaced. "Sorry, but you don't look well."

Maggi smiled but it was sad, pain-filled, as she adjusted her seat, like a hundred-year-old woman trying to find a position where her bones didn't ache. "You do not look so well yourself, Zamira. Rather like something the cat dragged in."

Another cawing laugh from the Raven.

"Touché." I gave her a careful nod and fought the roll of nausea that climbed my throat with that slight movement. She was not wrong. I felt about as bad as she looked, and worse by the second. "Why did you bring me here? I assume not just to exchange pleasantries about how we both look terrible and could use a spa day with a cute pool boy bringing us drinks."

17

"No, not that. We have business, you and I." She drew a slow breath and closed her eyes as her hands fluttered in the air between us like captured birds, right down to the too-long nails. "Ishtar is drawing my life away. I . . . am not long for this world."

I could believe it, based on how she looked. I wasn't sure how I felt, though, about her dying in front of me. We had been enemies at first, then she'd tried to help me. Now . . . was she was trying to help me again?

"Are you sure?" I asked the question even though I could practically see death at her shoulder, looming over her, waiting to snatch her last breath away.

Her icy blue eyes opened, faded but as sharp as ever despite the rest of her body failing. "I am sure. I've used the last of my power to make you two things, Zamira, the reckless one, the Wall Breaker, alpha of her pride and jungle cat of the deepest hidden forests. I wish I could stay with you and help, but I cannot do both."

I swallowed hard as her words made me shiver. "Why? Why would you help me?"

Around us, the ice cracked, and the temperature rose, blowing the cool breeze away. I looked around to see the edges of the oasis melting as her power faded. As she faded.

"Because, despite what so many tell you, there is no certainty that you will accomplish anything in regard to the Emperor. The seers that tell prophecy, they do not truly know. At best, they guess. Even your mother was making guesses." She clasped her shaking hands in her lap. "The only certainty is that things are changing, and you are a pivotal player in those changes. One with a heart and a mind that would do well to help direct our world's new path. At the very least, you have the best chance of stopping all this madness, and more than that, stopping my sister."

"Ish." I shuddered. "I do not want to face her."

"You won't. I don't think, not yet." Her hands trembled, fluttering again. "That time will come soon, but it is not now. I will, no I *must*, give you two things that will help you. They have the last of my abilities and strength poured into them. The last of all I am."

From her side, she pulled out a silken, icy blue purse—the fabric the same color as her eyes. Understanding rushed over me. "If you hadn't made these two things, would you be able to fend off Ishtar?"

Her smile was fleeting, gone in an instant. "Too smart. You are too smart for your own good, I think, but perhaps that will save you in the end. *Perhaps* that will help you survive. Or perhaps, you will outsmart yourself."

Maggi held up the silken pouch. "Here. This is yours now."

I stepped forward and took the pouch from her,

staring at her while I did so. "What is it you're giving me?"

"One of the items is a ring," she said softly, "woven to hold a curse at bay, the spell woven within it nearly identical to the one you wore from Ish most of your life, only this one has no backlash found within it. There is no pain to taking it off." She grimaced. "My sister is truly a bitch. That was dirty pool, what she did to you and your brother. I'd have just killed you and been done with it."

Her words were sharp and sweet at the same time. She recognized that what had been done was wrong. But that it had been done at all was a true burn along the edges of my heart. I shook the bag, whatever in it clinking, metal on metal. "I am not cursed any longer, at least not with being condemned to fail at everything. And why would you care anyway?"

"You are not the only one who has carried a curse. Even what my sister is doing to me," she touched the center of her chest, "can be considered a curse. And perhaps you could use more help than you realize. That is what happens when you are put on a pedestal to be a hero but are nothing more than a mere house cat." Her tone and eyes were not unkind, but I bristled anyway, feeing the sting of her words.

She wasn't wrong, and that was always the issue for me. I was not meant to be much of anything, not meant to be anything more than a house cat.

No matter how hard I fought, no matter how

many battles I survived, no matter how many jewels I'd brought back from impossible odds, I was and always would be the bad luck black cat. The one everyone underestimated. Just like Lila.

Just like . . . Lila. My mouth dropped open and I stuttered the words as my brain caught up. "Lila is cursed. This could free her?"

Maggi tipped her head to the side and frowned, but the frown was put on. "Is she? I had no idea. But yes, it does block a curse on someone, for a period of time."

A slow smile slid over my face. Lila could hold the ring. She could be the dragon she was meant to be. We could get to the crossroads where Ollianna and Trick waited, break the curses on us both and stop the Emperor. We could do this; we could survive what was laid out before us with Lila in her full size.

Lila would finally be what she was meant to be, and there wasn't an ounce of jealousy in me. For her, I would never feel like she didn't deserve to fly on wings that spread across the sky and darken the sun's light.

Lila would finally be a dragon of power and size —a force to be reckoned with.

She was totally going to shit herself when she saw this.

2

MERLIN

"We have to send Marsum away from the Emperor. If those two get their acts together and start working in tandem, we won't be able to stop either of them." Flora was ahead of him, her shapely ass swaying as she strode across the rocky beach. Merlin sighed. He was never going to get a shot at seeing what was under her skirts at the current rate of his epic screw-ups.

Behind them lay the island where the Emperor—his father—was bound. Or sort of bound, if he was going to be accurate. The truth was the chains that held the Emperor tightly were weakening, and his touch on the world grew more and more with each passing day.

Worse, Merlin was not sure if all he'd been doing had been the correct path to keep his father bound and the world safe. Initially he'd thought that having

Zam take down the wall was the first step. That would have freed the Emperor, but with Ishtar having the stones back, Merlin had thought that would be enough power to face off with the Emperor once and for all.

Then when he saw that the stones and their cumulative power and violence were making Ishtar a true-blue psycho, he thought that perhaps his plan wasn't quite on point. Zam seemed to be unaffected by the violence in the stones, but she was not strong enough to carry that kind of magic and face the Emperor. Then there was the Falak, the monster that had brought the Emperor to his throne in the first place. If that big bastard was set free, and the Emperor was dead, who would face the serpent that could destroy a continent?

Merlin rubbed his face, wishing there were better answers. Wishing for so many things. Like a latte. A latte right then would have been nothing short of amazing.

"Yes, I know we have to send him away, but if you haven't noticed, Marsum is powerful with the stone he holds. And while I am good at what I do, I'm not sure how to stop him without killing him. Killing him and the body that he holds would destroy any hope Zam has of bringing Maks back from the deep. Not to mention, I could end up becoming the bearer of all that Jinn nastiness."

Flora paused and looked over her shoulder, bright

green eyes flashing. "Then we have to kill him by some other means and not tell her."

"Did you not hear me? One of us would end up becoming the new master of the Jinn! The power of that stone and the memories that come with it would drive either of us mad." He blew out a breath as he hurried to her side, tugging his horse behind him to keep up. They'd slipped out of the Emperor's prison, crossed the water to the mainland, and now were hurrying to intercept Marsum, master of the Jinn, before he arrived to join forces with the Emperor.

The Jinn had always been tied to the Emperor in some way, but Merlin wasn't sure exactly how deep those bonds went. Or how the two parties benefited. What he did know was that if they truly decided to work together, then the world as they knew it was done. There would be no stopping the two of them, not with Ishtar, and not with Zam.

"Marsum said he was drawing power through the standing stones that the Emperor created," Merlin said. "That's enough to piss the old man off and make him kill Marsum." But that would mean allowing the two powers to meet, and that was a very dangerous gamble.

"You don't want to get your hands dirty?" Flora shook her head. "There are hard decisions ahead, Merlin, and dirty hands are going to happen whether you like it or not."

"I like the boy," he said, hands tightening on the

reins of his horse. "And he is a match `for Zam, a match she needs. And again, the Jinn master issue." It was like she wasn't even hearing him.

"She *wants* Maks. What she *needs* is Ford," Flora said. "He's solid. He won't argue with her. He'll follow her lead completely."

He snorted. "That does her no favors. She needs someone to challenge her, to push her out of her comfort zone and help her be her best. Maks is the one who showed her how strong she was by being her friend and partner, but by holding her accountable too." He snapped the words, irritated that she could be so blind to the love those two unusual shifters had for each other.

Her feet slowed and once more she looked at him. "Is that what you think? That he's good for her?"

"I think that love is more than just giving in to the other person, making yourself what they want you to be. Zam . . . that would kill her in the end to realize she'd become what she hated in Steve. It wasn't his cheating that burned her the most, Flora. I can almost guarantee it. It was his desire to make her something she wasn't. A doormat.

"Someone who took orders and didn't question him. She tried to be that for him. You can see that in her indecisiveness even now. And when she didn't fit into the mold he wanted, *that* was when he cheated on her. When he thought he could get what he wanted from another woman.

"I can't . . . no, I won't do that to her. I won't make her into what she hates by taking away the man who is the best for her. At least, not if I can help it." A huge breath slid out of him and he found himself in a staring match with Flora. The woman he wanted in his bed more than any other. She challenged him the same way Maks challenged Zam. And he'd walk away from her if she asked him to do this, to compromise what he truly believed when it came to matters of the heart.

He knew it was his downfall, always had been.

"Well, well, *Dr. Phil,* what do you think we should do then? How do you propose we deal with this new conundrum of helping Maks—who, by the way, has voluntarily put himself to sleep to keep her safe— come back to her side without having Marsum, who is currently in control of Maks's body, destroy her body and soul?" Her tone was drier than the desert in the middle of the summer and he didn't miss the sarcasm lacing every word.

What he wouldn't give to put her over his knee and spank her till she begged for more. His lips twitched. "I have an idea."

"You have an idea?" Her eyebrows raised. "Truly, fill me in. Your ideas do always work out so well." Again, he didn't miss the sarcasm.

Merlin smiled at her. "I had a chat with Maggi while I was trapped in the dreamscape with my father. She's going to help. She was there when I put the Emperor to sleep. She knows what is at stake now that her mind is not consumed with power."

He walked past Flora, forcing her to hurry to catch up to his side. The farther they got from the Emperor's prison when they fought Marsum, the better. On a flat stretch of ground, he mounted his horse and held his hand out to Flora. She took his offer and he pulled her into the saddle behind him, enjoying the way her arms went around him, holding him tightly.

Easing the horse into a ground-covering trot, he finally told her his plan, laying it out carefully. Minus a few details he wasn't entirely sure of, but she didn't need to know that.

"That is quite possibly the worst idea I have ever heard!" she shouted at him when he was done. "The worst idea I've heard in a long time, and I've heard more than a few bad ideas fall out of your mouth lately. And to involve Maggi? Can she even be trusted? She held the sapphire for a long time, Merlin. You don't know that she won't give Zam items that don't do what they are supposed to in an attempt to get that sapphire back! The stones are addictive, you know this! This is insane!"

He could feel her shaking her head and he shrugged, touching her hands that were clasped around his middle. He didn't tell her that Maggi would have to give up her life to fulfill the task that Merlin had given her. Either she would help, or she wouldn't, but he was leaning toward her helping. Zam had that effect on people. They ended up wanting to help, wanting to go to the ends of the earth for her. He had a suspicion he knew why—the blood in her veins that no one else had identified. She had a charm even she didn't realize.

Merlin was pretty sure he knew what it was, and that was the ace up his sleeve.

"Do you have a better plan? Besides killing Marsum, that is, because we've already discussed that not being a viable solution."

An intake of breath behind him was his only answer, because no words followed on the exhale of the same breath. He smiled to himself. "Then we are agreed. We will do what we can to slow Marsum down, to tie him up and put him to sleep if possible. That will buy us all some time."

"Ridiculous. Putting men to sleep has not worked well for you, idiot," she said under her breath, but she was so close, there was no way he could miss the words. He didn't mind, he was used to being called far worse by her.

"It will work out, Flora. You just have to trust me," he said.

"Trust you? I've trusted you all along and look where we are. I had to haul you out of the Emperor's hold. You were trapped by Marsum in that box. I ended up captured by the Jinn because you couldn't be honest with me!"

"Agreed." He nodded. "We are far farther ahead than if you hadn't trusted me."

The strangled squawk she let out made him grin. Yes, she kept him on his toes, that much was true. Even with all that, she tightened her hold around his middle and that was good enough for him.

She was with him still, both in body and in their new plan.

An hour slipped by before their target came into view.

The oversized desert falcon that held Marsum in his talons winged toward them. The flying pair were still a speck in the distance, but Merlin tensed regardless. "There he is."

"So, we are going to spell him, try to put him to sleep." Flora nodded and lifted her hands. "I can bring him toward us, spinning in a whirlwind; that should keep him busy and rather on the dizzy side."

"Good idea." Merlin slowed the horse and they both dismounted. Better to have your feet on the ground when fighting a Jinn master. Looping the reins of the horse around his arm, he slowed his breathing. The time spent with his father had drained him to some degree, but he was sure he could still create a sleep spell.

At least, he hoped he could.

Flora lifted her hands above her head and the mid-afternoon sky darkened, deepening to a heavy gray as clouds rolled in. Sweat broke out on her brow and a tiny burst of lightning cracked across the horizon. "Spin it," she whispered. "Spin it."

The wind picked up with her words, curling around and around, faster and faster. Merlin leaned into the weather, narrowed his eyes and kept Marsum and the falcon in view.

When Merlin had still been in thrall to his father, he'd been forced to possess the desert falcons and attack Zam and her friends. At the last minute, though, he'd been able to use the falcons to scoop up Marsum and carry him away from Zam to give her a respite. To give them all a momentary chance to figure shit out.

Because Merlin needed to buy himself time to try to fix things that he had set in motion. And now, here, he was about to reverse everything he'd put into play so far. For love.

For Zam and Maks to find their way back to each other. Because he couldn't help but believe love was the answer to all this mess, even if he wasn't fully sure how it would work out in the end.

"Maggi, don't fail me. You need to do what I asked of you," he whispered to himself.

Flora spun both hands in the air as if she were a belly dancer, then snapped her fingers, and lightning cracked across the sky followed by a boom of thunder that made their horse shy to one side. The wind doubled in speed and Merlin watched as the oversized falcon spun in a whirlwind, caught up and unable to escape the weather the priestess of Zeus had produced.

Flora slumped to the ground, down to her knees, her hands pressed against the sand to balance herself. "That is all I can do. The rest is on you, Merlin."

This was going to happen fast. He leapt onto the horse as the weather died down, and the falcon spun out of control, crashing into the hard-packed earth, wings crumpled a good football field length away from them.

Merlin put his boots to his horse's sides, and they took off at a dead gallop, straight toward the pair Flora knocked out of the sky. The wind around them was gone, and he had only minutes at best to put Marsum under and send him in the other direction.

To send him to Zam.

Ahead of him, the Jinn pushed himself free of the still-stunned bird.

"Shit," Merlin growled. He pulled his horse to a halt and leapt off before the beast was even fully stopped.

Marsum wobbled, obviously still feeling the effects of the whirlwind. Even so, his eyes locked on Merlin. "You? You did this?"

"About to do more than knock you out of the sky," Merlin said. He gathered his power to send Marsum onto his ass. But the Jinn was no fool. The black mist integral to the Jinn's power swirled out around Marsum, hiding his body.

Merlin grimaced and threw the sleep spell he'd rolled together directly into the mist, hoping to hit Marsum.

The mist dissipated, gone, and so was Marsum.

Merlin spun as Marsum appeared behind him. He managed to get an arm up as Marsum swung hard. "What is this? You want to spar?"

This made no sense. The Jinn should have been using his magic, not his fists.

Unless . . . "Maks, thanks, pup." Merlin caught the blow with one hand and yanked the Jinn off balance, dropping him to his knees. Blue eyes stared up at him.

"Hurry, whatever you're going to do, hurry. I can't hold him—" His eyes rolled in his head and he screamed, full bodied and full of pain that seemed to rip out of his middle.

Merlin clutched Marsum's head with his hands and pumped his power into him, quieting his brain and putting him into a deep sleep. One that would last until Zam touched him.

The Jinn's body slumped to the ground and Merlin breathed a sigh of relief. This was where things were going to get tricky. He grabbed Marsum by the hands and dragged him toward the oversized falcon. The bird was exhausted, but Merlin threw a spell at the bird that re-invigorated it. Mind you, the thing would likely drop dead when that spell wore off, but as long as it got Marsum to where he was sending him, Merlin didn't really care.

"Oversized, overstuffed turkeys," he muttered, thinking of Zam as he shoved Marsum toward the bird and directed it to pick up the sound-asleep Jinn.

Running footsteps behind him told him his time was up. Flora was back on her feet. There was no way she'd be okay with this last step of the plan.

Trust was a funny thing: he needed it from her, but didn't trust her enough to trust him. A quandary if ever there was one.

He wove a spell and sent it deeply into the falcon, through its bones and blood and mind. "Take him east, and to the south, take him to Zam."

The bird launched into the air, package gripped in one talon.

"What is happening? Where is it going?" Flora stumbled into him, out of breath, chest heaving.

"Well, Marsum is asleep now," Merlin said.

"I know, that was the plan! But the rest . . ." Flora's face was brushed with light pink across her cheeks and her eyes were wild and full of confusion. "Where are you sending him? You said we'd put him to sleep and then tuck him away."

"Away, yes, he's going away. Somewhere safe." Merlin was unable to look her in the eye for fear she'd know.

Flora glared at him, the heat of her gaze making

his skin prickle. "You didn't. Merlin, tell me you didn't!"

He tried to look innocent, though to be fair, he wasn't sure what that would look like on his face. What did innocent look like on a mage known for deception? And he should have known she'd figure it out. She knew him too well.

Her eyes narrowed and she smacked him on the arm. "You sent him to Zam, didn't you? *Didn't you?*"

"How—"

She threw her hands up and paced in front of him. "I can read you like a damn book, Merlin. What is it with you and a happily ever after? This isn't going to help her. It's going to break what's left of her heart into pieces. She *can't* save him! No one can!"

"Yes, she can," he said.

She stopped her pacing and looked at him. "How?"

"Well, the details are fuzzy, but I believe she can save him. Maggi and I discussed it at length. There is always a way back."

He didn't think Flora could narrow her eyes and still technically have them open, but he was wrong. Lasers might as well have shot out at him and he realized that she was . . . jealous. He grinned. "Maggi's not my type, Flora. It wasn't that kind of a discussion."

She sniffed and spun away from him. "You're going to break Zam's heart. Or kill her. Because

Marsum will not let her go again. He'll kill her first to make sure no one else can use her before he lets her go."

Their conversation might have continued on in that vein if not for one thing: a horse and rider running parallel to them, racing toward the east. There was a flare of skirts, the blur of hair as it swept out behind her, running her horse as if her life depended on it.

Flora paused and pointed. "Who is that?"

"I think that's the person who's been helping the Emperor." Merlin leapt up onto his horse and held a hand to Flora. "And it's about time you and I had a talk with her."

ZAMIRA

I clutched the bag Maggi gave me a little tighter, thinking of how I would present the ring to Lila. I mean, a ring that would allow her to be a full-sized dragon with no backlash or pain? It was what she deserved. "Lila would kiss your feet for this, even if they were covered in shit, you know that, right?"

"There is something else in there for you, something you will need—and soon." Maggi sighed and her body slumped, folding in on herself, inch by inch. The small oasis warmed quickly now as her power faded, the frozen sand turning mushy under my feet, no longer covered in snow, no longer covered in ice. A quick look showed me there was nothing but a few ice chips floating on the surface of the water, reflected by the moon above us.

Had that much time passed?

Shit, Lila and Ford would be freaking out by now wondering where I was. No doubt they were looking for me.

Maggi motioned for me to open the bag, her hands trembling as though she were cold. The silver bracelet on her wrist shimmered and danced in the light. "I have not many moments left as Ishtar's curse tightens around me. Continue on. Quickly, please."

I reached into the bag, my fingers brushing against the ring, the contours of it familiar, right down to the nick in the lion's ear. Shock stole my breath and I took a second to pull it together. "You found my father's ring?"

"It seemed fitting to put a proper spell onto it, rather than that garbage Ishtar put into it originally." She whispered the words, and for just a moment, she looked ethereal, transparent.

"Hurry, Ishtar will have all that is left of me soon and be stronger for it," she added, breathy, her eyes watering.

I pulled the ring out and stared at the familiar lion's head. I let it go, grabbing the chain as it fell, dangling it from my fingers as a thought rolled over me. Maggi's death would strengthen Ishtar. It would be a loss of knowledge. Could I afford that? Even for Lila, I couldn't deny that Maggi had information and an understanding of what I might face that I could use. Things happened for a reason in this world, and I was not ignorant of that fact.

Which left me a single choice.

"You first." I stepped close to her and slid the necklace over her head. If it was a blocker of curses as she'd said, and what Ishtar was doing to her was a type of curse, then surely it could save her.

Maggi stared at me, her hands—already not shaking as they were before—going to the ring as if to take it off. "No, that is not what this is for. I cannot take this. It is meant to help you, not me."

"I need what you know, which means you cannot die on me, not yet." I slapped her hand away from the ring and her mouth dropped open. She spluttered and I slapped her hand down again. "You gave me the ring, and I put it on you. I'll make you a deal. You can give it to Lila yourself when you're ready to die. How about that?"

Maggi stood, her body filling out even as I looked on, and her skin improving in color with each second that passed. "You are as stubborn as any cat and just as likely to ignore commands. How my sister kept you on a leash for so many years is beyond me."

The words were sharp and full of irritation, but they made me smile because at least she wasn't dying. "Well, to be fair, she didn't really keep me on a leash with much success. That was the problem. I was a shit disturber. Too reckless."

Maggi snorted and stretched, her joints crackling as if throwing off chains. I thought the ice would grow on the oasis once more, but it didn't.

"I have very little power left," she said, catching me looking at the melting cold. "I will be of no use to you other than what I know."

Good enough for me.

"What else—" I moved to stick my hand into the silken bag.

Maggi beat me to it and snatched the bag away from me. "No. You will not have this then as long as I am alive."

I laughed even though the sound hurt my head, though I tried not to let it show. "See? You're as stubborn as me. You weren't ready to die."

I reached for the bag again, my reflexes still fast even if I did feel like shit. I snagged the bag and she snapped her fingers at me. I braced for the impact of a spell, but nothing happened.

She closed her eyes and blew out a sharp breath. "Damn it."

"Really, you did give me this. What's wrong with me looking?"

I reached into the silken pouch and my fingers brushed against something metallic, something much larger than the ring. I took hold of the item and pulled out . . . a pair of . . . "Handcuffs?" I held them up with one finger, not sure what to make of this particular gift. I could imagine Maggi using them on someone to keep them bound, but what would I need with them?

Made of copper, the handcuffs were flecked with

a black stone that I guessed was some sort of quartz. The inner edges of the cuffs that would rest against the wrist were lined with silk, as if they were meant to be worn a long time in comfort. One cuff had more of the black stone than the other. I snorted and couldn't help the low chuckle. "Kinky. Not sure that—"

"I will know when to use them, Zam. That is all *you* need to know," Maggi snapped. "They are powerful. Do not mock the gifts you've been given."

She held her hand out.

"I thought these two items you made were for me?" I frowned and then thought about what she'd said. *She* would know when to use them. *She* would know . . . as if . . . no, oh no.

Her eyelids slid to half-mast like a self-satisfied cat who'd just lapped up a bowl of milk. "I will be coming with you, now. Seeing as you've spared my life, I am in your debt." That smile deepened and I realized right then and there I'd been played. And played well.

Had she known I would give her the necklace?

She tipped her head to me. "You are still a protector, a caretaker of all those in this land, just like your father. I took a gamble with the odds in my favor."

Even though I knew I was fighting an uphill battle, I tried to change the course of what was happening.

"No, that's not really what I was thinking. I can just call on you if I have a question. Or maybe . . ."

"Maybe what? *Phaw.* I will come with you. As you said, I can give Lila the necklace when she is ready. When I am ready." Her smile was sharp, and I kicked myself for giving it to her. Kicked myself for being so easily manipulated.

Idiot, I was an idiot.

She took the handcuffs and put them into the silken bag, then tied it to her belt.

"Tell me," she said, "have you killed Steve yet?" There was a definite twinkle in her voice, if there could be such a thing.

"How could you possibly know about Steve?" I spluttered.

Her eyeroll was nothing short of epic. I was surprised both orbs came back to center again.

"He was in my dungeon." She spread her hands wide as if that explained everything. "I watched how he was with his women. Watched how he treated you and them when you were trying to save him." She shook her head. "He is not done making your life miserable, Zam. Be wary of him. And if you get a chance to kill him, honorably or not, do it. I doubt you will get another chance. So, do it."

She turned and faced me, changing directions once more. "Are you ready to go then?"

"No, you tell me what you mean about Steve." I folded my arms, staring her down.

Maggi clasped her hands in front of her and placed them against her thighs and the gauzy material of her dress.

"He needs to die, that is all there is to him. There is power in him, as there is in many alphas, and if he figures out how to use that power, you will have a fight you will not be ready for on your hands. If Ishtar realizes what she could actually use him for, then there will be no saving you or your pride."

I frowned. "You think me weak, too, then?"

"In some ways, yes. Your size is against you. More than that, I think he will wait until you are beyond broken, *then* he will attack you."

I snorted again. "That is not news to me. He's a coward. He's waited for me to be injured before."

"Then be wary of him." Maggi opened her eyes, just a slit so the blue glowed in the darkness. "You and I should have had tea together long ago."

"Except you would have tried to kill me," I pointed out, a smile of my own catching me off guard. Smiling at her while discussing killing one another. What a strange night. My body protested that I was still standing and not resting at camp, but I stilled the tremors in my muscles with effort.

"Perhaps. But you must embrace death, Zam, if you want to be successful in your journey, if you want to survive." Her eyes were thoughtful. "Promise me you will . . . embrace . . . death. Hold him tightly when he comes for you. Promise me."

I shrugged. I'd never cared for word games and that's what this felt like. "Let me guess that you can't flat out tell me what I need to do any more than Merlin or Flora?"

She bobbed her head once. "It is the price of knowing some, but not all, of what can be in the future. Sometimes I do not even know why I say what I say, and see the truth of it only in hindsight."

Great, just bloody awesome. "I will do what I can to embrace death," I said, and even I could hear the fatigue in my voice. Bone tired wasn't a saying for nothing.

"The Oracle said to embrace death, did she not?" she said. "And I am saying the same thing. You *must* do it."

I threw both hands up. "Fine. Fine. I'll embrace death. At this point, I could use the fucking sleep. And how the hell do you know what the Oracle said to me?"

A sigh slid out of her. "I know much. It is the price I pay for seeing the threads of lives around me."

My turn to roll my eyes. "Great, but I still don't think you should come with me. We are going to be moving fast, and we don't have enough horses for all of us."

Maggi blinked rapidly, her eyes moving left and right. "Yes, yes, I can see that will be a problem."

Was she reading the threads around us like she'd said she could? I shook my head. I didn't really care.

All that mattered was that she realized she didn't need to come with me.

"Well, this has been lovely, but I want to go back to camp and get something to eat." A grumble rolled through my belly as if to accentuate my point.

With a twitch of her hand, she spun her skirt out around behind her, the gauzy material floating on the icy air of the still slightly frozen oasis. "Excellent idea. I am rather peckish myself."

My feet stumbled to a stop between one step and the next. "Pardon, what?"

"I think a meal would do you good. That you are still standing is truly a miracle as far as I can see. And I could use a meal myself."

"Yeah, but you said that you could—"

The former Ice Witch twitched an eyebrow upward. "I can see that you mistook my consideration of a problem for not wanting to come with you. I am coming with you, Zamira. That is final."

The step of talons on the sand behind me turned me around. The White Raven stared down at us both, but those eyes locked on Maggi. "You swore you would release me when this was done."

Maggi linked her hands together. "I am not dead yet, but yes, I will still release you, demanding creature. As soon as you perform a final task. We need you to take us to Zamira's camp, and *then* you will be free."

My first thought was that this was not happening.

44

There was no way Maggi was joining me, Lila, and Ford as we hunted for the Wyvern's Lair and a way to bring my brother back from the dead. The exhaustion that had been dogging my footsteps came back in a flood and the world spun a little. I braced my legs wide and breathed through the vertigo that hit me seemingly out of nowhere.

The White Raven clacked her beak and bobbed her head, feathers luminescent in the moonlight. "I can do that. Seeing as you will be dead soon and then I will be truly free of your machinations."

I spluttered and Maggi snorted. "I'm not dead yet; do not count your eggs before they hatch, bird."

The Raven spread her wings wide. "The magic you pushed into those items would have kept you alive for years yet. But you are too fascinated by this one and her path, and so for that curiosity, you gamble your life. All to give our world a chance, according to you. So, you will die, and soon. That is enough for me."

Once more my jaw dropped, and I gaped at the two of them quarreling like an old married couple, as though I were a fish yanked out of water. "Wait, what?"

"Stunning. You chose this pithy one to save the world?" the Raven drawled. "She's not even—"

"Hush." Maggi snapped her fingers and the Raven's beak clacked shut as though wrapped with a rope. The anger in those midnight-dark eyes was not

45

lost on me. Perhaps there was a little magic left in Maggi after all.

The air around us thickened, and there was a distinct crackle on the ice behind us that covered the meager water source.

"You are not the power you once were," the Raven said.

"No, but I do believe that Zamira would defend me should you decide to attack me, seeing as I am defenseless at the moment." Maggi didn't look at me or even include me in the weird-ass conversation between them.

"Damn shit fuck." I hunched my shoulders. She was not wrong, but that didn't mean I had to like it. I reached up and touched the handle of my flail, the wood warming under the tips of my fingers, eager to be used for killing and mayhem.

From the corner of my eye, I saw Maggi smile. "You see? Do not push us. I doubt you would survive this time."

The White Raven fluffed up her feathers. "I will be glad to be rid of you. Both of you."

"You and me both, birdbrain." I let go of the flail, though it tried to stick to me.

"You shouldn't speak like that to your ride." The Raven's wicked sharp beak clacked and she jabbed it in my direction. A thin layer of cold sweat broke out along my spine. Sure, we could fight, we'd probably both be wounded badly, and that was just stupid, especially here in the desert. You didn't fight unless you had no choice. Because wounded, the desert would finish you off in no time.

"Sorry, it's been a long day." I rubbed at the spot above my eyes that throbbed with an ache that wouldn't give me even a measure of peace.

The Raven crouched and tipped her back for us to mount, far better than riding in her talons. "Thanks."

She fluffed her feathers again. "You are not well. There is sickness on you, desert cat."

I noted that she ignored Maggi. So be it. I could pretend the sister of Ishtar wasn't with me too. At least until her hands settled on my shoulders, tightening, digging in.

"I'm just tired," I said. And heartsick. And anticipating what was to come with Ford when I told him I couldn't lead him on and that I was putting him firmly in the friend zone no matter what he said. "Let's go."

The White Raven launched straight up as if we weighed nothing, her wings coming down with a swoop that sent the last of Maggi's snow fluttering into the air before the flakes touched on the sand, melting away. Pretty and nauseating at the same time as my stomach dropped, rolling hard with the change in G-force.

"I'm gonna be sick," I whispered as we shot through the sky, the Raven's wings taking us quickly back the way I'd come.

"Lean to the side." Maggi scooped up my long hair and held my head as the Raven tipped her wings and I hurled what little food and liquid that had been in my stomach. Maybe Maggi wasn't all manipulative. "Thanks," I managed as we straightened out and I forced myself to sit upright.

All I wanted was to get to camp, curl up, and sleep for a week. But I couldn't do that.

We had to move; we had to get to the crossroads and break a spell, find the Wyvern's Lair where, apparently, he would tell us how to bring my brother Bryce back from the dead, and stop the Emperor. Yeah, no problem.

I must have dozed off because the Raven woke me with a sharp caw, startling me almost right off her back if not for Maggi's hands on my shoulders.

"Zam, there is an issue."

I blinked rapidly, looking around the bare sky, the twinkling stars and moon lighting up the desert below us. "What is it?"

The White Raven pointed with the tip of her beak. "There is something coming up fast behind us."

I twisted where I sat on her back. Thank the goddess for the night vision of a cat, or I would have missed the figure winging toward us—moving quickly as if it were trying to catch us. I squinted, noting the shape of the wings and body, recalling it easily. "That's one of those falcons. From the Oracle's Haunt."

"I will not fight for you, Zam." The Raven's words did not surprise me. "And certainly not for *her* any longer."

"Turncoat," Maggi said. "I have no power, Zam. I cannot help either. You must face whatever this is on your own."

Of course I would.

"Then land, and I will do just that," I said.

The White Raven banked her wings and we coasted toward the sand. This was just freaking awesome.

Just how I wanted to end my night, fighting with an oversized desert turkey.

W hile I knew it wasn't fair for me to be pissed that the White Raven left me to face the desert falcon winging our way with nothing more than Maggi at my side, who apparently was no good to me either, I was pissed, nonetheless. Maggi and I were dropped to the sand, and the Raven never even touched down. She just swept upward again with a hard beat of her wings.

"Be brave, Zamira," she cawed, her wings cutting through the air, the downdraft swirling sand and bits of brush into my face. I covered my eyes with my hands.

"Don't get caught by another wicked witch, how about that, birdbrain?" I yelled back. Her wings stuttered in mid-flight and she shot me a sharp glance with those midnight-dark eyes.

Me and my big fat mouth. I grinned and waved as

if it were a joke. Shit, at this rate, I was going to have to deal with the desert falcon and the White Raven at the same time. I was an idiot.

"You do have a knack for diplomacy, don't you? And even with that, people still like you." Maggi fluttered her skirts to knock the sand off.

"Life is a tale told by an idiot full of sound and fury, signifying nothing," I muttered to myself, feeling like an idiot and wishing Lila were there to point out that it was yet another *Macbeth* quote instead of Maggi who just raised an eyebrow at me as if she agreed that I was the idiot in question.

I sighed and turned to face the desert falcon still coming upon us fast. I had my flail, and I reluctantly pulled it out. Reluctant in most part because I was so damn tired. I could lie down right there and sleep if not for the incoming winged issue and the likelihood that it wanted to peck my eyes out. At least it was just a falcon. It could be worse.

The bird shot straight for me, flying hard and fast, something clutched in one talon. I squinted my eyes, the darkness hiding the thing the bird carried until it was much closer, and I could see the blond hair and limp body.

"Oh no." I clutched my flail harder, the handle warming, sticking to the palm of my hand, my heart simultaneously dropping and picking up speed as if it didn't know what to do any more than I did.

"What is it?" Maggi asked, and her tone said it all. "Someone you know?"

"Did you know Marsum was coming this way?" I yelled the question, not caring who heard. I mean, hell, she obviously knew he was headed this way. Fuckity damn it all right up a camel's ass, I was not in the best shape to deal with him.

Marsum, who held Maks's body in thrall. Marsum, who'd been the bane of my family's existence. Who'd wiped out the lion shifters of the desert. Who'd killed my father. Marsum who'd taken Maks from me.

He was loose-limbed in the falcon's clutch. I watched in fascinated horror as the bird touched down, flipped the Jinn out of its hold and promptly fell over to the side. The desert falcon shuddered a few times, its wings spreading wide and chest heaving once, twice, before it collapsed completely, going still. Dying on the spot.

I stood staring at the still-limp form of Marsum, unsure of just what to do. Marsum lay on his belly, unmoving but breathing steady as if he were asleep. Could that be right?

"Perhaps you should check on him?" Maggi suggested, and I whipped around—wobbling a little —to stare at her.

"How about we run for the damn hills?"

"You can't run." Maggi shrugged. "There is no running from him this time."

"Why do I get the feeling you are up to something?" I glared at her, but the effect was ruined by the way I struggled to stand upright.

I looked around as if there would be some other clue, some other tip as to just what I was supposed to do with this new turn of events. Where was Shem when I needed him? Or Lila? Or even Merlin? I'd take that idiot mage in that moment to give me an idea of what the next step was.

I couldn't kill Marsum, but I couldn't leave him here either. And Maggi was not to be trusted no matter how much she tried to help me—I wasn't that big of a fool. I took a few steps back and then forward. Once more, the indecision I'd lived with for so many years cut into me and I grimaced. I was not that person anymore. I put my flail into its holder across my back and let the handle go.

"Maybe he's dying," I whispered to myself as I crept forward for a closer look. I couldn't let him die. He had Maks's body. Though how I would save him if that was the case, I had no idea.

"Perhaps you'd better check," Maggi said again, and motioned for me to move forward.

Damn it all to the desert fires and back. I swallowed hard and made myself cover the distance between him and me before I could change my mind again. His face was turned to the side and his body gave a quick twitch as he snorted . . . in his sleep. Yup, definitely sleeping.

I frowned.

"What the hell is going on here?" I spoke loud enough that a normal person would wake up.

Marsum didn't move. Not an inch.

I bit my lower lip, worrying at it.

"I do believe he's been spelled to stay asleep until a trigger of some sort awakens him," Maggi said. "At least, that is what the spell on him looks like to me. The spell will have a time limit, I'm sure. Whatever you wish to do to him, now is your chance." I turned to look at her, and she shrugged her thin shoulders as if it mattered not, but she would not meet my eyes. Yeah, something was up with her. Back to him, I looked.

He'd been spelled to sleep? All well and good, but leaving him here was dangerous because who knew what trigger would wake him, and then I'd have no idea where he was. Dangerous, wasn't it? That question and its potential answer were snatched from me.

A wave of vertigo hit me, and I swayed where I stood, groaning. I sidestepped, tried to catch my balance, but the dizziness was too much coupled with my current state of fatigue and I crumpled to the ground, landing on my knees. The world swayed even there on my hands and knees, and my body swayed with it, rocking like I was on a bucking colt until I couldn't hold it off any longer. I fell to the side, hit the ground next to Marsum, and squeezed my eyes shut as the ground seemed to roll beneath me in waves.

"What the hell is going on?" I'd never been sick like this before, not even at my lowest points. I had to have contracted something, maybe in the witch's swamp—that water was damn filthy and no doubt riddled with disease. Another wave below me that was not real—I knew it was all in my head—and I rolled with it.

"You are very sick," Maggi said, "and this is the only thing that will save you. I thought to use them myself, but it is not to be. This will work."

What the hell was she talking about? Was I supposed to hear her?

My hand brushed against Maks's forearm, along the muscles I wanted so badly to touch and to hold me. I couldn't help it, being near him was like a reflex. I grabbed him tightly and clung to his arm like a life raft in rough, dark waters that wanted to suck me under the waves. His arm trembled, flexed, and I forced my eyes open. Even lying on my side, the world heaved and swayed, and my stomach rolled with nausea, bucking at what was left in my belly. I dry heaved a few times but that was all I had left.

He groaned, his body flexing as he shifted to push to his hands and knees.

I was flat out, barely able to open my eyes, and Marsum was waking.

"Oh, dear," Maggi said. "This is too fast."

"That all you got? It's a fucking shit show," I groaned.

"I don't plan on engaging in the sailor talk your generation enjoys." She sniffed.

Another grumbled moan from Marsum, but he hadn't looked my way yet. I didn't dare let my hold on him go, because it would change the pressure on his skin and that would be as noticeable as if I hadn't been holding him and suddenly grabbed him. Filthy damn luck that I had, I didn't see a way out of this.

He would fight me. Or he would take me with him if I didn't do something, and that something had to be fast.

Kiss him. That was always a good distraction. And Marsum wanted me. Well, he could have pukemouth me, then.

I forced myself to my knees as he turned his head to me, his eyes clogged with sleep as though he was still half out of it. That made two of us. I launched myself at him—and by *launched*, I mean I fumbled over to him and pushed him to the ground with zero finesse.

There was a moment of surprise, or maybe confusion in his blue eyes, and then he was flat on his back, and I was lying on his chest, my head on his shoulder, unable to do more than that.

So much for kissing him senseless.

"What are you doing?" His hands were on my hips as if he wasn't quite sure if this was real or not. Hell, I certainly was beginning to wonder myself if this wasn't some sort of weird-ass dream.

"Beating you up?" I offered, unable to lift my head. It felt like a cannon ball on top of my shoulders, heavy and unwieldy.

A sharp laugh escaped him. "Piss poor job, cat."

"Oh, I know." Maybe I could just lie here and hold him down until Lila and Ford came to look for me. Or Maggi could knock him out. Totally the stupidest plan I'd ever had, but there it was.

I just had nothing left in me, and I wasn't willing to pull the flail on Marsum as long as there was a chance I could bring Maks back. The same as I believed there was a chance to bring my brother back from the dead, there had to be a way to bring Maks back from the power of the Jinn masters.

His hands slid over my hips to the curve of my ass, his fingers tightening over me, digging in with a more than pleasant pressure. "You make this too easy. I should have let Maks take my head long before."

Maggi let out a low hiss.

I closed my eyes. "What do you mean I make this too easy?" I shimmied, moving one hand to my side to try to push off him. "Little help?"

Maggi said nothing. I managed to twist my head to look for her, but she was gone. Damn it, I was on my own again.

"I want a child. The next of the Jinn masters will be yours and mine with more power than any other."

He grabbed me and flipped me over to my back in a smooth movement that knocked the wind out of me.

"Hardly gentle. You should work on that. Lady skills are lacking," I wheezed.

I fumbled to get my hands between us, to hold him off, but he was doing the same. Only Marsum reached between us to unbuckle his belt.

The nausea hit me hard and I didn't try to hold the vomit back. I turned my head and spewed chunks, mostly fluid at this point. Stomach acid laced my mouth and I dry heaved where I lay, wishing I could just close my eyes and sleep. After the puking, that was.

"Disgusting," he snarled, his voice and tone deep and totally not Maks. He pulled back, his weight leaving me.

I didn't for a second think he was going to let me go that easily. There was the sound of a buckle closing and then he pulled me to my feet.

"Stand up," he snapped as I wobbled. I draped a hand over his shoulder.

"What's wrong with me?" I mumbled more to myself than to him.

Marsum grabbed me by both arms and shook me straight until I was looking at him. His eyes locked on mine and despite what had to be the worst puke breath, he slid his hands up to my face and held me close enough that our noses were touching. I closed my eyes, wishing for all the world in that moment that he'd just kill me and get it over with.

"Keep your eyes open," he snarled. Maks's voice, Marsum's tone.

"Unless you want me to hurl all over you, I think it's best—"

"Something is wrong with you, woman. Open your damn eyes!" Was that panic I heard in him?

I reached up and held onto his forearms and forced my eyes open. "Why do you care?"

Those blue eyes raked over my face, studied my eyes as he pulled one eyelid open, and then he shot a hand to the center of my chest between my breasts and pressed hard. I wanted to know what he was looking for, what he thought was wrong, because I suddenly realized that the longer he looked at me, the more worried he was, the worse whatever was going on in my body probably was. Bad mojo indeed if a Jinn master was worried.

"Goddess be damned," he finally muttered. He let me go and my legs buckled, sitting me right back down. I lay back and stared at the black sky above, watching the stars move and heave with each breath I took.

"What's the verdict?" I managed to ask, wondering just how strange of a world it was that Marsum was suddenly, weirdly, concerned for me. Or maybe that was Maks coming through?

"I can't get a child in you right now, not until your

body has been cleansed," he growled. "That is going to be a royal pain in my ass, you know that?"

I drew a breath and formed the words slowly. "What do you mean, cleansed?"

"You . . ." He was suddenly there, over me in a crouch, once more peering into my eyes. "Something happened to one of the stones you were thieving for Ish. What happened to it? You broke it, didn't you?"

I blinked once. "Yes, I shattered the diamond with the black lightning in it. The witch stone."

He grimaced. "You were holding it when it broke? Which hand?" He picked up my left hand, dragging it away from my side, and then the right, looking them both over. "No scars. Where was it when you were holding it?"

I couldn't fathom what he was getting at. What he was trying to tell me.

"Yes, it was . . ." Was it under my shirt when it had shattered? "I think under my shirt."

He pulled my shirt up, exposing my bare flesh. The night air actually felt good on my flushed skin. "Here? You have a crystal pattern scar, and it's new by the color of it."

Marsum touched the spot between my breasts where the stone had lain inside a pouch, not a single moment of sexuality to his inspection. I frowned up at the sky and pulled my shirt down. "Yes, but what does—"

"You absorbed the power of the stone, you idiot."

He grabbed both my hands and pulled me to a standing position. "You need another stone from the same cut as that black-flecked diamond to push all that power into or you're going to die. And die very soon."

He paced a tight circle, obviously deep in thought. This was the moment I could take my flail and smack him, kill him. But that wasn't going to happen. He knew it, and so did I.

"There is another," he muttered, his tone changing once more, deepening, aging. "That one you had with you, the witch. She has the Emperor's lines too. She will do." With that he turned and started away from me.

Leaving me there.

To die.

So he could impregnate Ollianna.

5

The idea of Marsum in Maks's body getting a child on Ollianna was enough to fire my muscles past the sickness that was apparently killing me. Again, where the hell was Maggi? Had she really just fucked off on me after saying she would help if she could?

"You are not going to touch Ollie." I stumbled after him, hating how weak I was.

Marsum looked over his shoulder and grinned. "Jealous?"

"Not of you, shithead. But Maks is mine." So okay, maybe a little jealous.

"What are you going to do about it? Nothing. He let himself be shoved to sleep like the coward he is," Marsum said. "I need an heir, one that is stronger than all the others, and a woman with the Emperor's bloodline is the answer—" He snapped his mouth shut as if he'd said too much.

Then he continued. "But I suppose I could take you with me. Just to be sure." The mist of the Jinn began a slow swirl around his feet. He moved like a damn snake, striking out and grabbing me, throwing me over his shoulder and then striding forward.

Upside down was not a good place for me to be. I heaved and gagged as though my entire stomach was trying to push itself up and out of my mouth.

We weren't moving very fast, that was about the only good thing I could see. "Where are you taking me?"

I had to stop him; I knew that much. Stop him from getting to Ollie first. "Ollie isn't the Emperor's child. Me or nothing, sweet cheeks."

A blatant lie, but maybe he wouldn't realize it.

The string of profanities that escaped him told me that maybe he *did* believe me. One point for the liar.

"Then we need to get a stone," he growled. "This one won't do." He touched his hip and I realized he was carrying the Jinn's stone, the amber stone. I reached for it.

"You sure?"

He slapped my hand away. "Stop touching it."

I snickered, words popping out of my mouth I couldn't stop. "That's not what you said a few minutes ago."

"Are you drunk?" There might have been a hint of

laughter in his voice. Marsum didn't have a sense of humor. That was Maks coming through, it had to be.

"I feel like I'm dying," I said. "Makes me crazy funny. Want to go out with a fucking *bang*." I clapped my hands together though it was a weak clap at best.

He stopped and pulled me off his shoulder to my wobbling feet. I couldn't stand without his help and I clung to him, clung to Marsum, the worst enemy of my family and the Jinn who'd destroyed so much.

"Then we need to fix this. Because I need you still, at least long enough to give me a child if indeed you are the only granddaughter of the Emperor." His jaw flexed and there was a glimmer in his eyes that I *knew* was not Marsum. I lifted my hand and touched his jaw, for just a second the world standing still. "Maks?"

His throat bobbed and he leaned his head in. At first, I thought he was going to kiss me, but that would be disgusting—puke-mouth that I was. But he didn't kiss me. His hand cupped around my face, digging into it. "There is a way to keep you from being overwhelmed by this."

He shook his head. "No, don't you dare, boy! Don't you dare tie us to her. We'll both die!"

What was happening? "Maks, what way?" I whispered those words, hoping against hope.

Hands on the side of his head, he tried to step back but I hung onto him, holding his wrists. "Maks, don't leave!"

His eyes closed, pain rippling across his face, his tone deepening past even Marsum's sound. "For that, I'm going to leave her to die now, boy. That's enough out of you. If you can't behave, you get nothing."

With a quick motion, he pulled one hand free, leaving me standing there, hanging onto his other wrist. His eyes were dark and his tone deepened once more. "I think I'll just kill you and be done with it. That will end his fight."

Despite the dark of the night, black mist swirled up around us. The magic of the Jinn raced around us, faster and faster, like a whirlwind of darkness even here in the heart of the night.

In the distance, a voice screamed my name, called for me, searching for me.

"Lila." I said her name but couldn't call back. The magic rushing between Marsum and me was too much, too thick, and it was choking me.

Of course, there was one more player in the mix. One I'd given up on.

"I think not today. We need her still." Maggi stepped into view, her gauzy skirts swirling up in a gust of wind, almost as if she still had her own magic.

The sound of something clicking, metallic and sharp, cut through the air and the black mist dissipated on a breath of the breeze.

The first thing I noticed was that the nausea was gone, and my body relaxed. Something shivered through me, soothing like honey on a throat raw from coughing, easing away the sick feeling, easing away the pain and fatigue until I was on my own two legs easily, standing there, hanging onto Marsum. His forehead pressed against mine, hands holding my face, thumbs tracing the curve of my cheeks. That was not Marsum.

"Maks?"

"He needs you. I'll do all I can to keep him in line," he whispered.

"Maks!" I yelled his name and grabbed him hard, the clinking of metal chains something I should really have paid attention to. "You have to fight! You have to fight him!"

He blinked once and then gave me a slow wink. "He can't fight me, pussy cat. And you won't kill me because he's in me. What a glorious conundrum. That being said, you need to die, I think. That will be the only way to keep him truly in line."

I took a step back, and before I could think better of it, I snapped a fist upward in a perfect uppercut, smashing it into his jaw. His blue eyes rolled back, and he slumped away from me to the ground. But I was going down with him, pulled along by the hand-cuffs connecting us.

Oh, shit.

"Maggi!" I yelled for her.

"ZAM!" Lila screamed my name and I looked up in time to see her dive-bombing me. She pulled up at the last second, blue and silver scales iridescent even in the night, small wings stretched as wide as they could go. "Holy sheep shit, where have you been? And who is this? Freaking hellfire on a candle stick, is that *Marsum?*"

Her words were rapid fire and I shushed her with a wave of my hand. Already an idea was forming now that my brain wasn't addled by the nausea that had taken me over so fully. Much as I wished this night was over already and I was sleeping in my bedroll next to Balder's feet, I knew that was more than a few hours off.

"Yes, that's Marsum, but Maks is in there too. He . . . saved me, Lila."

"No, *I* saved you." Maggi moved to stand in front of where I was crouched over Marsum.

"You handcuffed me to him. How the hell is that saving me?" I tugged up the hand attached to Marsum, cuff to cuff. "Seriously? Something in you thought this was a good idea?"

"Those cuffs connect you in more than a physical sense. They blend your magic and lives together. He wasn't wrong about the stone and the damage it was doing to you—I just didn't see it until he pointed it out—but leaning on his strength and power, you will survive. If you hurry." She smiled as though she thought I should thank her.

"Are you freaking kidding me?" I stared up at her, unable to fathom what had just happened. "He wanted to kill me. How will this," I held up my cuffed hand, "stop him now that he is literally within arm's reach from me and I can't get away?"

"Well, for one thing, he would die. And that would be the end of the Jinn masters. Such is the bond of those cuffs." Again, Maggi smiled, only this time, there was a hint of malice in the look.

Damn it, had this been her plan all along?

Lila was completely horrified if the way her mouth hung open—with nothing coming out despite the way her jaw flapped—was any indication.

My winged friend finally seemed to pull herself together.

"Oh." She dropped to the sand next to Marsum and jammed two claws up his nose, pulling on the nostrils. I batted her away and she pulled her claws out, and wiped them in his hair. "So, no cubs for you and Ford then, I guess? 'Cause I see that look on your face. I know it. You love him, of course. Even if he is a jerk right now."

I wanted to say I had a feeling there would be no cubs for me at all—ever. But for right now, I didn't need Marsum thinking I was useless to him too. I needed him to need and want me. To believe I had value to him.

"Maybe this is not the time for that discussion." I sat my butt in the sand there beside Marsum. Maks. Whoever he was.

"Marsum, looks like you're coming with us."

"WHAT?" Lila's screech lit the air, and the hair on

the back of my neck stood. I held up the hand cuffed to him and then pointed at Maggi. "You see her?"

Lila turned and then gave a quick nod. "Yeaaaaaah."

"I'd bet both horses that she's not taking these cuffs off until she gets what she wants. And she won't tell us what she wants, will she?" I quirked an eyebrow at my unlikely savior.

Maggi tipped her head in my direction. "Correct. The only way to find a path that will stop the Jinn is to keep him close."

I swallowed hard. Keeping him close was dangerous for a hell of a lot of reasons. Time to change directions a little.

"I'm guessing Ford is out looking for me too?"

"Yeah, he went another direction," Lila said. "Why?"

"Good. We're going to need to get our story straight before we see him." I touched the handcuffs and tugged at the chain that now attached me to Marsum and by default, Maks. "Because no matter how this goes, Ford is going to be pissed."

6

The only good thing I can say about Maggi having put one handcuff on the Jinn and attaching the other to me was the leverage it had given me for the uppercut I'd delivered. It kept him out cold for a few minutes so we could discuss what was going to happen.

I only hoped that when he woke, there would be no wrestling with him. I'd already tried to outmuscle Maks once, and it had ended with me on my back. That strength would still be there, even though Maks was not the one in control of the body.

Lila hopped around my feet, a seriously agitated dragon in miniature. "You have got to be kidding me. You want to take him with us? Why? I mean, I love the Toad, too, but we know he's not exactly in charge of this body." She pointed at him with the tip of one sharp little claw as I lifted his left hand to stare at the cuff around his wrist.

I twisted around to look at Maggi. "You aren't going to take them off, are you?"

She shook her head. "I didn't know why I made them, why my power chose that form. But when I saw him coming toward us, I knew their purpose. Magic is funny that way, sometimes it acts on its own for our best interest."

"Doubt it. I think you knew all along what you were making and why," Lila said. I agreed with her.

He moaned, stirring. We were almost out of time here. Even so, I answered Lila.

"I was dying, I think, and he did consider saving me, Lila. He needs me because he wants a child out of me. As long as that is the case, then he won't hurt me." I think. Maybe. Hopefully.

He'd seemed to truly want to stop me from dying —at least for a moment—and while Ollianna would have probably agreed to give him a child—seeing as that was what she wanted—I wasn't about to tell him that. I was the granddaughter of the Emperor, and that was a powerful bloodline the Jinn master wanted to take advantage of in the worst way possible. I just had to keep him from realizing there was a whole swamp of witches related to the Emperor. I grimaced at the thought of Maks with them, any of them.

Lila looked between me and Maggi. "Okay, so he

thought about saving you so he can knock you up and make cute little bastard Jinns, but that doesn't explain why you want to take him with you, with us. I hate to say it, but cut his arm off. It'll regrow and we'll be free." She leaned in and poked at the cuffs. A tiny spark of magic zapped her and she leapt back, hissing, her lips curled back over her teeth.

Marsum groaned again and lifted his hands to touch the underside of his chin, dragging my hand with him.

Maggi spoke quietly. "To be clear, whatever injury happens to one, happens to the other, little dragon, so hurting him will hurt your sister."

I wasn't sure that was true. My own chin felt just fine. I touched it to be sure, and found a bump there growing. Damn it. I was going to have to be careful about how I handled Marsum.

Lila snarled and dug her feet into the sand. "Lord, what fools these mortals be."

"*Midsummer Night's Dream.*" I gave her a tired smile. "And yeah, I'm probably being a fool."

Lila hissed. "Damn it all!"

I moved back as far as I could being attached to Marsum. I should have been freaking out, melting down, raging at being tied to him. Maybe I was getting older and wiser, but I could see that Maggi was doing what she was for a reason, even if she didn't know exactly how it was going to work out. I had been dying, that much I knew. And, now, I wasn't.

My body still tingled with the magic that connected Marsum and me, dampening the sickness that had raged through me only moments before. But for how long?

Lila flew up so we were face to face. "No, no, we need to get to Trick and Ollianna. She is part of our triad, remember? She is the one we are going to work with to make things happen that will bring Bryce back and stop the Emperor. How the hell are we going to drag dipshit along like this?"

I held a hand out to her, welcoming her to my shoulder. She landed lightly, still agitated if the shivering of her wings was any indication. "And!" she glared at Maggi, "just because you put handcuffs on him, how is that going to stop him from hurting us? I mean like me and Ford and anyone else?"

"They diminish his power, little one. They were made to completely shut a person's power away from them." Maggi sighed. "I foolishly thought they might be used on the Emperor. They can only be used once, though." There it was, she'd had an inkling as to what the cuffs would be used for.

Lila groaned. There was silence for half a beat before she flew off my shoulder and around my head to once more stare me in the eyes. "What the hell have you been doing tonight? Not hunting for dinner! I can't leave you alone for a second, can I?"

I laughed, because it was kinda funny in a twisted, warped world sense.

Marsum took that moment to sit up, one hand between his knees, his other hanging midair attached to me. He lowered that arm a little more so he stared at me over the links of the handcuffs.

"Really? I never would have pegged you for the kinky kind." He licked his lips, nerves showing.

I shrugged. "You aren't exactly trustworthy. Can't touch your magic, can you?"

"I could have saved you."

I pointed at him. "But you didn't. Maggi did." I pointed at her with my free hand.

She smiled at Marsum. "Hello, Davin."

Marsum's face contorted. "No."

Okay, now this was interesting. "You knew—"

She tipped her head at him as he stared up at her, shock written clearly on his face. "Marsum's uncle, I suppose. Cousin maybe? He was a friend of mine, fighting the pull of the jewel into the darkness the longest. When he was killed, it seemed to speed up the violence in all the jewels. Like a cascade effect."

The moon was on the downward spiral of setting and the urge to move, to get our feet going, was strong. "One last question." I turned to Maggi. "Did you know that Marsum would come to me?"

She shook her head, but her eyes didn't quite meet mine. "I did not."

Then how had . . . the answer came through my

74

now-clear skull in a crack of understanding. "Wait!" I held up a hand and the words poured out of me as I pointed at Marsum. "The falcon you were being carried off by after the Oracle's Haunt, it was being manipulated by Merlin, who was somehow in thrall to the Emperor. Let me guess, Merlin intercepted you somehow and sent you back this way?"

Those blue eyes narrowed. "He did. There was a woman with him."

That had to be Flora. So she'd gotten to Merlin in time to help him, and now they were meddling again. I couldn't help the tight smile as I snapped my fingers. "Damn you, Merlin. What are you up to now?"

The reasons behind Merlin's actions were rarely clear, but it looked like he was in his own way trying to help me make it through this journey I was on—at least that was what I believed. I paced back and forth in front of Marsum, dragging his arm with me, thinking fast. I could see no way out of this.

"Okay, fine. Let's go."

"You are kidding me," Lila said, doing her own version of pacing as she circled my head. "Please tell me . . ."

"Look, do you see him doing any magic? Trying to kill either of us?" I pointed at Marsum.

Lila turned her back to him. "He was a brute to me. And he called me names."

75

"I know, but he can't do anything." I turned my back to him too, as if to prove a point.

He snorted and a hand slid over my ass, his fingers tightening on my cheek. I reached back and grabbed his fingers as hard as I could. The smile on his face said it all. He wasn't in the least bothered by coming with us. Maybe he even wanted to.

What if he and Maggi were somehow working together? Sweet baby goddess, I just didn't know.

"Excellent," Maggi said, a smile on her lips. "Let us go."

I twisted Marsum's hand and turned him toward our camp. There would be no dinner tonight, but we could sleep and be on our way in only a few hours. Already, the energy I'd been missing the last few days was coming back, and I was ready to move. Ready to get to the crossroads, to Ollianna and Trick, and then on to the Wyvern's Lair.

I had shit to do, and very little time to do it in.

The three of us walked and Lila perched herself on my shoulder. The campfire wasn't far ahead. Not far enough indeed.

Because once we were there, I was going to have to explain to Ford that not only was Marsum coming with us, but so was Maggi. I grimaced, thinking about how we were going to manage that conversation. Then again, Ford was not Steve. He would likely just take what I said and be good with it. That was how he did things.

Already I was planning how this would work. Ford would have to stay in his lion form. I'd have to ride with Marsum on Balder and Maggi would ride Batman.

Nobody was going to be happy with this new setup.

We walked together up and down the rolling dunes for fifteen minutes, maybe a little longer before Lila broke the silence, echoing my earlier thoughts. "Ford is not going to be happy about this. None of it."

I shrugged, knowing she was right. "Ford is not in charge."

"Lover's spat already?" Marsum said. "Terrible start to a new relationship. It won't last; I can tell you that."

Lila shook her head, then ducked her mouth close to my ear to whisper. "I will back you up on taking the two of them along, you know that, but I'm afraid of what will happen if *he* gets loose. And it will happen. You know it as well as I do."

"He can't," I said, without hesitation. "If that happens . . . there is only one answer."

We'd run. There was no way we could stop Marsum with all his knowledge and power. I was pretty sure Lila thought I meant I'd try to kill him, but I didn't want to share my body with all those miserable Jinn masters either.

"As long as we are in agreement," she said.

"We are." I sighed. "But right now, I'm exhausted."

"That's because you are still fighting the power that is trying to eat you from the inside out," Marsum said.

"How do you know that?"

"I have the knowledge of the Jinn masters at my fingertips. I know a great deal more than anyone realizes."

Maggi lifted a hand, drawing my attention to her. "He is correct. There were several before Marsum, and they all had great knowledge. Including Davin."

Marsum grunted. "Davin is not in charge now, any more than Maks is."

"That does not mean I cannot appreciate him," Maggi snapped. "He was a good friend."

"You were not *friends,*" Marsum drawled and I choked on nothing. Sweet cherry pie, that was information I wasn't sure I ever would have guessed. Maggi had a fling with a Jinn master?

I wanted to ask to be sure I was hearing this right —curiosity and the cat and all that shit.

The conversation might have gone on but for one itty bitty thing.

To my right came the sound of big cat pads running across the sand, and through my bond to the pride I was the alpha of, I could feel Ford as he approached. Worried and then furious as he caught a glimpse of Marsum next to me. I couldn't really see him in the darkness. There was just a shifting of movement as his dark body rushed us. As an extremely rare black lion, the night was a perfect camouflage for him as it was for me in my cat form.

I stepped up and blocked him from tackling Marsum at the last second, putting my cuffed hand on the captive and holding the other out to Ford. "No, he's bound and can't hurt any of us. Stand down."

Marsum burst out laughing. "Oh, the blinders of the naïve. It's quite something to see up close and personal. Stand down, what a crock of shit."

Ford shifted from four legs to two in a blur, which, of course, also left him completely naked. Not necessarily a bad thing seeing as he was built like most male lions, well-muscled and stacked with not an ounce of extra fat on him. He pressed toward me to get closer to Marsum.

"He's not Maks anymore, and you know it!" Ford snarled the words, the testosterone in the air thick like an old lady's flowered perfume. I pushed him back, easily, as he didn't try to use his size and weight against me like my ex-husband Steve would have.

Time to be the grownup here, the alpha, the reasonable one. Even if inside I was freaking out a little. "I know. But he's bound with these handcuffs . . ." I held up my hand that was literally attached to Marsum, "and his life is tied to mine now. You hurt him, it hurts me and vice versa. I would have died had Maggi not done this. Also, say hello to Maggi."

Ford took a step back and then forward again, his eyes darting to me and then to Marsum, then sliding to Maggi. He'd never met the Ice Witch, so there was no recognition from him. His emotions were all over the map, but at the front of them all was fear. He was afraid for me.

Damn it.

"And if he breaks the handcuffs?" Ford snapped. "What then? He's letting this happen for a reason. I don't care who made the cuffs!"

"If he breaks them, then I will deal with him," I said. "Everyone does what they do for their own purposes, Ford. I'm not stupid. I know what he wants from me. You'd do best to remember that. And the cuffs are magic. Maggi slapped them on us, and it *saved my life*." He needed to get that through his head, that I would be dead if not for the cuffs.

Ford held his hands up and then slowly dropped them to his sides. "This is not happening. It can't be. This is ridiculous. A damn nightmare!"

"It's happening," I said, knowing with those two words I was hurting him. Something I didn't want to do, but I was anyway.

Goddess, I was an asshole.

To be fair, I was in the same boat as Marsum. I didn't have a choice with the cuffs on.

But I . . . almost didn't mind, because it meant that

maybe I had a better chance at getting Maks back. And it was easier than telling Ford I didn't want him the way he wanted me.

I tugged on our cuffed hands, pulling Marsum toward the camp. We weren't far now, only a hundred feet or so. The fire had been banked and had only a faint glow in the darkness, and the horses stood sleeping with their heads down, their forms just barely visible against the dim embers of the low burning coals.

I slowed my feet as just the faintest of smells caught me by surprise. I grabbed the back of Marsum's belt and pulled him to a stop as he tried to pass me. Ford moved to my other side, scenting the air the same as me.

There was something—or had been something—checking out our camp.

Humans.

That couldn't be right. "Ford, you smelling that?"

"Yeah, that's weird." He looked at me and I gestured with my chin for him to move ahead of us. Tied to Marsum as I was, fighting would be tough. Humans, this far out and away from the wall? That was beyond strange. And strange was rarely good in my traveling of this world. Strange meant that something was up, something that could kill us.

Maggi dropped back a little. "Lila, watch her," I said.

Marsum said nothing, but I could feel him flexing

against the cuff, testing it. I stopped and waited for Ford to clear the campground. He did a few passes around, wider and wider, then finally waved for us to come in. "All clear. Whoever it was just passed through. They didn't even touch anything."

Not that we were afraid of humans, but they were, on a good day, unpredictable. They often carried weapons that evened the playing field against any supernatural. A bullet could kill any of us as surely as a spelled arrow, or a well-placed knife. I'd heard rumors that on the other side of the wall that separated us from the main human populations were weapons like we'd never seen.

As we approached, Ford tugged on a pair of pants, shirt, and boots and set to getting the fire going higher, not that we had anything to cook over it.

"Dried jerky again," I said. "Sorry about that. Between Maggi and this one, I've been preoccupied."

There was no response from Ford. Hell, he didn't even look my way. Another time I would have said he had every right to be pissed off at me, every right to hold me to task. But not tonight. Not with Maks's life on the line here, or mine for that matter. Not with Maggi having done what she'd done. Hell, I didn't even have it in me to be mad at her.

"Ford, are you going to walk around sulking all night?" I asked.

Marsum chuckled. "Oh, this is going to go well. Why not just kick him in the balls while he's down?

You just brought the body of the love of your life back to camp. What's he supposed to think? And rightfully so."

I didn't look at Marsum, but instead kept my eyes on Ford. His back slowly stiffened, and he turned to look at me, the hurt in his eyes etched there as if I'd tattooed it. And now I felt like even more of a shit. I slumped a little where I stood. "Ford—"

"I'm going to get us something to eat. I'm tired of jerky." He turned away from the fire and stalked out into the darkness. His emotions came through loud and clear to me through our pride bond. Anger, hurt, confusion, love.

Damn it, that last one would be the death of me. I was sure of it.

"You don't have a real soft touch, do you? I'll give you that. You're a classic Jinn and a right bitch when you want to be." Marsum sat against one of the saddles, stretched out his legs and crossed them at the ankles. He lifted his arms up and behind him so that his biceps flexed as he cupped the back of his head, dragging me a little closer.

I arched a brow, choosing to ignore him and his words that were meant to be weapons. "That move work on the ladies?"

"With Maks's body, yes." He grinned and there was nothing in my mind but an image of Maks in bed with Nell, taking his pleasure with her. I wasn't sure if I was seeing something real or just a picture that my own head made up.

I took a step in his direction, hands fisted at my sides before I could catch myself. Lila zipped in front of me, holding her little clawed hands up, waving them rapidly. "He's doing this on purpose. He's pushing your buttons. Already."

"Easy buttons to push, just like yours," Marsum drawled, the words thick as though he were tired.

I forced my fingers to relax as I stood there, breathing through a combination of rage and hurt that was thick enough to choke me. I counted in my head to ten, then twenty, then to thirty before I was able to move properly again.

"Maggi," Lila turned her head to the witch, "why did you really do this? It can't just be out of the goodness of your ice-cold heart."

Marsum's blue eyes slid to the tiny dragon as she landed on my shoulder and dug her claws into my scalp. Her idea of a massage was not the same as mine, but I said nothing as she raked my skin as gently as she could in what could only be an attempt to soothe me.

"I'd be curious as to the answer myself," Marsum said. "You are not known for being helpful, at least not without your own reasons."

I wasn't sure that I liked Marsum agreeing with me.

Maggi spread her too big for traveling skirts and

sat on the sand, crossing her legs beneath her body. The firelight flickered, dancing over her pale skin. "Her bloodline alone is worth saving. And there is something she needs you for yet, I believe."

"What do you mean she needs me?" Marsum rubbed at the back of his head, a move I'd seen Maks do how many times as we sat across the campfires as we traveled to the Witch's Reign? Too many to count and it tugged at my heart strings.

"I bound your lives together. That's how I stopped the magic from eating her. That being said, it will only last a short time before it will start destroying you both. At that point, if you haven't found what you need in order to expel the destructive magic from her body, you will both die. But I have faith that at least Zam will survive." Her eyes lifted to mine and I didn't like what I saw there—that Maks would take all the magic into himself to save me. As clearly as if she'd spoken, the truth hovered between us.

"Well, that's comforting." I stood next to Marsum, not really sure what to do with myself. Did I sit next to him? Did I smash him in the head and knock him out again?

Did I kiss him and hope love was enough to break the spell like some fairy tale?

"Nope," I said and everyone looked at me. "Never mind. Just talking to myself."

"Is that the magic making you crazy?" Lila asked.

"Nope, just my own head." I sat as far from

85

Marsum as I could get, which left our arms reaching for one another.

He laughed and yanked me to him so hard that I ended up in his lap, straddling him. "This is far more comfortable."

"Doubt it, by the way the front of your pants are stretched, Toad," Lila drawled.

I shoved myself off Marsum. "Oh my gods. Keep it in your pants, man."

"A comedy of errors, perhaps. I shall amuse myself with watching you two dance around the ties that bind you together," Maggi said, and I could hear the smile in the words.

"This is not fucking funny!" I snapped.

Lila snickered. Even Marsum snorted, his lips turning up in a wry grin. Not funny, this was a damn mess.

A shout broke the brief moment of silence. Loud, sharp, and not anyone from around the fire.

I froze where I was, half crouched. "That was a human."

Marsum pushed to his feet, the chain between us tugging me toward him again. "Where is your lion?"

I reached for my connection to Ford and found him a couple miles away already. He was moving awfully fast for being on foot. Two feet, to be exact, and supposedly hunting. But what I got from him through our pride bond was that he was *asleep.* That made no sense.

"What the . . ." I blinked, not sure what I was feeling was right, because how could Ford be asleep and moving that fast?

He couldn't.

Which meant someone had him under a spell.

7

"Lila, someone has Ford." I ran for the saddle Marsum stood next to, dragging him with me. I grabbed it and the saddle pad and threw them both onto Balder's back in a single motion.

"Marsum, be a dear and saddle up Batman." I stretched out my arm attached to him. With the horses this close together, he could do it. Awkward, but doable.

"I don't know horses."

"Maks did, so let him do it," I snapped. I didn't have time for this. No matter what happened between Ford and me, he was still part of my pride, and mine to protect. For him to be moving away from us that fast, and be *asleep,* there was no other answer except that he had been snatched by someone. Or something. The list was long and didn't only include ophidians, giants, mages, gorcs, hyenas, sand wraiths, another Jinn, or Goddess knew what else.

On a normal day, it took me less than thirty seconds to get Balder ready, kick dirt over the campfire, and be up in the saddle. But not tonight. Every time I tried to do something, my hand attached to Marsum was pulled.

Lila sat clinging to the base of Balder's neck, watching, clicking her tongue. "Another time I'd laugh my little ass off, but this is pitiful. Work together."

I looked across to see Marsum finishing tacking up Batman. Maggi approached him. "Thank you, I will ride this one."

Which meant Marsum and I were riding together on Balder. Damn it. He could take our weight, but it would be better if I were smaller, as in my four-legged form. "Maggi, can I shift while cuffed?"

"Not yet," she said.

Not yet? I didn't want to waste time asking her just what she meant. "Mount up." I pointed to Balder and gave Marsum a tug in my direction. He winked at me. "Any time."

A tongue-in-cheek response rolled to the front of my mouth but Lila leapt across the small space between us and smacked the top of my head before winging away.

"No flirting with the prisoner," she said. *"He's not Maks."*

I bit back the words and put my foot into the stirrup to mount behind Marsum. "Right. Let's go."

Balder leapt into a ground-covering canter, and Batman did the same as if tied to us by a string. Maggi rode easily, and Batman didn't seem bothered by her.

"Why are you being so well behaved exactly?" Lila asked as we rode into the night. "I mean, you are a Jinn master, a bow-to-no-one kind of satyr's ass. What gives?" She flew around us, doing her trademark barrel rolls. Those rolls, the flashy moves, were her tic. She only did them when she was anxious or stressed.

Marsum didn't look at her as he spoke. "I don't have to answer you."

"Answer her," I snapped. "You answer her as if I asked the question."

He grimaced and miracle of miracles, he did answer. And more than a few pieces of the puzzle fell into place.

"I don't know."

Maggi laughed. "You two are quite something to watch, but let me fill in the blanks." She cleared her throat. "The handcuffs are spelled, connecting you in more ways than the obvious physical one. The copper cuff that he wears makes it so he can't use his magic except to protect you, Zamira, and he must follow wherever you go until either he is released by you, or he dies. The black cuff you wear makes you the master."

He shot a glare at her and Maggi smiled right back. "And you must obey her as if she were your literal master, Jinn. That is what you get. What you deserve." I felt like she was jabbing him for something we didn't understand.

I about fell out of the saddle if not for the fact that I clung to his back.

I had a Jinn in my back pocket with enough power that he could make even Merlin wary. "So, he has to tell me the truth about anything I ask of him?"

The grimace on his face deepened and he shook his head once as if fighting not to answer.

Maggi laughed softly. "Yes. Ask away."

Three little words that changed everything.

"Hell, yeah!" I pumped a fist into the air. "Come on, *Pet*, let's go find our lion!"

Lila burst out laughing. "Pet, can I call him that too?"

"No," he said even as I said, "Sure thing."

"Pet. Oh my goddess, I think I might pee myself." Lila barrel rolled right in front of him and then swept back to land on the front of my saddle.

"We are going to have a long conversation when we stop," I said.

He didn't answer. I didn't care.

For the first time since I'd stepped out of the Stockyards and headed to the Witch's Reign to save Darcy, I was going to get some answers straight out of a person who could actually answer them. A person who held hundreds of years of answers *in his damn head*.

I leaned into his back and eased my heels into Balder's side, urging him forward. Up ahead was movement in the dark. Several figures I could just make out. Horses and riders, a large black lion in the middle of them. Ford had shifted? That was all well and good, but still didn't answer how he could be running and fast asleep.

"Someone spelled him," Maggi said. "That's how."

"You in my head?"

"I can see the question on your face. You don't hold your cards to your chest well; I don't recommend you ever play poker," she said.

Not the first time I'd been told that. I settled back and reached for the shotgun in its sheath under my leg. No need for the flail here. These were the humans we'd been smelling earlier. I was sure of it. But how the hell had they snagged Ford, convinced him to shift into four legs and then go with them? The whole situation was crazy to me. A spell, to be sure. But what human had a spell like that? None that I knew.

"Hey, shit heads!" I yelled as we drew close. The four horsemen spun, startled if their wide eyes and freaked out horses were any indication. "You got something of mine there. I want him back."

Marsum turned Balder so we were sideways, and I could look the humans in the eyes as well as sight down the barrel of the gun.

"No, the lion belongs to the goddess of the desert," the man closest to me said. I frowned, recognizing him even in the dark with his shining bald patch and bug eyes.

"Gerry? What in the actual hell are you doing here?" Gerry had been one of the humans in the Stockyards, one of Ish's slaves . . . Oh shit. "Oh, no you don't. She can't have him." I lifted the shotgun and pointed it at Gerry's chest. "Not happening."

The click of weapons being cocked filled the air and three other guns were lifted, pointed right back at me. I didn't move. "Gerry, Ishtar is not having him. Over my dead body are you taking Ford. And we both know who will come out of this alive, and it ain't going to be you."

"Zamira, please. I don't have a choice," he whispered, his hands raised in surrender. "She has my wife and children. I can't go back without a lion. She swore she'd kill them. Please, you of all of the shifters understand family."

The pain in his voice was real, and I knew he had a family. I'd seen them together. Seen him throw his daughter into the air, to catch her squealing with laughter. "You can't take Ford," I said, but I couldn't help the lack of conviction in my own voice.

"Ford would not want you to kill a family," Marsum said. "Would he?"

I whipped around to stare at him. "Why would *you* care what Ford wants?" Of course, the second I said it, I knew the answer. Ford was in the way. Ford would try to stop Marsum from fucking me at every possible turn.

Ford held a piece of my heart, and even as small as it was, that was enough to make him competition.

"I agree, you must let the lion go," Maggi said as she and Batman caught up to us. "His path diverges from yours now. His fate is not yours."

"No." I shook my head. "No, Gerry, we will figure out a way to make this work, so that you and your kids will be safe—"

Marsum laughed, cutting me off. "We have limited time before you and I die, and now you want to add dealing with Ishtar to the list? You are a fool. She will wait for you, injured as she is."

My grip on the shotgun slid and I slowly lowered my weapon. "Gerry, what does she want with him?"

He looked to the other three men first before answering. All of them I recognized, even if I wasn't sure of their names.

"She's collecting the lions. She's hurt real bad, I think, like Maks says." Gerry shook his head and made a motion for the others to lower their weapons too. I looked past him to the humans I knew from the Stockyards. All enslaved to Ishtar. Though for years that was not what I'd been told, and I felt a fool for believing anything that ever came out of that bitch's mouth.

"I'm surprised she's not dead," Marsum muttered.

"Close." Gerry tipped his head at Marsum. "She came home barely alive on the back of Steve."

A moment of shocked silence was about all I could hold onto.

"STEVE?" His name burst out of me. "*Steve* is helping her?"

Gerry shrunk away from my violent outburst. "I don't know exactly for sure. You know she tells us very little. We saw her ride in on his back, flat out as if she were dead. Next day, Darcy came back, then Kiara with some others I didn't know."

Panic clawed at me. Ishtar had my entire pride. She had them all. How had I not known?

The only answer was she'd blocked me from feeling them. I reached for Kiara through my connection to her. Even at a distance, I should have been able to pinpoint her, to tell if she was injured or not.

I got nothing.

"That fucking bitch," I growled under my breath, anger rising through me like a growing storm.

"She'll syphon off their strength until she is at full capacity again," Marsum said. "It's what I would do if I were hurt like she is."

Like shit all over my clothes, there was no way to get out of this situation without getting covered in

more of it. I looked at Lila for some sort of sugges-
tion, and for a moment wished that my crazy uncle
Shem were there. But of course, he was with Kiara
and the others, being syphoned off by Ishtar.

"You don't have time to save them and yourself,"
Marsum said. "We have time—maybe—to get a stone,
and then if you survive that, you can save your pride
later. That is the only way to do this."

"Don't you even dare think you are going to tell
me there is only one way to do this!" I snapped, and
the humans cringed. I worked to get my emotions
under control. Freaking out would do no good for
anyone. Certainly not for my family.

Maggi sighed and moved Batman up, so she was
well within my line of vision. "We do not always like
the choices in front of us, Zam. That does not mean
we can avoid making a decision. These men's families
are depending on them. You must choose now."

The string of profanities that escaped me flowed
like a river on a downhill slope. The alpha in me
wanted to race toward Ishtar and fight her for my
pride, to save them.

"Goddess damn it all! That's what she's banking
on." The realization was painful and so sharp that I
might as well have been stabbed with a knife in the
belly.

"Lila?" Just her name, but she knew what I
wanted; I was sure of it. I knew the answer already,
but I had to be sure and she was my second-in-

command, sister of my heart, and I trusted her more than anyone else in my life.

"I hate to say it, but I don't think either of them are wrong." Her mouth twisted as if she were about to spit acid from agreeing with Marsum. "You can't save our pride if you are sick, if you are dying. Whatever is wrong with you, we have to fix that first. And if you go after Ishtar at half speed, she'll have you for sure."

"We have to go," Gerry said, all but jigging in his saddle. "I really am sorry, Zam. I just can't risk my family. She has a time limit on us."

I held up a hand, stopping him. "I know. Let me say goodbye to him. At least give me that much." I slid off Balder's back, tugging Marsum along behind me, and went to Ford. "Marsum. Wake him up."

A strangled growl escaped Marsum before a pale blue mist wrapped around Ford, tightening and then sliding into his jet-black fur. Ford growled and shook his head, his eyes clearing quickly. I stepped into his line of vision and his eyes locked on me. "Zam? What's happening?"

I cupped his face, waiting for the last of the sleep to fade from his golden eyes. He blinked a few times and then butted his head against mine.

"Zam, what are you doing here?"

I forced a hard swallow down my tight throat. "Listen to me, Ford, and listen carefully. I need you to go with these humans."

His jaw dropped. "Wait, these shits? They threw a *pre-made* spell at me!"

"I know they did." Goddess, I hated that I was sending him away, because despite knowing he wasn't the one for me, I cared for him deeply. He was family. He was my enforcer, and I wanted him to be safe. And I felt safer with him around. "Ishtar has our entire pride. She has Steve and Darcy, too, and she is syphoning off their strength to heal herself."

I paused and looked at Marsum. "How long do you think it might take?" To get the stone, to get back to the Stockyards, all of it. I didn't say it, but he knew. Damn him, even with Marsum in charge, he knew me too well.

"A couple weeks," he said. "Assuming it all goes as planned. Which with you is—"

"Shut it," I snapped.

I tightened my hold on Ford's face, forcing him to keep me in his line of sight even with Marsum beside us. "I need you to go with them. I need you to be in the Stockyards and I need you to protect Kiara and the cubs. Ishtar will draw from them and you are strong enough to stand in their place." Goddess of the desert, I was asking him to lay his life on the line for them.

"No, my place is with you," he growled.

My jaw ticked. "Your place is where I ask you to be for the safety of this pride. You will go with the humans or I will have them spell you again. I will come for you all as soon as I can." I stood and took a step back, right into Marsum. He slid his hands up to my shoulders.

"You lose, lion."

Crap on a cactus, this was going to bite me in the ass.

Ford snarled and lunged forward. I shook my head. "Stop, he's taunting you on purpose!"

The lion's shoulders slumped, all the fight going out of him. He'd lost this round. We all knew it. "This is not right. You aren't safe with him."

"I'll spit acid on him if he acts up," Lila said, dropping a barrel roll in front of Ford as she spoke. I pushed backward, forcing Marsum to take a step or stumble. I yanked my hand down so at least one of his hands was off my shoulder.

I walked back to Balder, keeping my hands to my sides so I wouldn't touch Marsum even by accident. "Go with them, Ford. I will be there as soon as I can."

"You're just doing this because he's here," Ford snarled. I turned to face him as he spun on his haunches, his body tensed for a lunge. I looked to Gerry and nodded.

With a flick of his wrist, the human lobbed a round sticky-looking ball at Ford, hitting him square on his shoulders. The black lion blinked once, then bowed his head, turned and trotted away to the west without so much as another growl.

"We didn't have any thought you'd be here," Gerry said. "I have to tell her I saw you."

"You do that," I said. "And tell her I'm coming for my pride."

Marsum mounted Balder first, and I followed suit, ignoring the hurt in my heart, ignoring the sting in my eyes as we turned my horse to the south. "Seeing as we're all so freaking wide awake, let's go."

"Pithy as always," Marsum muttered.

Lila landed on Balder's saddle once more. "I'm sorry. I know you care for him."

"Don't want to talk about it."

Because just like that Ford was gone, and I was stuck with Marsum. Marsum who held Maks in thrall.

Maggi and Batman trotted along behind us, not a single word sliding from her.

Was this what Merlin had wanted all along when he sent Marsum back toward us in the falcon's talons? Did he think I'd figure out how to save Maks if I was *literally* stuck with him? I snorted to myself. Merlin had never liked Maks, and had, in fact, encouraged me to stay away from him, had warned me that the man I thought was a human was more than he looked to be.

I frowned, thinking about the possibilities. Maybe Merlin thought I could do something to stop Marsum. At the very least, he had the final stone with him. I could make him give it to me.

Only I didn't want to. As soon as I took that last stone, the wall that held the line between supernaturals and the human world would come down, and with the falling of that wall, the Emperor would be free. That was what I'd been told, at least.

This—this whole goddess damned journey—was not going as I'd planned. In a matter of an hour, I'd been handcuffed to one man who'd as soon kill me as fuck me, and sent away another who would lay his life down for mine and never ask anything of me but to love him. The worst part? I wasn't sure that it was the right choice either, despite what my heart wanted to say.

My head was much more reasonable about the situation. I rubbed a hand over my face as the horses trotted along. They, at least, were happy enough to be moving despite the late hour. My stomach grumbled loudly, and I pulled out some jerky, chewing on it, handing some to Lila as she swept by, and basically just doing what I had to do to keep moving.

"Do you even know where you are going?" Marsum asked over the steady cadence of the horses' hooves on the ground. We were able to skirt some of the worst of the dunes which meant we were on hard-packed dirt instead of sliding through the loose sand.

"South, toward the crossroads," I said. "It'll take us just under two weeks to get there, so get ready for some serious saddle sores on your ass."

Maggi caught Batman up to me and Balder so we were side by side.

"I am going to suggest a third horse," she said. "I do believe that would be prudent."

"Great, but the two of us are still stuck together." I held up my hand that was still very much attached to Marsum.

"Just like old times," Lila whispered, burrowing deeper into the folds of my cloak on my lap between me and Marsum until just her violet eyes peered out, tiny jewels that caught the light of the stars.

I tapped Marsum on the shoulder. "So, tell me then, Jinn master, where do *you* think we are going?"

His answer was without hesitation. "The Blackened Market. It's the only place we'll have a chance to get a stone that can contain the power you sucked down like the foolish git that you are. And I suspect that's what this one," he motioned a thumb at Maggi, "wanted all along. One more stone she can steal." His words were sharp and sounded less and less like Marsum's voice even.

I shrugged. "Nope, we can't. There is only two weeks minus two days until the third golden moon, and we are going to be at those crossroads in time for it." That was what the Oracle had said, and that was what we were doing.

"You'll be dead before then," Maggi said. "He is right. The Blackened Market is our best chance."

"Her being dead is fine by me at this point,"

Marsum said, his voice dipping low. Damn him and his moody moods. First, he wanted to bed me, then kill me, then laugh at me.

I slowed Balder just by shifting my seat, and Batman followed suit. Good boy that he was. Batman, that is, not Marsum.

"Right, because you'll just let me die?" I asked, and he nodded. I smiled and lifted my wrist, which lifted his wrist. "You sure about that?"

He looked down at the cuffs and muttered a string of profanities that made me grin. Maggi was a freaking brilliant genius. If I ignored the point he made about her wanting a stone. For now, I was ignoring that. Marsum had no choice but to keep me alive. I lived, he lived. I died, he died.

"Yeah, that's what I thought."

8

The four of us rode south for another couple hours, moving slowly seeing as I made Marsum dismount and walk beside Balder. My horse didn't need to be packing us both all the time.

"Enough of this shit," Marsum growled as the sun began its slow rise on the eastern horizon. "Maggi, you can make this bond ethereal, can you not?"

Maggi sighed. "Wait for the sun to hit the chains."

I raised my eyebrows. "What?"

"I like my quirks when it comes to spells," she said with a shrug. "Did you not see that with my pets? Under the light of the first day wearing them, your chains will fade."

The sun rolled over the horizon and as the light hit us, the handcuffs just flat out dissolved. Marsum stumbled away and rubbed his wrist. I touched my own wrist, but it felt as though the band was still there. Just softer somehow. I squinted and could still see the faint outline of the metal on my wrist. Apparently Marsum did not see that same mark.

He grabbed Maggi, yanked her from the saddle, and leapt onto Batman.

"Hey!" I yelled and Lila zipped toward him.

He was barely in the saddle when he booted Batman and they leapt forward, running hard though Batman tried to turn around and come back to us.

I moved to follow but Maggi stopped me with a wave of her hand and a short, sharp laugh.

"Why are you laughing?"

"He's about to get a shock." She laughed again. "I have not had this much fun in years. Just you wait and see."

"Shouldn't we go after him?" I asked even though part of me didn't want to. Riding behind him, feeling the heat off his body and everything about him was still Maks, right down to the smell rolling off him. We'd lost Ford, Marsum was gone, and we still had enormous tasks ahead of us. I could have used some Jinn magic on hand for the tight spots I knew were coming.

Because let's be honest, me and my black cat luck were not exactly known for being stellar at the best of times.

"No, he'll be back. You'll see," Maggi said, her eyes staring after Marsum and Batman.

I cleared my throat, trying to put what we faced into perspective. "Look, the Blackened Market is practically on the way to the crossroads. We'll go hard and see if we can't get there and get the stone and deal with this." I motioned to my body with a wave of my hand up and down. "But the farther south we go, the worse the heat is going to be, so we're better off to travel at night if we can, and sleep during the day. Which means we need somewhere to hunker down for the day. As in right now." I looked around, hoping for a cluster of trees, or a bunch of rocks, or something that would act as a shelter.

And then I looked at Maggi. "Can you help us out here with a little magic shelter maybe?"

"No, I have literally no power left to me. Knowledge is all I can offer now."

Great. I was packing a two-legged library with me. One full of riddles.

A yell cut through the air and Batman and Marsum blasted by us at full speed as he cursed rapidly in several languages by the sounds of it.

I cringed to the side. "What is he doing?"

Lila shot into the air. "What's happening?"

"He's on a tether." Maggi giggled. She damn well giggled. "He can only get so far from you before the tether begins to tighten on him, drawing him back to your side. Did you not notice him riding in a circle around us?"

I hadn't. I'd been too busy looking for somewhere to rest for the day.

Another loop around us and Marsum pulled Batman to a halt next to us. "Stupid horse won't leave you."

Now it was my turn to laugh. "Oh, please. He's better trained than you are. We need a shelter, and there's nothing on hand. As you can see."

He glared down at me. "I am not a *slave* to do your bidding."

I grinned up at him. "I beg to differ. *Pet*."

Lila snickered and covered her mouth with her tiny claws. "Being her slave what should you do but tend, upon the hours, and times of her desire? You have no precious time at all to spend; nor services to do till she require."

"Boom, that's a good one," I said, racking my brain. Not an insult, so I wasn't quite as familiar. "Sonnet 57?"

"Damn, I can't stump you," Lila said. "I'm going to find one, just you wait!"

I pointed at a smooth, flat area. "Make us a tent big enough for the horses to stand in too."

Rage flickered like a storm across his face, his eyes darkening to a jet black before they faded once more to the blue I knew so well. "Heaven would that she these gifts should have, and I to live and die her slave." He bowed from the waist, slowly straightening, his eyes never leaving mine, raking me from toe to crown.

I swallowed hard, unable to tell him which play it was. Because this was a game Lila and I had played with Maks. Not Marsum, and my voice was lost to me.

He curled his hands out in front of him, snapped his fingers on his left hand . . . and nothing happened. He frowned, made a flicking motion with one wrist as if he were trying to light a fire, but again there was no response.

I rolled my eyes. "That's it? That's all you've got?"

"This makes no sense," he growled, staring at his hands as if they'd offended him greatly.

Maggi lifted a finger, her mouth pursing slightly, like a grimace she didn't want to show. "I believe this might be a quirk I didn't perceive for the cuffs. You, Zam, are not in immediate danger. You aren't even afraid. So he can't use his magic. At least that is what I put into it. As a precaution. I thought I would lock him to me, but it was far more interesting to put one cuff on each of you."

My mouth dropped open and Marsum spoke for both of us as the truth was laid out.

"Fuck off!" He roared the words, dismounted and tried again with his wrist flicking for the magic. If it weren't for the fact that we were going to get fried by the heat of the sun, it would have been funny to watch him wave his hands around and produce nothing.

Who was I kidding? Shit, it was funny. I grinned. I was going to die one day, laughing my ass off. "Keep trying. You look constipated."

He stopped moving and stared at me, then to Maggi, his voice deepening. "You two, you *both* did this to me."

I nodded and winked. "You know what? Even being tied to you like this, seeing you all ragey and mad, I'd do it again. Hell, I'd put the cuffs on us myself. You bet your ass I would. Mount up, we have to keep moving until we find shade, seeing as you can't *erect* a single thing."

Lila belly laughed, grabbing at her sides. "Oh, snap, you didn't!"

He threw a fit, kicking the sand and yelling at the sky. And while amusing, it was wasting time. "I said, mount up!" I yelled at him, and he moved as if I'd lashed him.

He mounted Batman and I motioned for Maggi to ride with me on Balder. Things were better that way in my mind. Better because of . . . reasons. Like a hard chest, and a body I wanted to touch a little too much, a little too close.

Reasons like wanting to bury my nose against his neck and bite down on the muscles along his shoulder while he did the same to me. Yeah. Reasons.

Maggi rode behind me, and I was sure I saw her

smirk when I glanced back at her.

That smirk wouldn't last, not with the way the sun heated the world exponentially with each passing minute.

We rode in silence all day, finally finding a small stand of shrubby trees that gave meager shade.

Four days we rode in almost silence, or at least silence from Maggi and Marsum. Lila and I spoke as we always did. We managed to ride at night for the most part and find shelter for the worst of the day's heat. Not ideal, but it was what we had.

Maggi's dress stayed impossibly clean and lovely.

I was sweat and dirt-covered as was Marsum. I tried not to look at him, tried not to feel him there, just a few feet away from me and think about all the things I wanted to do with Maks. Damn my libido, maybe I was coming into a fertile stretch or something because the images of rolling across the sand with him played over and over in my head.

Or maybe they were his thoughts? I couldn't tell. Maybe I didn't want to know if it was him or me.

On the fifth day out, Lila stretched out across Balder's rump, soaking in the heat. "I don't know what the dragons were thinking making their home in the cold north. This is glorious."

"The Jinn held this land first, and they don't share any better than the dragons," Marsum said. He rode a few strides behind us, but as I turned to look at him, it was obvious that he was still trying to make his magic work—as he had for the last few days—with no success. I had him here, literally at my mercy, and I needed to make the best of the time. No more silence, it was time to talk.

I twisted in the saddle, using my hood to shade my eyes from the sun. "I want you to tell me about the Jinn. What are their weaknesses?"

He froze in the saddle, his eyes widening. "I . . ."

"Oh yeah, get him, Zam!" Lila giggled. "Maybe he'll give you Maks back if you pester him with enough questions." She lowered her voice to a wicked whisper. "*All the secrets, Jinn.*"

Marsum's jaw flexed over and over as he worked to get the answer out. "The surest way to kill a Jinn is to take their head."

"Not what I asked," I said. "I asked what are their *weaknesses*. I'm aware of the decapitation rule when it comes to killing them."

I thought he was going to throw up all over poor Batman.

"Different for every Jinn." His mouth turned down into a hard frown.

That actually made sense. "Is that because the bloodline is becoming diluted?"

He made a strangled sound that turned into a laugh. "The Jinn blood doesn't dilute, Zamira. The Jinn blood always comes through strong in the males. Females born of the Jinn—which despite what you have seen in yourself and a few others—are rather rare. And most can't carry a child, their bodies are at war with producing another Jinn with the history we have."

"Then why bother with me if you think I might not be able to produce?" I threw at him, even though it was stupid. I needed him to need or want me, whichever way I looked at it; the more he needed me, the safer I was. Kind of. Maggi tapped me on the thigh, the side that he couldn't see, as if warning me off this line of questioning.

"You are different." He swiped his hands across his face, wiping sweat away. He wore a white swath of cloth that I'd given him on the first day. I'd dug it out of my saddlebags and tossed it to him without a word. He'd wound it around his head and created a sun-blocking hood. I'd have done it for Maks, which meant I had to do it for Marsum as long as he held Maks's body.

"How is it that you are even speaking to me civilly when you know that I killed your father, that I put the spear through your brother's back?" He asked as nicely as if we were on a first date.

"Because I can use you," I said.

"Blunt," he threw back.

"Truth," Lila tossed in.

Death.

The word hissed through the air around us and I hauled Balder to a stop. "You three hear that?"

"Yes." Lila shivered. "What is it?"

I looked to Marsum. "That what I think it is?"

His jaw flexed. "Yes. We need to move. Even if I had full control of my abilities, I could not stand on my own against them. They are somewhat immune to Jinn magic and there is no creature I know that can control them."

"What?" Maggi asked. "I do not know the desert like I knew the north."

"I'm with her. What is it exactly that I'm hearing?" Lila repeated, agitation making her wings shiver.

I wasn't sure that Marsum was telling the truth about his magic, but I knew I could not fight what was coming. And the horses would be the first to be taken down, and I was not going to let that happen if I had anything to say about it. I dug around into the saddlebag and pulled out the sapphire, slipping the leather thong that held it over Lila's body like a harness. Maggi reached for it and I threw it into the air for Lila to snag.

"I need your eyes in the air. The creatures coming for us travel under the sand, and they move like snakes. Look for the ground to slide side to side, just like a serpent." A really, really big serpent. Sand snakes were thirty feet long at adulthood, their bodies made with an armor-like scale not dissimilar to a dragon's, and they were venomous. They had a knack for sucking down entire caravans, leaving nothing behind but the wagons.

She gasped as she grasped the stone and her eyes

immediately glittered with what I could only say was malice. "I can freeze them."

"I don't know if you can, Lila. They are desert creatures and heavily armored. Don't even try unless they are fully above the sand. They're too fast otherwise." I watched her as she flew up and then I leaned into Balder, urging him into a gallop. Batman kept pace easily, but the horses were tired, they'd been going hard for the last few days as we tried to make good time. I shifted to four legs without hesitation, lessening the weight on my horse. I clung to the front of the saddle and Maggi took my place in the seat.

"How far back?" I yelled up at Lila.

She swept back to us. "Hundred feet and coming fast. What do we do?"

"Hard ground." Marsum leaned forward over Batman's neck, urging him faster. "We need to get to rock. That will force them above ground; they're slower on rock should they try to traverse it."

"That's not a hell of a lot better!" I said.

"No, but it will give us a chance. You have the flail, that will kill them. If you don't get bitten first."

Maybe it would, but I'd have to get close to them and I was not going to put my horses or us in harm's way.

The soft sand beneath the horses' hooves sucked them down, slowing their strides and making them work twice as hard than if they were on hard-packed earth.

"Hurry!" Lila yelled, panic in her voice, and then she shot down and behind us.

I glanced over my shoulder to see the sand shifting, whipping side to side, and counted four ophidians.

Four.

"You listen to me, Marsum, when I say go left, you go left!" I said. "I know these horses and how they can move! Maggi, don't do anything, I'll direct Balder."

Marsum looked at me like I'd lost my mind, but he nodded. I waited, urging Balder, whispering to him that I would let him rest for a year if we could just get this current shit storm handled. I kept where I was, watching the ground right behind the horses' back feet. "Come on, you little fuckers. Come on." The ground at Batman's back foot shifted and I yelled, "LEFT!"

Marsum drove Batman to the side as the ground sunk where he'd been standing. I drove Balder to the right with a touch of my claws on his neck with the same effect—they missed us on the first two strikes. The snakes were quick, but not good at sideways moves. We'd slowed them down, but it wouldn't last.

Lila shot ahead of us, flying like a blue streak of lightning. Her wings were a blur and she was far ahead of us when she yelled.

"I've got hard ground here, and water!"

"Is it close enough?" Marsum yelled at me.

115

I didn't know, and it was weird that he would ask me that. Had he never fought them?

"Never on horseback. Always with my magic at hand. I've never been weak like this," he said, once more picking up far more than he should have without me even saying a word. The bond between us was something else.

All around us, the sand seemed to shimmer and shift, the individual sand specks tinkling and glittering in the hot sun. With a growing sense of horror, I realized it wasn't just four sand snakes. I whipped around, all but spinning on the front of the saddle as I counted, my horror growing with each subsequent number. I gave up at twenty.

"Oh sweet baby goddess," I whispered. "Marsum. It's a nest, we woke up a goddess damned nest of ophidians!"

The sand to my right shifted and I drove Balder to the left. He dodged the ophidian as its head shot out to grab his right front leg. I got my first good, close up look at one of the nasty beasties. I'd run from one of them once before but that one had already snagged a meal and had given up quickly, full of whatever wretched creature it had found. Darcy and I had been lucky that it had been only one and we were too much work for it. So fucking lucky.

The ophidian's head was diamond shaped, the scales overlapping heavily like armor, and they were the color of the sand so the camouflage was near perfect. Tiny eyes that were bare pinpricks of red glared at me, a set of four horns protruded from its head curling back over its neck, and the fangs . . . the thing hissed at me, flashing its fangs as it sank back into the sand. Fangs the size of my forearms, far bigger than was needed for the size of its head in my opinion.

I watched the ground around us, yelling to Marsum. Moving both horses left and right, faster and faster the sand snakes came, like a wicked fast game of chess that we could barely stay ahead of.

"Slow them down!" I yelled at Marsum. We were close to the hard ground, close to what could be a measure of safety.

"I can't! They aren't directly attacking you. They're attacking the horses. And for some stupid reason, you aren't afraid!" he yelled back. "Remember the cuffs you two brilliant ladies put on me? I am literally hog tied!"

"I wouldn't have put them on you if you hadn't stolen Maks from me, you fucking piece of work!" Never mind that Maks had been the one to take his head. Those were semantics, in my mind. And he was right; I wasn't afraid, not yet anyway.

Balder stumbled and I looked down to see him dodge a snake on his own. "Good boy, keep going!"

Lila was on the ground ahead of us, the sapphire glowing as she scooted across the sand, whirling about like a dust devil. What was she doing? A split second later, I knew.

"Damn it, she's smarter than I gave her credit for." Marsum yelped as we hit the frozen sand and ice. It wasn't slick because the sand itself made for a perfect grip under the horses' hooves and we flew across it, our speed increasing, putting distance between us and the nest of ophidians.

Better than that, though, was that the frozen ground was hard enough to do some serious damage to the creatures who had no idea it was even there. The first wave of ophidians hit Lila's booby trap head on, at top speed, cracking it and their skulls as we raced away to safety. I watched over my shoulder to make sure none of them came to the surface.

The sand bubbled up red, the blood melting away portions of the frozen sand, showing the armored scales of the ophidians. Tails flipped and thrashed in their final death throes as the others from their nest slowed their pursuit. One by one, the bodies of the dead sand snakes were tugged downward, sucked below.

"They're going to eat them?" Lila barked the question.

"You do what you have to in the desert, dragon," Marsum said, turning away from the image. "Be glad we aren't their meal. We're safe."

Only we weren't all safe. I just didn't realize it right away.

9

We slowed our gallop along the hard ground that acted as a refuge from the ophidians behind us. Lila spun around us, grinning like a giddy little monster. "Did you see that? I froze the ground and the snakes rammed it head on!"

"That was brilliant!" I yelled, and below me, Balder stumbled again, and pitched my ass out of the saddle. I grabbed at his mane with my claws, hanging there against his side. Sweat frothed along his neck, far more than there should be even for that sprint.

Oh goddess, no.

"Whoa, whoa, boy." I slowed him quickly and leapt off his back, shifting in midair. I landed on two feet in a crouch, stood and grabbed for his reins as Maggi slid from his back. His head hung low, mouth frothing with white foam all around his lips. Every inch of his skin flicked as though he were being eaten alive by a thousand flies. I put fingers under the throat latch of his bridle, finding the pulse in his neck. Rapid, erratic, fluttering. Slowing.

"Shit, shit." I ran my hands over him quickly, looking for what I already knew would be there.

A bite.

Balder had been bitten by one of those fucking ophidians, and he'd kept going like the huge-hearted horse he was even as he was being killed from the inside out. I was shaking as hard as him as I searched for the wound, knowing what was coming. And there it was, just above the pastern bone on his right front leg, I found the marks. Two punctures, barely there, as though they'd scraped him instead of getting a full-on bite. "Marsum, help me!" Panic clawed at me. Marsum was here. We could heal this. He'd healed me before.

"I don't have to," he said. "And to be fair, it's not your life so I couldn't summon up a pinch of magic even if I wanted to. Did you not heal the black lion? Do the same here."

"She is in some ways as bound as you by the cuffs. Whatever magic she has is damped down," Maggi said softly. "I'm sorry."

I ignored them both, already trying to connect with my magic, but whatever, however, the cuffs had bound us together, it had put a block on me. Maggi was right about that. A block I didn't understand and didn't have time to figure out. "Take them off, Maggi!"

"They will come off when they come off. I have no control—"

"Take them off!" I yelled at her.

"I can't!" she yelled back. "That is not the spell!"

I shook my head, fear racing through me. I had no time to wonder if she was telling me the truth or not. Not this, not now. I'd lost too much, the price we'd paid to get this far was too steep as it was. Fear laced every part of me. I couldn't lose Balder. Too much had been taken from me, I couldn't go on without him.

"What if . . . what if we work together?" I looked at Maggi. "Would that work?"

"It might," she said. "But I don't know for sure."

"Marsum." I took a breath, my voice cracking. "Maks. Please. Try."

Balder groaned, his legs trembling. I yanked off his saddle and bridle, getting them free of his body before he crashed to the ground. I cried with him as I caught his head, keeping him from smashing it on the hard rock, cradling him as I sat on the ground, holding him. "No, no. Marsum . . . I need your help, please!" I would beg him. I would give him anything he wanted if he would help me now.

"I couldn't help you even if I wanted to with this cuff on." He shook his seemingly bare wrist at me.

"I'll give you anything you want if you will at least

try to help me." I looked up at him, not caring that he was seeing me cry, that he was seeing my pain and fear. "Anything."

Lila didn't argue with me. Not even a peep. To save one of my family members, I would make a deal with the devil himself. She would do the same; she understood.

Marsum squatted beside me as Balder shook, seizing as the venom coursed through his body. "For a horse? You would give me this for just trying to save a horse?"

"For my friend," I whispered through the tears. "For family. Maks would understand."

He lifted his hand and brushed my tears away, frowning. "You can heal him. You have it in you to be a healer, Zam."

"I can't reach it," I said. The more I thought about using his magic, too, the more it felt . . . right. "I need your help."

Balder groaned and gasped, his head thrashing against me. I clung to him with one hand and reached for Marsum with the other. "I don't know what I'm doing or why it won't work this time, but—"

"You will die one day, trying to save someone who shouldn't be saved," he said, but he took my hand, lacing his fingers with mine. He scooted around me so that he sat behind me, me in the shelter of his arms.

"Lila, you too," he said.

She didn't hesitate but dropped onto Balder's neck as he began to slow in his seizures. Dying in front of me. Batman drew close, and lowered his nose to his friend's face, then went to his knees, laying his face on Balder's neck. Comforting him the only way he could. He gave a low whinny, as if to call his friend back from the brink.

Just a horse.

Just an animal.

But one of my truest friends, and I would fight for him as I would fight for Lila, for Ford, or Kiara. I would not turn my back on him, even though it would cost me something. My body was a small price to pay.

"Open yourself to your magic, both of you, with whatever that is," Marsum said, his voice resonating through my body with the magic that was uniquely a Jinn's. "The only chance we have to work through this, is if it is all of us." I didn't think that was true at all, but this was not the time to argue.

Dark blue and black mist spooled up around us as I leaned over Balder's face, my lips against the curve above his eye. Marsum's hands tightened on mine and then Lila's little claws were there too. A spark slipped through us, a spark of lightning and fire, of acid, and a love so fierce that I didn't understand at first that it wasn't me or Lila.

It was Maks.

He was the one driving this. Using Marsum and the Jinn master's knowledge to help me heal my horse. I didn't think I could love that man more, but I was wrong. He understood me and the importance of saving Balder.

I gasped as his arms tightened around me and his chin rested on my shoulder. One hand laced with mine, the other pressed against Balder's neck, Lila touching us both as she sat with Balder.

This was more than when I'd healed Ford, more than when I'd healed Batman on my own.

All that power that had been blocked rushed through the three of us, growing and shifting, becoming more than any of us could ever have accomplished on our own, and it wove through our hearts and into Balder.

Maggi gasped.

Batman whinnied again, softly, his eyes fluttering closed. "He's getting the backwash," Maks said.

Maks, not Marsum. There was a different cadence to his voice that I'd not heard before. Subtle, a gentle touch that took the edge off what he said.

"Will it hurt him?"

"No." He rubbed his face against the side of my neck and let out a sigh. "This feels amazing."

Hell, yeah it did. Damn amazing. The magic swirling between us was sweet and soft, and despite how strong it was, there was safety in it.

Love, this was love inside the magic.

I massaged Balder's neck and he lifted his head, blinking a sleepy eye at me. He gave a long, low snort and lowered his face back to my lap. I ran my hands over his neck to find his pulse.

Strong, steady, and very much alive.

Lila looked up at me. "The Toad is right, this feels amazing. Should we stop?"

I stared at her, really looking at her, and I tightened my hold on the hands laced with mine. Toad. Maks. Marsum. I wasn't sure who I was holding, not really. The thing was, with all this power coursing through us, I could see something on Lila that I'd never been able to see before. A layer of magic that was ugly and hard.

I could *see* the curse on her. I wanted to reach out and snap it open.

"Do you see what I'm seeing?" I reached out with my hand still linked with his and ran a finger through the layer of magic that looked as though it were tied to her with hooks that burrowed under her scales.

He leaned closer, his chest pressed hard against my back. "The curse? Yes, I can always see it."

Lila startled as though we'd shocked her. "You can see my curse?"

"Yes," I whispered, then grinned as Balder blew out a huge snort against my legs. Horse boogers . . . I'd never have thought I'd be happy for them. "If we can see it, shouldn't that mean we can break it?"

He sighed. "Maybe, but not today. You aren't feeling the lag yet, are you?"

"The lag?" I twisted around to see those blue eyes so damn close, close enough to kiss him, and I knew that it wasn't really Marsum talking to me. Sure, he was there, but not as bad as he could have been. Maks was sitting with me.

He licked his lips and squinted against the sun. "We saved your horse, Zam. There is going to be a cost to that."

I couldn't help myself. "Was there a cost when you healed me?"

He gave a half grin. "Maybe. But I count it a good cost to keep my mate alive."

My heart thumped and Lila gave a tiny gasp. I motioned for her with my fingers to be quiet. Marsum had never called me his mate. And I didn't want to draw attention to the fact that this was not Marsum, for fear that he would push Maks down again.

I wanted to kiss him so badly. I wanted to wrap myself around him and breathe him in until we were both drowning in the sensation of skin on skin, of hearts beating in sync and love conquering all. Believing that a kiss could break Marsum and the Jinn master's hold on him. But that was the fairy tale, not reality.

Of course, that was when the lag, as he called it, hit me. I slumped where I was and the power faded from our fingers even though we were still hanging onto each other. Lila sighed. "I have to go to sleep."

"We all do. Dangerous damn time to fall asleep," he growled and there was Marsum again, the tone sharper, harder, meaner.

I didn't care. Maks was in there, and he was trying to come to the surface without Marsum realizing.

For the first time since Maks had taken Marsum's head and we'd been forced apart, hope lit me up from the inside. Real hope, hope based on more than just a dream and a wish, but on tangible evidence that Maks was not lost. And if he was not lost, I could bring him back.

I touched his face, drawing his eyes to mine. "If I would go to this length to save my horse, what do you think I'm willing to do to save Maks?"

I smiled as I spoke, smiled as I slid into the oblivion of sleep, the last thing I saw being the shock on his face, the shock and an echo of my own emotions.

Hope.

10

MERLIN

Flora and Merlin rode hard after the fleeting figure on horseback that he was fairly certain was another bastard sister of his. A bastard sister who was trying to free their bastard of a father so he could take over the world and most likely kill a whole swath of people Merlin cared about.

He didn't doubt that a family reunion amongst his relatives would be nothing short of horrendous, full of daggers and deadly spells hidden in the dark. Or maybe more accurately put, made of devious spells and more devious plots to take one another down.

"Any idea who she is?" Flora asked. They'd been riding hard for days, using their magic to boost their horses' endurance. A second horse bought from a caravan going west made some difference, but not enough if they kept this up. In the short term, it would help, but if they didn't give their steeds a break soon, the magic would drain them, and they'd drop dead under them in mid-stride.

There was always a price to pay with magic, and the user or the one used would bear the brunt of that cost one way or another.

He wove another tiny spell through the horses as he thought about it, fueling them for the next hour. Flora shook her head. "It will be a matter of who can keep their horses going the longest unless we do something else to slow her down."

As if that were the cue the other woman had been waiting for, she pulled her horse up and spun it to face them.

"Looks like you just got your wish," he said, his mind already working around just what his sister was thinking. What was she up to?

They slowed their horses to a blowing, snorting trot, advancing still, but not racing forward.

Merlin took the lead. "You blew out all your magic on Marsum, so let me do the talking."

"Your 'talking' can cause more damage than my magic," Flora muttered.

He grinned back at her. "You are not wrong, my love."

"I am *not* your love," she said, but there was very little heat in the words.

"Let me have my dreams," he said and turned back to face his sister. Half-sister, really. As they drew close, he wasn't sure this was a good idea at all. Because he recognized her, this half-sister he'd never met. She was the spitting image of her mother and that gave Merlin heart palpitations, ones that made him want to turn and run the other way. He wasn't a coward exactly, but he also wasn't always the bravest of men.

What if she wasn't a half-sister at all? What if she was . . . something more? Something closer to him?

"Fuck." The crass word escaped him before he could catch it and he saw Flora's eyebrows raise. While cursing wasn't beyond him, he usually stuck to the light words. The thing was, a string of hard and soft profanities lined up to fall out of his mouth the closer they got to the woman.

Long, straight, jet-black hair, bright blue eyes, and the heart-shaped face that came from her father's line no doubt, as her mother had a more angular long face. She wore a red dress split at the sides, riding leathers underneath. Her eyes flashed and she lifted a hand, magic spooling out around her.

He lifted a hand, palm to her in a sign of peace. "Daughter of Ishtar?"

Flora gasped but otherwise remained silent.

The other woman's glare did not ease. "How do you know me?"

"Well, to be fair, I do not know your name, but I can see the stamp of lineage on you as clearly as a nametag."

Her frown deepened and again he was struck by the likeness to her mother, and distantly to her father. His stomach rolled. "Do you have a name?"

"Shara."

"Princess," he laughed and she bristled. "I mean, it is suiting, to be the lineage of the Emperor and all."

She flipped her hair over one shoulder. "And you are my half-brother. Merlin, the mediocre."

Flora burst out laughing. "Oh, that's funny, if untrue."

A little bit of warmth fuzzed down his spine that she would defend him.

Shara looked down her nose at them both. "Why are you following me?"

Merlin shrugged. "You look like you are on a mission, headed for somewhere important. Perhaps we want to come with you."

Her eyes popped wide. "You can't."

"Why not?" He shrugged. "Perhaps I want to get to know someone in my family."

"Bother someone else then. You are below me." She turned her back on him.

He looked at Flora. "I think I'm going to have to bring out the big guns."

"Oh gods," Flora drawled. "What now?"

Shara spurred her horse forward and Merlin followed, cutting her off. "I think perhaps I should make this clearer. You are on a mission for the Emperor. A mission that is likely dangerous and could end with you dead, him free, and the world in danger. For a man who isn't your father, seems a pity and a waste of a good life and talent."

His words hauled her up short like nothing else would. He'd timed that right and gave himself a pat on the back. She turned her horse and stared at him. "And just who do you think my father is? I carry the Emperor's bloodline, and Ishtar's. It is proven in the prick of blood in the scrying mirror."

Merlin cleared his throat. "How many sons did the Emperor have again? I forget, with all the women he's spawned over the years."

Flora drew in a breath slowly, but it was the closest thing to a gasp she was going to give him. She didn't like being shocked. To be fair, neither did he, but he found a perverse pleasure in making her realize she didn't know everything. Even if he was in the same boat, Flora didn't have to know that.

Shara stared at him, the blood slowly draining from her face. "No."

"Well, you can say no all you like, that doesn't mean the word applies." He shrugged. "To be fair, I had no idea. Ish and I haven't been close for some time. If you get my drift." He winked at her. She shook her head.

In hindsight, he could have handled the situation better, maybe with less desire to "drop the bomb and shock and awe" the two women. Maybe a gentle discussion over a nice hot tea would have been better.

Shara let out a scream and slammed her hands together. He should have expected it, really, but he'd been stupid to think she'd be happy to meet her real father (who she considered mediocre) over the Emperor himself. But that meant, at least for some reason, she believed him. A burst of power rippled out from Shara's hands, which sent Flora, Merlin and their two horses hurtling backward.

End over end, they went until the four of them crashed against the ground, sliding to a tangled, bruised and amazingly still alive heap.

Merlin was the first to his feet and he reached for Flora. She pushed his hand away. "That was poorly done, even for you. Why didn't you tell me you had a child?" There was hurt in her voice he didn't like.

She went to the horses first and helped them up to their feet. They stumbled a little, shaking, but there were no broken legs. Merlin dusted himself off.

"Yes, well, I foolishly thought she'd be happy to meet me. I mean, as soon as I realized that she was mine and not his . . ."

"And when was that?" Flora barely spared him a glance.

"Oh, about two seconds after I met her."

He rubbed at a bruise blooming on his side. That was going to hurt later something fierce. "He took her, to use against me," he said softly, the ramifications settling in.

"He thinks you won't hurt her." Flora tossed him his horse's reins.

"I won't," he whispered. He'd never had a child, never had a desire for one, mostly because his family was so damn messed up. Who wanted to bring an innocent into that god-awful cluster of bad behavior? He'd always known that a child could be used, and his father knew that he had a softer heart than most.

Flora sighed. "I do understand that, and while she might very well be your . . . daughter . . ." she shook her head as if she was having as difficult a time as he was believing what she'd seen, "you can't assume that she won't try to kill you. Or me."

She was likely right, and Merlin wasn't *fully* sure that Shara was even his daughter. There was a definitive likeness there, but that could be because they were siblings. But even that half fib didn't stick with him. Ishtar had never had a child with the Emperor. He would have known. He did his best to keep tabs on all his father's women. "We have to go after her, regardless. She is working for the Emperor, doing his bidding. That is enough to stop her."

"And how would you like to do that? Do you have any idea of where she might be going?" Flora had her hands on her hips, ready for an argument. He went to his saddlebags with a slight limp of his left side. Yes, that was going to be tender for a few days.

Rummaging around his bags, he breathed a sigh of relief as his hand slid over the cool-as-glass crystal ball he used for scrying.

"I think we can assume her direction is to the east, and for some reason she is going hard. Being drawn away from the Emperor. Enough that she wouldn't even bother to fight us." He held the scrying ball in his left hand and slid his right over it in a quick wave. The image wavered and the Stockyards came into view.

"What is that place?" Flora asked.

"Ishtar's home." He frowned, wondering why the scrying ball had shown him this when it was the girl, Shara, he'd been scrying for. He tried again, forcing a little more of his magic through the clear crystal until it shivered in his hand, the sound of it cracking singing through the air.

"Not so much," Flora said softly, putting her hands over his. "You'll break it."

She was right. Merlin tried to breathe through the desire to shove his magic deep into the crystal ball to force it to hurry up. He softened his hold on it and eased back in his power. It occurred to him, briefly, that he'd never been strong enough before to even come close to cracking a crystal ball. That should have tipped him off to some rather important changes in himself, but his mind was focused on one thing. Finding the young Shara. But again, the image that appeared seemingly had nothing to do with her.

As the image cleared, it showed them the Stock-yards again from another angle, as a set of four horse and riders came into view, a prisoner in the center of their group.

A rather large black lion as said prisoner, his head down and feet padding along as if he were drugged.

"Oh, dear," Merlin said. There was no way this was good.

"That's Ford!" Flora gasped, her hands cupping the crystal ball around his fingers. "What has happened? Is Zam . . ."

"No, we would feel the repercussions of magic being loosed from her death if she had been killed." He was at least fairly certain of that fact. If again, not fully certain.

There was a flash across the crystal ball and the image of Shara riding hard to the east. Merlin sighed, exhausted already, as he saw the head-on collision long before it even happened.

"What is it? What do you see?" Flora stared up at him and he sighed again.

"The Emperor has sent her to Ishtar." He smoothed his hand over the crystal orb and the images slid away.

"But why?" Flora frowned, and then her face cleared with understanding before he could answer her, and she gasped. "To retrieve the stones. Zeus's thong in a wicked twist, that is going to put her on a head-on collision with Ishtar. Ishtar will kill her. She won't care that Shara is her child, not with the state she's in."

"Yes. The stones that Ishtar took into her body to keep them from being stolen again are what she's after. I'm sure of it." He put the crystal ball into the saddlebag and mounted. "We need to get there before Shara."

Flora nodded, her face grim as they turned the horses east and rode as though the devil himself was at their heels.

The thought crossed Merlin's mind as he turned his head to look back toward the prison he'd created for his father, a distant laughter curling toward them, that perhaps that was exactly the case.

11

ZAMIRA

The hard ground below me was far from comfortable with the points and jags of the stone jamming into my ass, reminding me that I didn't have a ton of cushion there. I opened my eyes, my arms still locked around Balder's neck as he lay with his head across my lap. Another set of arms were still around me, hands that I knew all too well. I blinked once, drew a breath and found Lila staring back at me, her violet eyes wide.

"Marsum is still asleep. Maggi wandered off, and I don't know where she is," she whispered and then shoved the sapphire back at me. I took it and tucked it under my shirt. She went on. "We have to talk about this situation. About him."

The *him* in question was slumped against my back still, his breathing in and out smooth and even. All of us—the two horses included—had passed out after the massive amount of magic we'd run through our bodies to heal Balder from the ophidian's killing venom. I sat up a little straighter and Marsum's arms tightened around me, but otherwise he didn't stir.

With a bit of a wiggle, I slid his arms down around me and stepped out of his hold. Again, he stirred but settled back to leaning against Balder's neck. By the set of the sun, we'd been out for a few hours, nothing more. Good, we couldn't afford to lose more time. It would be dark soon and we could keep going—albeit slowly. Much as I'd like to lie down, the nights had proven restless for me, my dreams full of Maks.

Batman lifted his head and gave me a big yawn and a sleepy blink as I took a few steps away from the three males of the group.

Lila flew to my shoulder and put her mouth close to my ear. "I know we can't really trust him, but . . . it was Maks in there, helping, wasn't it? Marsum wouldn't have helped, he said he wouldn't and then he did. Maks came through, I think. I'm sure of it. It felt like him, didn't it?" As quiet as she was, the words were still rapid fire. Fueled by excitement and hope, no doubt.

I nodded. "Yes, that was what I got too. But . . . I don't think Marsum realized he was being manipulated by Maks."

"I thought Maks went to sleep. Isn't that what he told you?" Lila's question was not unwarranted. When

I'd last seen Maks in a vision, after we'd visited the Oracle's Haunt, he'd told me he was putting himself into a deep sleep so Marsum couldn't use his love for me against me. So there was less attraction there, less desire to be with him. We'd said goodbye and I'd thought I could turn to Ford to be the rock in my life.

Look how that had turned out.

And now, Maks was coming through without Marsum noticing, trying to help me still. "I think we just take this as it comes each day. I can't fully trust him, and neither can you." Maybe never really, if I was being honest with myself. Unless there truly was a way to remove Marsum, there was no way I could ever trust the person running Maks's body.

"Do you think this is a ploy of Marsum's to get in your head? To give you what he wants? Could he be faking it?" Again, her question was a good one, and I had no solid answer.

I looked over my other shoulder at the sleeping form of Marsum. "I don't know. We have to be ready for that to be a possibility. Maggi might know; if she were here, I'd ask her." I did a slow turn, sweeping the horizon for the Ice Witch. She was nowhere, like she'd just disappeared. Had she taken the opportunity to run away? Wearing the necklace that blocked Ishtar from taking energy from her, she could have done just that and been free of us. But I had a feeling she wasn't done with her meddling, not yet.

"For now, we need him to help me survive this mess." I touched my chest where the magic coursed through my veins, too much power for me to hold on my own. Even just standing there, a shiver of nausea caught me off guard and I wobbled where I stood. I swallowed hard.

I was no magical vessel to hold the magic within me, no mage like Merlin or Ishtar to use the power in its rawest form. The fact that Marsum and Maggi had come upon me when they had and saved my life was nothing short of pure luck. Good luck for once. "It's amazing that Ishtar can hold all this magic from so many stones without dying," I said.

"She can't."

We turned as Marsum stood and stretched. "The power was hers originally, and if it was still in that form as when it was taken from her, she'd be fine. Or at least not losing what sanity she has left."

"What do you mean? What happened to it?" I asked as I went to where the horses lay. I urged Batman up first and then Balder.

Marsum spoke while I rubbed Balder down, currying off the worst of the dirt and sweat, beyond grateful that he was still with me.

"The power of the desert goddess was within her in all its forms, from the rawest of elements to the most ethereal powers. Merlin convinced the other lesser powers of our supernatural world that if we all had a piece of her magic, we could contain the Emperor, stop him from his rampage.

"Ishtar even agreed to it, according to what I recall, but none of us really understood. Not even Merlin knew what would happen when we stripped her of most of her abilities. In many ways, he was right; we contained the Emperor, but the cost of that was a ripple effect that is even now being seen and felt."

I carefully checked Balder's leg where he'd been bitten, feeling for any swelling or residual reaction to pressure. He was fine, though, as if he'd never been bitten.

Marsum crouched beside me and ran a hand over Balder's leg as if he cared that the horse was well. "So, with Merlin's help, we took Ishtar's power and split it into—"

"An even ten stones," I said. "I know this part. The stones went to the giants, Swamp Witches, Jinn, dragons, Ice Witch, Northern Shrikes, Southern Trolls, hyena shifters, Middlings, and the Tribe of Death." That last had been one of my first hunts for stones, quite the scene trying to get away from them without an extra couple of curses laid on my head.

I looked around again for Maggi. "Lila, do a loop around. See if you can find her."

Lila launched into the air. "On it."

"Ah, but that's where you're wrong." Marsum smirked and mounted Batman. I took Balder's reins and led him forward, walking at his side. "There were three other stones created from her to hold the most dangerous of her power and abilities. The power of creation was one of them. The ability to make new monsters."

"You have that ability," I pointed out. "You made the gorcs."

He waved a hand as if dismissing me. "No, I didn't *make* them. I bred them out of two species that were compatible. Very different than actually creating something new from nothing." He looked down his nose at me, easy to do when he was on Batman.

"Three more stones?"

He shrugged. "That's what my memories tell me."

His memories were not something Marsum would share so easily. There was no way he would be so casual about information like that. It had to be Maks coming through. Didn't it? Or was I just being hopeful? Or it could be lies, that was a possibility too.

He continued on ahead of me. Lila swept back to me a few minutes later, landing lightly on the pommel of the saddle. "Maggi is up ahead of us. She's found something to ride."

I jogged to catch up to Marsum and Batman. Balder trotted with me, the cadence to his hooves steady and even.

"Tell me," I said, "what are the other stones capable of?"

He grunted. "Destruction is the second, and it is enough to tear the world apart in the wrong hands."

Lila looked up at me, eyes wide as she mouthed his name. Maks. I'd asked Maks to answer me and he did. "And the third?"

"That one is more complicated. It has the ability to bestow gifts on others. Like creation and destruction, it has the power to be incredibly dangerous in the wrong hands. Before you ask, I only know where one of the three is." He glanced over his shoulder at me. "The Wyvern carries one of those final stones."

My stomach tightened into a hard lump. "The Wyvern holds the key to bringing my brother back."

He shrugged. "That's what you've been told, but who was the one who gave you that information?"

The Emperor had told me the Wyvern held the answers. But the Oracle had spoken the same words to me. "Two sources."

"Either one trusted?" He raised an eyebrow. As if he really cared. But was it Maks or Marsum making a play for my sympathies? Damn it, I hated guessing games.

Ahead of us, an image wavered, and Maggi trotted toward us on the back of a camel. I grimaced. Faster than a horse in many cases, sure, but they stunk like rotting food and had a tendency to spit, not to mention they could be stubborn as a freaking mule on steroids. "Really?"

She tipped her face and gave me a cold look. "It's

all I could find on such short notice. So unless you wish to continue riding double with me or our prisoner, I suggest you be grateful."

I wanted to ask her where she'd found the camel with all its gear, but I noticed her silver bracelets were missing. She found a trader then. At least she hadn't stolen the beast.

Marsum choked as if she'd punched him in the belly. "Prisoner? I thought I was a slave."

"Well, you surely are not either of our friends, are you?" Maggi said as she turned her floppy-footed mount around so we were all headed in the same direction.

He glared at her. "I am no one's prisoner."

"Then you are here by choice? You wish to be with us?" she asked, and I watched his face carefully. The response was immediate, fueled by anger. His eyes narrowed and his mouth tightened before he turned his face away. No matter what he said, the truth was there.

A prisoner he was, and once he was free, he would kill her. I was sure of it.

"Marsum," I deliberately didn't speak to him as if he were Maks this time, "the other two stones, what happened to them? Even a rumor can give a hint as to the placement of those things." I'd learned that in my years gathering the other stones for Ishtar. I frowned, wondering how she could have been fooled into believing there were only ten stones instead of the thirteen Marsum believed there were. I looked to Maggi. "Do you know about the three missing stones?"

"Not missing," she said. "No, they were never missing. But hidden, yes, I was aware of them. Some of us were. Except Ishtar. Merlin kept that information from her, and those of us who received a stone with a portion of her power were not supposed to know. Merlin never could play cards. His face always gave it away."

"How did you find out?" Lila asked. "My father doesn't know."

"Goddess, no," Maggi said. "If Corvalis found out, I can only imagine the hunt he'd put on to take any one of those three stones. The most powerful three. That is why only a few of us knew."

I looked from Marsum to Maggi and back again, trying to put the pieces together. How could both Maggi, the Ice Witch, and the polar opposite, the Jinn masters, both know?

Holy crap stuck in a camel's ass hair.

"You really did sleep with one of the Jinn masters?" I blurted it out before my brain caught up and thought better of my words.

Maggi shrugged. "Davin and I were friendly, a long time ago. We kept each other company in a world where our power made us feared."

Marsum snorted. "He thought he could use you and he stupidly fell—"

He cut himself short and shook his head, his jaw flexing and tensing. Holding back whatever that last bit was he was going to say.

"Fell in love?" Lila offered, helpful as always. "So what happened? Davin fell in love, and Marsum took his head?" She gasped. "Oh my, that's exactly what happened, isn't it? The ties that bind. Boy, do they mess you up when they are sticky with power and sex."

He shot her a look and then shook his head. "He's gone, dead. That's what happens when the heart is involved. That is why I am still in charge."

"His consciousness is not gone, nor are his memories," Maggi said, a softness to her voice that turned my head. She was looking at Marsum in a way I wasn't sure I liked.

As though maybe she wasn't interested in Marsum, or Maks, but that like me, she thought she could somehow bring her long-gone love back.

Like I needed something else to worry about.

Don't worry, though, those concerns were wiped out in three . . . two . . . one.

12

M arsum barked a laugh at Maggi as we rode along, three abreast, me in the middle.

"Davin has zero control here," Marsum said. "And even if he did, I doubt he'd want a dried-up, no-magic witch as a lover."

The hurt on Maggi's face was immediate and though she turned away, I saw the glimmer of tears. Awesome, just what I needed, a heartbroken Ice Witch.

"I would not want him back," she said, her voice far harder than the tears would have led me to believe. "He was weak. As you can see, he lost his head." She laughed then, and I could swear I heard the sound of the White Raven. I checked the sky just in case, but there were no telltale white wings.

"He was not weak," Marsum snapped. "He was a damn brilliant man who very few people understood, including you, witch."

"Too bad he didn't pass those brains on," Lila muttered.

I grabbed her and pulled her close as Marsum turned an icy glare on us, his eyes going nearly black with anger. "You best watch yourself, dragon, before I find an accident for you to stumble onto."

"Don't you *dare* threaten her!" I turned my glare on him and his eyes bugged wide as his throat flexed. Of course, I'd given him a direct command and was about to give another. "Apologize to her. Now."

His face darkened along with his eyes, and slowly he opened his mouth. "My apologies."

I held Lila close, feeling her shake against me. Marsum scared her, and I understood. At his full power, he could have wiped the floor with either of us.

I found myself reaching for the two stones I still had. The emerald stone taken from the Dragon's Ground, and of course, Maggi's blue sapphire. The sapphire cooled under my fingertips, but I felt nothing with the green stone, not even a faint flicker of magic. Good enough by me, I didn't need it right then.

But if Marsum decided to attack, that would be a different matter altogether.

"Look, can we just deal with one thing at a time?" I said. "Wyvern's Lair, Blackened Market, and the crossroads, not necessarily in that order. Then we can discuss who is going to claim his body and mind?"

"Actually, the Wyvern's Lair is not far from the Blackened Market," Marsum said, and then clamped his mouth shut like he hadn't meant to say anything at all.

"But is there time to go there?" Maggi shook her head. "I do not believe so. If you must be at the crossroads when the golden moon rises, then there is no time to diverge."

The Oracle's words came back to me.

The Wyvern is only part of the answer, the most dangerous part. You must embrace death to find what you seek. A child waits at the crossroads. A spell is broken on the impaling stake on the third golden moon. An Emperor dethroned. It comes for you three. Three. Three. Three.

The fire in you will burn until it can burn no more, the curse will be offered a cleansing, the magic, the child, the spell, they are tied . . .

I spoke the Oracle's words quietly, over and over as I tried to make sense of them. Because I couldn't throw the feeling that if I could figure them out, then I would know what to do, where to go. "Damn it. If you're so bloody smart, what does it mean?" I looked at Marsum and spoke the Oracle's words one more time, loud enough for him to hear.

His eyes faded to a blue I knew and went thoughtful. Maggi drew closer.

"The Wyvern being the most dangerous part makes sense. He is territorial like the dragons in the north," she said. "And his magic affects the surrounding area so that the land bends and shifts at his will. It could be an offshoot of his power through the stone."

"You mean the landscape adjusts to his needs?" Lila asked. Maggi nodded.

Well, that sounded fun.

"I don't know what child could be waiting at the crossroads," Marsum said. "But the Impaler's Stake is the mountain range near the crossroads. Dethroned can also mean displaced, so not necessarily what you would immediately think it could mean. Could just mean the Emperor will be moved." He tapped his fingers across the front of his saddle, drumming out a steady beat. "Embracing death. Golden moon. Fire in you burning." He mumbled the words out of order.

After a solid hour, he finally grimaced and rubbed a hand over his face. "None of it quite fits right now. Whatever comes, will come in threes?"

"Seems to be the gist of it," I said.

"Then we need to watch for that. Attacks in threes. Enemies in threes."

I glanced at him, then to Maggi. "Well, I've got two of you already. So I need a third enemy?"

Maggi sniffed. "I am helping you now."

"Well, then . . . enemies who were enemies, now friends?" I laughed.

That seemed to mollify her some.

A sharp pain ran through my back, stiffening me in my seat. Like a wave, it crested, stealing my breath and then slowly faded as I struggled to get my wind back. Little black dots warping into miniature lightning bolts danced across my vision.

"Zam, what's wrong?" Lila tugged on my face and I realized I'd slumped over my saddle.

"Just some growing pains," I groaned.

I pushed myself upright to see Marsum in nearly the same position. "Damn it, that was unpleasant," he said.

"Yeah. That's the magic still?" I took a breath, breathing out the last of the pain. My skin and bones felt all tingly.

Marsum gave me a terse nod. "Yes, which means there is only one choice. We go to the Blackened Market first. If we are already feeling this power cut through us, then we are only going to be less and less able to handle it with each passing day."

And then he clamped his mouth shut and stared straight ahead. I wondered what was going on in his head. What sort of war of his memories was happening? Because each time I looked at him, his face was twisted in a grimace, or he'd be shaking his head ever so slightly like he was arguing with himself. Maggi said nothing more, and Lila fell asleep in my lap, snoring slightly.

We rode like that for the rest of the day and then set up camp near a trickle of water sliding down a slope of rocks. Without a word, I dug out a pit at the base of the slope for the water to gather, lining the melon-sized hole with a chunk of oiled leather from my saddlebags. The horses drank their fill slowly, draining the small bowl I'd made several times before we could get our own refills.

"Clever," Maggi said as her camel drank—after us, I made sure of it. I wasn't drinking camel washback.

"Desert life teaches you to survive." I shrugged and turned around to see the horses untacked and Marsum currying their hides. He'd laid a fire and even got it going.

Just like Maks would have.

I bit my lower lip to keep from pointing it out. Lila, on the other hand . . . "Damn, can you make dinner too? Maks did that for us. Though I'll say he always had to have his food cooked through, couldn't stomach it even near to being raw." She shook her head and sighed. "What a terrible sin to overcook a steak."

His face greened a little and I grinned to myself. Maybe would have even had a quick laugh at his expense.

Except I swayed where I was, suddenly so tired I

literally couldn't keep my eyes open. Someone cried out my name.

"Zam."

My knees buckled and I could do nothing to stop it. Lila yelled for me, and Maggi might have stepped toward me, I'm not sure. I only know I stood there in the desert with them one second, and the next I was somewhere far more dangerous than a land of heat and Jinn and ophidians.

I was in the dreamscape world that the Emperor had created to keep his fingers on the waking world while he lay bound in his prison.

I lay on the sand, the same place that I'd fallen in the waking world, the sky above me black and without stars. There was no Marsum, no Maggi, no Lila. Both horses and the camel eyed me as I rolled to my belly and stayed where I was, thinking about what had happened.

I'd never had the dreamscape come over me like this, dragging me in when I was awake. Did that mean I'd been drawn here by someone? But who could have done it? The Emperor, I supposed, and maybe Merlin. Someone had called my name, but the voice was far away and I couldn't even tell if it was male or female.

Could it have been Maggi? Had she shoved me here so that she had time with Marsum and Davin? That rang far truer than I wished it did. Which meant I would wake when she let me.

"Just freaking awesome." I pushed to my feet and did a quick check of what I had on me. The flail was on my back and warmed instantly when I touched the handle. A knife in its sheath on one thigh, and my pouch with the two stones. Good enough, at least I wasn't weaponless. That being said, I needed to go as quietly as I could while I was here. The last thing I wanted was to draw attention to myself.

I shifted to my four-legged form. With fur black as night and a body that was a tiny little house cat, I could keep my stay here hopefully unremarkable.

"Zam. Hurry. Please hurry." My name was called, coming from the south from a voice I knew this time, one that was full of fear. Ollianna.

Low to the ground, I scooted forward, the land flying under my feet as I raced toward her. Was she the one who'd called me to the dreamscape? Somehow, I didn't think so. Which meant she was in trouble.

The world twisted and jumped around me as I went as fast as I could, all but flying over the desert. After a few strides and off to my left was a place of darkness and water that slowed my feet a little. The water frothed and turned, and a set of eyes peered at me from the depths. I made a mental note of the place that could only be the Wyvern's Lair and then continued on to the crossroads.

At the base of the Gashishum Mountain range were the crossroads where the three golden moons would rise and the power to do big ass miracles would happen.

Trick—Lila's dragon-crush who ruled the power of storms and lightning—had taken Ollianna, a witch from the Swamps who'd joined with us, to prep the crossroads. I wasn't sure what to expect when I arrived there, but not what was in front of me now. Especially since Ollianna was not at the crossroads. Or at least, it didn't look like it to me. She sat by herself, sobbing into her hands within a stand of trees well off the road to the north of the mountain range.

"Zam, hurry," she whispered, rocking where she sat.

"Did you call me here?" I slid to a stop, kicking up a flurry of dust. She shot up, her hands out, magic curling around her, thick and dangerous, her tears gone in a flash.

"Zam, you should not be here." She lurched toward me, catching me in a hard hug, squeezing me as if she was afraid to let me go. I shifted to two legs, and held her tightly, feeling the tremors go through her body. I patted her back and worked to unpeel her arms from around me. "I didn't plan on being here."

She pulled away from me. "You have to go. The Emperor is hunting you." She shook her head. "And he is not the only one."

"Who else?" Ishtar, most likely.

"Trick says there is another dragon sniffing

around here. He's not sure who, though, and every time he goes to see who it is, they fly away before he can see."

"A loner then?" I didn't know if that was possible. I'd have to ask Lila. "As strange as that may be, it's not a reason for—"

"Where are you?" She cut me off, shaking me a little. "Right now, where are you in the waking world?"

I blew out a breath. "We aren't far from the Wyvern's Lair. It's to the east of us."

"You need to go to the Wyvern," she said. "You need to ask for his help before you come this way."

Like I needed her to remind me that I had more than one task on the table. She didn't know about the other stone, about the magic absorbing into me, and slowly killing me. She didn't know Marsum was with me.

"Look, it's not that easy—"

"The crossroads are being held by the ophidian queen," she said, cutting me off once more. "We cannot get closer than this, ten miles away. Trick has tried to fry them with his lightning, but it just makes them laugh."

"SHIT FUCK DAMN." The words shot out of my mouth like bullets from a gun. "We've already dodged ophidians once and not well." I rubbed a paw over one ear. What else could go wrong? No, strike that, I didn't want to know.

157

"Our time is slipping by," she said. "What do we do? Will you go to the Wyvern's Lair first? I think you should."

She couldn't know that the Wyvern had a stone, one that embodied destruction. That could be useful against the ophidians and their apparent queen. Goddess of the desert, since when did those creatures have a queen?

I didn't know how much time we had so I went with the simplest answer. "We can't. I'm sick. We need to get to the Blackened Market to heal me."

"But your brother . . . if you do not go to the Wyvern, how will you save him? And we need him to face the Emperor." Her green eyes were worry-filled and I didn't like it. All the pieces were tied together, and I couldn't separate one from the other.

"I know, but I can't save him if I'm dead!" I snapped.

"I understand." She shook her head slowly. "You must do what you must, as we all do."

"Ollianna, it's not that easy to just walk into the Wyvern's Lair and . . ." I almost said *take the stone from him*, "and ask him a question," I finished lamely.

"Perhaps it is that easy," she said. "And you are just more worried about your own life than anyone else's."

I stared at her, shock dumbing me. I spluttered, shame and guilt rolling through me like the waves of pain from earlier. Did she really believe that? Worse, was she right?

Her eyes widened, she spun and ran from me as what felt like a rope tightened around me. I looked down, but could see nothing, no rope, no magic spell. But that didn't stop the feeling of being squeezed.

I was yanked away from where I stood as though I had a string tied around my middle and I was pulled through the air, end over end. Breathing was not possible, the tension around my middle too much. Right as I thought I would pass out from lack of oxygen, I landed with a thump on a chunk of flat rock. The pressure around my middle faded and I sucked in a big breath, blinking rapidly as my eyes were all watery from the high speed with which I'd been pulled through the freaking air.

Clouds floated by. Clouds and a few birds. The rock below me was cold and slippery with condensation. I blinked and stood; the flat stone I was on wobbled precariously side to side until I found my balance, legs spread wide. Just how high was I? I couldn't see over the edge of my platform, but at a distance there were mountain peaks and they were on eye level with me.

Awesome.

"No dragon with you this time? Pity for you, seeing as I suspect you'll take a tumble before this is over." The Emperor's voice was not a surprise to me.

"You yanked me into the dreamscape?"

"Much as I would have loved to do so, no, that was not me. Someone is playing games with you, I think." He smiled as he stepped into view, his teeth even and white. He was on a flat rock as well, but his floated in the air and didn't wobble under his feet. Fucker.

His thick shock of white hair was pulled back from his face, and once more, he wore the light khaki-colored loose pants and top of the desert, a scarf around his neck ready to be pulled over his face in the case of a dust storm or extreme heat.

His eyes were not full of anger or hatred this time, and I realized then what I was dealing with—a split personality. "You're the good gramps today, huh?" I sat carefully, adjusting my butt on the flat rock. It felt as though there were a pivot point in the middle, and if I moved in any one direction quickly, I would send the whole thing toppling into the clouds. But if I just sat there, acting scared, he'd have the upper hand.

That was not acceptable.

"Perhaps." He smiled.

Yeah, this was not the same Emperor I'd dealt with before. But like dealing with Marsum, I didn't know how far to push him, how far to take the questions before I got the ugly Emperor back. This was going to be interesting.

He folded his arms and watched me. "You are fighting for your brother, correct? To bring him back from the dead. Why? Why him and not, say, your father? Or your mother? Why is his life so much more valuable to you than theirs?"

His words were as sharp as if he'd stuck me with a knife and I struggled to answer calmly. How did I explain that I knew it was possible with Bryce? That something in me said that he was not really gone? I didn't.

"Because."

There, that was as good an answer as any, and I refrained from sticking my tongue out at him, which was something as far as I was concerned. Not to mention that I didn't want to think about bringing my parents back from the dead. Maybe I hadn't because I'd lost them so many years ago, or maybe because their deaths were timely in some ways even though they were painful. Maybe because Bryce deserved another chance at life.

He laughed at me, teeth flashing. "Such a thoughtful and well-considered answer deserves a reward. I can give you your brother. For a price, of course, but I can give him to you."

I narrowed my eyes. "Right, like my ass on a platter?"

He shook his head, still smiling. "The flail. It's just a weapon. Give it to me, and I will free your brother."

I frowned. "What?" He'd said *free* my brother, not bring him back to life.

He snapped his fingers and my brother was just there, as surely as if he'd been alive and breathing.

Bryce looked tired, his face drawn and his golden hair a mess, but he was there on his knees. A cage around him, the bars glowing with a pale white pulse of magic, he stared at me. His mouth was covered with a similar colored cloth, glowing with the same magic. His eyes, though, spoke volumes, and he turned his head side to side ever so carefully in increments and slow enough that if you weren't watching for it, you would never see it.

Don't help me.

"Bryce!" I lunged forward and the rock I was on tipped, going nearly vertical. I scrambled backward, my claws digging hard into the stone. Perks of having shifted with the flail on my back. The connection to the weapon made my teeth and claws stronger than they would have naturally been and I used it to my advantage.

I worked to balance the rock once more until I was standing in the middle, shaking this time. Bryce was so close, there at the Emperor's feet on that platform. I could leap the distance, I was sure of it. Pull him with me as we woke. But that would put me into striking distance of the Emperor's hands—or better yet, the Emperor would move his platform and let me fall. Either way, I would end up in a not so good place.

My brother didn't want me to make the trade. Not that I was surprised. He wouldn't want me to risk my life for his.

"I don't need your help to bring my brother back. To *free* him," I said. "So you are offering me nothing for something. Not a good deal, especially not in the desert, which you should know."

"Ah, but that's where you're wrong. I can offer you more, if you will bring me the flail. I will give you your brother, and the form you were meant to have." The Emperor's smile didn't slip. "If you do not, I believe the ophidian queen will be happy to kill you and bring me the flail, and then you will have nothing for nothing. At least, I offer you something in exchange. Let us call it a family discount."

"So, she's one of yours?"

"They are all mine." His eyes narrowed. "All of them."

I didn't know what to make of that. All of them? Who was he referring to? The ophidians? Somehow, I didn't think so.

A shiver ran through me and I answered before I could think better of it. "No. No deal. I'll kill your snakes and fry them up for breakfast before I ever give you what you want." Even if it cost me my brother, even if it cost me my full form.

The taste of my full form, a jungle cat that was a force to be reckoned with, was still with me and I couldn't deny the desire to be what I was meant to be. But I said no, even if it was hard. Even if a part of me wanted to say yes.

"You will *never* break that curse without me," the

Emperor all but cooed to me. "You will always be the weak and useless cat you are now without me. Or dead. Dead is fine too. Either way, I'm going to win this. You will not stop me from freeing myself. Slowing me down puts you in a nasty place. A place that will cost you dearly."

I pulled myself together with some difficulty, locking eyes with my brother, not letting him out of my sight. I nodded to him, not the Emperor. "I'll find a way to free Bryce myself, and I'll find a way to keep my other form. Just. Fucking. Watch. Me."

"No, you won't," he said. "That is the sadness of all this. You will fail on both counts. But I could give them to you now. For the weapon. A mere weapon. And you would keep your life. Is that so much to ask? I do not think so."

I shook my head as his words burrowed into my skull, driving home the point he was trying to make. No one had been brought back from the dead before. Why did I think I could bring back Bryce? Because I loved him? Was love enough? Was love enough to save Maks? No. Bryce *wasn't* dead. The Emperor had said he'd *free* my brother. Freeing him meant he was alive but captured.

Part of me knew that it was the Emperor getting inside my head, feeding me doubts, making me believe he was the only path. Even knowing that I couldn't escape it, or him.

I had to do something fast or I would agree to his

demands, the words were there on the tip of my tongue to say yes.

"I will . . ." I shook my head again and again. "I will . . ."

"Say it. Say you will give me the flail." His voice hammered into my skull. He was trying to force me to agree. That couldn't happen. I shook my head again and took a step back, the rock beneath me tipping.

"I'll fucking die before I give you the flail," I snapped.

I did the only thing I could do. I let gravity take hold of me even knowing that whatever happened to me here happened to me in the real world. A fall like this could kill me. But agreeing to give the Emperor what he wanted was worse. And I was banking on someone to save me.

He shouted something, I'm not sure what, but his magic slid around to stop me, and I fought its hold, pushing it away.

I went limp, letting the wind take me, whistling around my fur and clearing my mind of the Emperor's magic. I twisted, thinking about hitting the ground feet first at least. The ground seemed to shoot toward me. I needed someone to wake me up. Someone who was bonded tightly to me.

"Maks!" I screamed his name, praying he'd hear me. It didn't occur to me to yell for Maggi or even Lila. Just him. Either he'd save me, or I'd die smashed on the rocks below. Maybe that was better, too. Maybe it would be the telling point of my story. I drew one last breath and screamed for all I was worth.

"MAKS!"

13

Dying in the dreamscape was not how I wanted to go out. In my head, I'd always thought it would be fighting a gorc, or some epic save-the-world shit, but not falling to my death while I was asleep.

But if someone on the other side of the dream-scape didn't wake me, that was exactly what was going to happen. A weird sense of peace flowed over me as I fell and fell. There was nothing I could do, whatever happened was out of my hands.

A soft breath escaped me, and I closed my eyes as the ground flew toward me . . . and a rush of wet cold splashed over me.

But I didn't wake.

I closed my eyes and my mouth warmed, lips against mine, softening and demanding at the same time. Arms around my neck pulled me back from the ground rushing toward me and I sat up, tangled with Marsum as he kissed me awake. I pulled back, staring up into his face. "Thanks."

Reality hit me hard a moment later. I'd left Bryce behind, again.

Water spilled down my cheeks, masking the sudden onslaught of tears, masking the pain rocketing through me from leaving my brother behind. I rolled, twisting to my hands and knees as I fought to breathe normally. So much for being in a state of calm and peace as I died.

"Fuck it all." I gasped the words, my mind catching up with what had just about happened to my body.

Lila was right there, touching my cheeks with her tiny claws. "What happened? We couldn't wake you! You screamed Maks's name and then Marsum threw a bucket of water on you and even that didn't work so I told him to kiss you and he did and then you woke up!"

I nodded and sucked in a shuddering breath. "Thanks. The Emperor dragged me under." Sure, he'd said he hadn't, but he also had proved himself to be a liar more than once.

"You saw him?" Marsum pulled me to my knees so we were face to face again. He was pretty much holding me up at that point. "You saw the Emperor? Did he try to kill you?"

"He's like a split personality." I shivered, colder

than I should have been from the splash of water that had literally saved my life. "I got the not so bad version. The happy gramps version."

Marsum's hands tensed on my arms. "What did he want?"

"The flail." I touched the weapon, making sure it was there. "He wants the flail."

Maggi stood to my one side and Marsum spoke, his words thoughtful. "The weapon absorbs magic. I created it that way on purpose. It could destroy the Emperor's throne and the entire prison he is held in with no help from any of the stones."

I nodded. "Makes sense."

Marsum didn't let go of me, and the heat from his hands sunk into my muscles. He looked to Maggi. "How do we keep her from the dreamscape? He could have killed her." Which, of course, would mean he would die too. Self-preservation at its best.

Maggi shrugged. "We don't. There is no protection against it. You saw her, twitching and moving. That is the only indication and then she must be woken. Immediately."

They talked over my head like I was a child, and I let them because my mind raced through what little I'd learned from Ollianna.

"We have to go the market before anything else," Marsum said.

"I don't disagree, but with the Emperor finding her—"

I interrupted them. "The ophidian queen, she's guarding the crossroads and keeping Trick and Ollianna from protecting the site. That is our goal, that is where we need to be if we have any chance of taking the Emperor down. It's supposed to be the power of the crossroads that will do that." And bringing Bryce back.

Maggi's shoulders slumped. "Then the queen wants the power of the moons that will shine down. Many creatures will, but only one major event can be accomplished."

Lila groaned. "You mean whoever is first gets their spell done? The first gets the magic thingy they want and everyone else is screwed?"

"Close," Maggi said. "The magic fades with the waning of the moons. So the first spell is the one that will take the majority of the night's power, and then less with each successive spell. Perhaps three or four spells at the most could be done. That is why holding the crossroads is so important." Her face tightened. "How well do you know this Ollianna and Trick you sent to guard it?"

"I trust them more than I trust you," I said.

"You should never trust a witch," Maggi smiled. "Not even me."

Marsum's hands tightened further and he dragged me up and away from Maggi. As if she *were* a danger. Lila flew around our heads.

"Maggi put us into the dreamscape once. Could

she have done it here?" Her question stopped us in our tracks.

The Ice Witch, once formidable and dangerous, the sister of Ishtar, watched us with obvious amusement. She folded her arms across her chest and laughed. "When you are done being foolish, we can discuss what should be the next step. You have seen, and you know I have no magic left in me. Unless you wish to give me the cuffs back."

"Yes," Marsum said at the same time I said no.

The next step. As if Maggi were in charge.

I turned my head so my mouth was close to Marsum's ear. "I've got a bad feeling about this." Maggi was up to something. I was suddenly sure of it. But what? Was she trying to get Davin to come forward, or was she going for something bigger?

Like the sapphire or emerald stone I carried in my pouch.

"Me too. I say we make a run for it," Marsum said under his breath, his eyes locked on Maggi.

"The camel can keep up," Lila reminded us quietly. "It'll run longer and faster than the horses."

"Then we need to find out what she's really about. Have you got any liquor we can use?" he asked, his breath soft against my cheek. Warning bells went off in my head.

Too close, I was too close to him.

"Ţuică," both Lila and I said together. His hands tightened farther, then softened and slid down my arms to my elbows, cupping them. He tugged me so that my back pressed against his chest, the feel of him solid, safe. I leaned into him, breathing the moment in—

"You two knock that shit off," Lila hissed. "We don't have time for it."

I blinked and realized that Marsum's mouth was only a sliver away from my own. He didn't pull back, but instead closed the distance and kissed me. Not hard, not aggressive, just a pressing of his lips to mine, a soft touch that reminded me of Maks. I pulled back, my heart hurting and hammering all at once. "Lila's right."

"Oh, the dragon is very wrong. But you'll see." He let me go. "Where's the booze?"

And just like that, the moment was gone. I blew out a breath, unable to keep my eyes off his butt, as he walked back to Maggi who quickly wiped a glare off her face. Damn it. "Thanks."

"He's bad mojo right now. You've got to remember that." Lila tapped me on the head with the points of her claws, like tiny pins.

"Yeah, I know. I know." I did know, but damn it, I was struggling with not wanting to bite that very fine piece of ass. Or let him do the same to me, bad mojo or not.

Marsum dug into the saddlebags and pulled out a bottle of țuică. "This the stuff?"

"What is this about?" Maggi asked.

"Celebrating." Marsum yanked the cork out with his teeth and spat it to the side. He lifted the bottle and chugged a few mouthfuls down, then handed it to Maggi. "We're alive for tonight. That's worth celebrating. I'm doubtful of our chances tomorrow, so let's drink."

To say that's where things got interesting would be an understatement.

The liquor was strong and agreed with me just fine on the way down my throat, sweet and hot as it trailed a burn line straight to my belly. We passed it around, and with each shot, the laughter increased until we were all rolling with it.

But one thing I was beginning to wonder about was just how many bottles of țuică were out there, and how they kept ending up in my saddlebags.

"Oh, that's me," Lila snickered, wobbling across the ground. She climbed up onto the back of the saddle and tapped on the bags. "When I do my flybys early in the morning and late at night and check out places, I also search for the booze. I like it way too much." She hiccupped and I laughed, and even Maggi laughed.

"A dragon with a drinking problem?" Maggi shook her head, her words only slightly slurred. "*Now* I've seen it all."

Marsum sat on the ground next to me, the bottle in one hand. "No, not a problem with drinking," he

SHANNON MAYER

pointed one finger off the bottle he gripped. "She has a problem with stealing. She's a damn klepto."

Lila and I both burst out laughing. "Fitting, seeing as she's with me." I snagged the bottle from him and raised it in a toast to the sky. "Queen of the jewel thieves."

Marsum's leg leaned against mine as he bowed at the waist howling. I fell against him and Lila sprawled out in front of us, flat on her back, claws over her mouth as if that would stop the giggle fits.

I had a flash of a moment of understanding that this was not something I ever would have done with Ford. As much as I liked him, I never would get sauced with him around. There was too much vulnerability to these moments.

My sobering thoughts did as much to my plum-liquored brain and I sat up, handing the bottle to Maggi. She took another swig and closed her eyes as she swallowed. "Lila has good taste in her drinks, at least."

"Are you here to get your man back?" The words burst out of me, untampered by any cognizant thoughts. Wasn't there one of the Jinn masters she was sleeping with? Or was my brain that far addled by the sweet nectar already? Wait, that wasn't the question I needed to ask her.

Maggi smiled. "Well, much as I do like the body that Davin is currently in, I think I'd have to fight you for him, and I believe I'd lose that fight. So no. I don't

174

think that's going to happen." She eyed the bottle and then shot a look at me. I barely noticed that Marsum slid his arms around me and pulled me into his lap. I was too intent on Maggi.

"Why are you *really* helping?" *That* was the question I was supposed to ask. "Maybe you're the witch we can't trust."

"I saved your life and you want to know my motivations?" She smiled instead of frowned, which I thought would be the case if someone was accusing me of not being trustworthy.

"Yes," Marsum said, only it wasn't Marsum's voice. It was Maks. "You might have saved her, but you tied her to me. That's not nice in the state I'm in."

"Merlin's idea," she said softly, "but I agreed, not nice, but necessary. Because you will eventually face my sister, and I cannot, and you need the power of the Jinn on your side. Also, I know something even Merlin does not." She put the bottle on the ground and stared at it. "You want to know what I know? Do you want to have the secret that is tearing its way out of me?"

We leaned toward her, all three of us, quiet, straining to hear what it was she had to say.

"Well, you can't!" she snapped, anger flashing through her so brightly that even the horses startled with her explosion.

Lila snickered and even I had to cover my mouth. It all shouldn't have been funny, but it was. Gods, it was funny. "Another secret? Like a secret baby?" I offered.

Maggi grimaced. "No babies."

I opened my mouth and Balder whinnied. Maggi laughed. "It looked like you were the one neighing!"

I turned to look at my horse who frantically pawed at the ground. I stumbled to him and he did it again, then dropped his head and touched his leg where he'd been bitten. Where the ophidians had gotten him.

"Mount up." I spat the two words out, grateful we hadn't taken the gear off the two horses and Maggi's camel. "Ophidians!"

That got Maggi and Marsum moving. Lila was passed out on the ground and I scooped her up into my arms. The night had fallen and we were going to be riding hard in the dark with no real idea of where we were going. No, that wasn't right.

"Marsum. Lead the way," I yelled as I scrambled into my saddle. As soon as I sat my ass down, Balder took off, partially unseating me. I took a moment to get myself together, then looked at Maggi and Marsum. The camel took a hard left, avoiding the ophidians as he took his rider up onto a rocky outcropping. Marsum and I, though, we were in the softer sand. Shit, this was going in the wrong direction, and fast. My head spun with the liquor, which wasn't helping at all.

"This way!" he yelled, turning Batman to the right.

Balder kept up easily and I kept looking back for signs of the ophidians cutting through the sand. Here and there in the darkness the ground behind us shifted, shimmering in the starlight. "Thirty feet behind," I yelled.

"We'll make it. There's hard ground up there," he threw back. My head was fuzzy, and I just let him lead. A few moments later, the sound of the horses' hooves changed from the dull thud of running on sand to the sharp clang of iron shoes on hard rock. We slowed our pace and I twisted around to see the head of an ophidian watching me. Resting its lower jaw on the first part of the hard rock, it yawned, showing off its fangs and forked tongue before sliding back into the sand.

"Are they even trying to catch us?" I asked. Because they'd moved much faster before, I was sure of it. Then again, I was drunk this time so I could be wrong. Marsum slowed Batman to a walk and Balder easily caught up.

"Of course they are. Why wouldn't they be?" He frowned at me like I was a fool.

I cradled Lila close to me and she farted in her sleep, then smiled like she damn well knew it. Crap, the ţuică was playing havoc with my ability to think straight. Marsum seemed less bothered by it. To be fair, Maks had been the same way.

"Ophidian queen. Never has been one, so this is a new player, and someone fucking strong if they can control those goddamned monsters." He rubbed the back of his neck.

"You've tried?"

"And failed. They can't be controlled. Or at least, I didn't think they could be." He pointed at a chunk of rock ahead that made up a bit of shelter. "We can wait here. It'll take Maggi half the night to reach us, staying off the sand."

I sighed, slid off Balder's back and loosened his girth. "Good boy." If he hadn't warned us, those damn sand snakes would have had us for sure. Especially more than half cut that we were. Was. Is. I squinted as if that would help my brain function.

Things were fuzzy and I watched in amusement as Maks loosened the horses' tack, fed them, and then set about putting a fire together. "Maggi will find us easier that way."

"Thought you didn't like her with the whole cuff thing." I held Lila in my arms, partially wrapped in my cloak as she snored. He lifted his head, took one look at me and turned away. But not before I saw the way he swallowed, and how his eyes had widened. "What?"

"I don't like her. But maybe she'll come in handy."

I put a hand to my head and a sharp pang coursed through me from the roots of my hair down through my body. "Ouch." I went to my knees, still hanging onto Lila. Hands wrapped around my arms, pinning them to my sides.

"What is it? The drink or the magic?" He was grimacing, feeling the pain too but unable to pinpoint it any more than I could.

"I don't know." I tried to look up at him, but it was hard, and the world swam. Most likely the drink, but I kinda liked how worried he was about me, so I wasn't saying that. Even if it was just to keep me alive so he didn't die. I tried to smile, but my lips were tight and it came out like a grimace.

His hands slid up to my face, cupping it as he tried to flip my eyelids with his thumbs. "Knock that off," I grumbled. But again, he had me at a disadvantage because I couldn't put Lila down. I mean, I was on my knees. I could have but didn't.

A teeny tiny part of me knew that if I put her down it would be like taking off a chastity belt. Hanging onto her reminded me I couldn't throw myself at him. Him. Maks.

"Hi." I blinked up at him, into those oh-so-blue eyes.

His lips quirked. "You are so smashed."

My grin widened and his fingers softened on my face. "What's my name?"

"Maks." I leaned toward him and he dropped his head so that we were touching foreheads.

"No. That's not my name."

He couldn't have sobered me up faster if he'd thrown another bucket of ice water on me. A flush of hot and cold rushed through my veins, and my damn eyes prickled with tears. "Yes, it is."

His lips quirked up to one side. "You can keep telling yourself that, but he's not strong enough to be in charge."

"That's not true," I said. "He just has more to lose than you." As soon as I said it, I knew those words were exactly the issue. I could be used against Maks, always me, always his heart. In my still somewhat inebriated state, I came up with the only solution that would work. I carefully laid Lila on the ground, feeling Marsum's—no, Maks's—eyes on me.

"What are you doing?"

"Proving a point." I slid out of my cloak and laid it on Lila. She cooed in her sleep and burrowed into the borrowed warmth.

I turned on my knees to face him, grabbed him by the ears and dragged him to me. If I had magic, I was damn well going to try and use it to my advantage.

14

I *can express no kinder sign of love, than this kind kiss.*

That was all I could think as I clung to Maks for all I was worth. Maks, not Marsum. With my lips locked on his, I reached for whatever strange magic I had in me. Maggi had said the cuffs dampened my power too, but I had to try something. Maybe I could work around them?

Like the doorway I saw in my mind when I shifted shapes, there was another doorway next to it now, one that seemed to glitter and beckon to me. I opened it and the magic poured through me and into Maks.

Score one for the girl who didn't know a thing about her own magic.

He grunted, maybe surprised, and then his arms were around me, the magic humming between us like

SHANNON MAYER

the drone of a honey bee hive and about as lazy as a summer day. Curling through us, wrapping us in warmth and with all the love I had in me, I opened myself to it like never before.

Partly the alcohol was to blame, I'm sure, but also partly to blame was Maks. With him at my side, I was braver, bolder, and I believed in more than I could possibly have considered without him.

I couldn't get enough of him. I couldn't kiss him deeply enough, long enough. Like I was hungry for him in a way that couldn't be satisfied. He groaned, or maybe I did. I'm not sure. His hands slid over my waist, under my shirt and along my ribs.

"You're too skinny," he mumbled as his lips left mine to trace a line of heat along my jaw and down my neck. The magic went with him and every touch tingled and danced. Yeah, that next groan was mine, for sure. I mimicked him, running my hands under his shirt and over skin that was flushed with heat and desire, muscles tensed and flickering with each brush of my fingertips. The need to pull clothes off and roll around naked on the bare ground was growing wildly out of control.

He bit at my collarbone, then lower, to the top of my breasts. I arched upward, his hands slid to the waist of my jeans and he yanked me forward so I was sitting on his lap, my legs around his waist.

"We've been here before," I whispered right before

I bit the side of his neck. He grunted, grabbed my ass and ground me against him.

"I know, and we never did get to see where this would lead."

Maks, this was all Maks. The magic was doing something. I knew it was. Could I free him from the other Jinn? I slid my hands around his face and into his hair, holding his mouth to mine as if I were under water and he were my only way to breathe. Time slowed, but the magic didn't. I'd opened that door again and I didn't know what I was doing with it, only that it was giving me this moment with Maks.

"Fight him," I whispered against his mouth. "Fight for me, Maks, for us."

"He'll hurt you," he whispered back, following the words with another kiss that left me struggling to think straight.

"No, he won't." I rubbed my cheek against his, marking him as any good big cat would do to her mate. "He won't hurt me."

Maks's lips brushed mine, fluttering kisses that were sweet and spicy and in every corner of me I knew him. "You don't know that."

The thing was, I did. The more I thought about it, about Marsum and all his interactions with me, I was almost certain of one thing. He wouldn't hurt me if he could avoid it.

"He loves me."

Well, that shouldn't have slid out, or at least, not

when I was enjoying Maks being with me, holding me. Maks pushed me back and stared at me. "What?"

Now was my turn to swallow hard. "As much as he can, I think he loves me."

"No."

Maks slid away and it was just me and Marsum once more. His hands tightened on me and he pulled me close, anger flashing in his eyes. "I don't love you."

You know when you look back on a moment and think, maybe I shouldn't have done that? Yeah, this was one of those moments.

I lifted a hand, slowly, to his face. Without hesitation, he pushed his face against it, rubbing the stubble against my palm. "Liar."

He froze as if he didn't realize what he'd been doing, like he'd done it by accident. He all but threw me off his lap despite the rather obvious arousal he had going on, stood, and without another word, turned and stalked away into the darkness. Even knowing he couldn't go far before being drawn back to me, a pang of worry slid through me. Because what if he *could* get away? What if that meant I would lose my last chance to bring Maks to the front of his mind to fight for me?

"Shit, you're a fucking moron." I put a fist to my head, seeing that glittering doorway in my mind's eye. I slammed it shut and the magic in me turned off. Well, at least there was that now, a way to access the magic even if I didn't know what the hell I was doing with it.

I scooped Lila up and went to lie between Balder and Batman. Curling around my little sister, I closed my eyes and begged the gods of sleep to bestow on me dreamless, safe dreams.

Sleep rushed over me too fast, and again, I could have blamed the țuică, but I doubted that was it.

I lay on the sand, still curled around Lila when I opened my eyes to the dreamscape.

"Fuck me," I whispered. Maybe if I just stayed where I was, the Emperor wouldn't notice me. I mean, who in their right mind would willingly go back to sleep so damn fast when they'd just had a run-in with that asshole in the dreamscape? No one. Except me.

Because I was a damned drunk fool.

What if I pretended to sleep? Maybe that would do the trick. I scrunched my eyes shut, thinking about Maks, and thinking about Marsum's reaction to my words. I mean, Lila had pointed it out first, so maybe I could blame her, but I didn't think so. Not with how he had looked at me.

Shock, but more like his own lightbulb had gone off, like he realized that I was right, and he was in love with me, and that meant I had the upper hand.

Thoughts in my head kept racing and the sound of sand crunching under feet made me want to tense. But I just lay there, trying to breathe normally, wanting everyone and everything to just go the fuck away and let me sleep.

"You think she's still asleep?"

"Could be."

That first one was Merlin. I almost rolled over to give him shit and tell him what I thought about all his damn schemes. But the other voice, I knew that one too.

Ishtar.

"I see your father finally convinced you to behave. How did he do it?" Ishtar asked.

"You get your brain rattled enough, you listen," Merlin said. "What are we doing here exactly? And since when are you working with the Emperor?"

Her laughter tinkled through the air and my skin broke out in tiny pinpricks of sweat made of fear coursing through me. "Oh, you never guessed, did you?"

"Guessed what?" Merlin asked, and it was the question I was dying to know the answer to as well. What was she talking about?

Another step closer and a hand I knew brushed over my cheek. "I loved her like a daughter, because I lost mine. I loved her too because I knew she would be integral to my husband being freed one day. I saw it in every line of seers' prophecy that she was tied to the Emperor and his freedom."

Merlin gasped and I nearly echoed him. Fuck shit fuckity fuck holy shit on a camel goddess of the desert, was she saying what I thought she was saying?

Merlin stuttered enough for the both of us. "He . . . you . . . are you . . . working with the Emperor?"

"I never really stopped. I gave you my power all those years ago because I had to. You'd aligned too many of the strongest powers against us. Against him. I knew that I would have to bide my time to find those who could bring the jewels back to me. Someone who resonated with my power but couldn't be seduced by the darkness." She sighed and her hand brushed my head, petting my hair back. "Zamira was the only one who could bring the jewels to me."

I wanted to recoil from her, to grab her hand and yell at her that she was one twisted bitch. How many lives had she ruined over the years?

"I almost had her mother," she said softly. "Almost. But she slid from my grasp. Someone who loved her very much killed her to protect her from me. But Zamira, she has been mine from the beginning."

Maks, Maks, Maks. In my head I called to him, begging him to wake me. Lila stirred in my arms but didn't wake. I clung to her, knowing that if she woke now, we were both screwed.

"And what now with her? You cannot mean to harm her here."

"No. She has tasks ahead of her that I need her to complete. You think I don't know, but I know." That hand I'd never thought would be raised to me in anger or malice pulled away from me. What tasks? I wasn't working for her. I wasn't doing what she wanted.

"And that is?" Merlin prompted.

"Never mind. You have your tasks. I have mine. Not that you'll remember yours when you wake." She laughed. "You are broken, Merlin, and you don't even know it. Pity, I always thought you were smarter than this. But you threw your lot in with the wrong crowd as so often you have done before."

"I did not," he grumbled, but the effort seemed half-hearted as if he knew she was right.

And all I could think was that I needed to wake up.

"I'm going to give her a nudge in the right direction," Ishtar said. "My husband's power does not seem to work on her mind, but she cannot deny me. She could never truly deny me."

A nudge. I needed to wake now.

If Maks couldn't hear me, maybe Marsum could.

Marsum! In my head, I shouted his name and held my breath.

Ishtar put her hand to my head and a fire lit inside my skull. A fire to obey her no matter the cost. A fire that wanted to burn away who I was and make me hers in truth.

Words cut through me, started to solidify—

And then I was being yanked awake, shaken hard enough that my teeth rattled.

"Is she in my head?" I yelled the words before my eyes were even open. "Marsum, is she in my head?" Panic laced my body and I scrambled to my feet, grabbing at his hands and shoving them against my head.

His fingers tightened and the fire cooled as though water was once more being poured over me.

"You're fine," he said. "Stop it, you're fine."

I was crying, I think, at least that was what the shaking felt like. "She was burning me away. She was taking away who I am. Is it me? Am I me?"

Panic like I'd never known left me shaking, broken out in a wild sweat that was hot and cold at the same time.

"I won't let that happen." His mouth was against the side of my head and he breathed those words into my hair. "I won't let her take you."

Those words, damn it, and then he pulled me into his arms, tightened them around me. I clung to him, knowing that for the moment, he had me and wouldn't let Ishtar's power into my head.

"Shouldn't the flail have sucked her energy in?" I dug my hands into the back of his shirt, hanging onto him and the power running through the two of us. Again, he was the solid rock in the wild waters bashing into me.

"If it wasn't a direct attack, it might not have been triggered." He blew out a breath and went to push me away. I held on, though, and after a moment, he

SHANNON MAYER

sighed and gave in, kept his arms around me, his hands splayed on a hip and shoulder as if to touch as much of me as possible. What would it mean to make Marsum love me? Would he give Maks back?

Was that the answer to this riddle of bringing Maks back to me?

"Don't take this like you mean anything to me other than—"

"A potential fuck buddy?" I had my face against his chest. "Of course not."

He grunted and I was the one who pulled away, looking up into his face. "You've never fallen for anyone, have you?"

Marsum frowned and looked away. "Why would I do that? You can be manipulated if you let your emotions take over. Look at you, fighting for a horse. Look at Maks, doing exactly what I want him to do. Just to protect you."

"You wanted him to cut your head off?"

He shrugged. "It was bound to happen eventually. Better that it be him and not one of the other Jinn with less power and less connections to power."

His hands slid from me, but we stood there, close enough that I wanted to touch him again. Crap, Lila was right; this was bad. Because I couldn't see Marsum when I looked at him. I saw Maks.

Confusion rocketed through me, and then a moment of clarity. He wasn't wrong about emotions allowing you to manipulate someone. But could I do it to him?

He'd killed my family; he'd wiped out the lions. Could I use emotions against him? Damn it, I was willing to try.

I shook my head and took a step back. "You're right. This is a bad idea."

"What is?"

"Feeling anything for you." I turned my back on him but not before I saw the shock in his eyes. Was it him or Maks, though?

I sat by the fire and flipped a few bits of grass into it, making the flames crackle. "We need to sleep in shifts, to keep me awake. I can't fall into the dreamscape again."

The pad of big flat feet on the stone turned us both to see Maggi riding in on that damn camel of hers. She lifted her hand. "They are driving us. I'm sure of it. They could have had me twice, but they backed off as soon as I took the direction they wanted."

"Not good," I muttered.

Maggi slid from the camel with a grimace. "I believe we are safe here for the night."

Easy for her to say. I shared a look with Marsum, and he shook his head. I didn't like that I agreed with him to keep my last encounter with Ishtar to ourselves. I'd tell Lila, but, of course, she was still sound asleep. I reached over and pulled her into my lap, still wrapped in my cloak.

Marsum sat beside me. "You can sleep. I'll wake you if you slip into the dreamscape."

"How exactly are you going to do that?" I asked. He grabbed me and pulled me down beside him so he was spooning me on the ground. The fire in front and his body behind.

"I'll feel you twitch and dance. The dreamscape scares you."

"Good idea," Maggi said. "The cuffs should connect you enough that even if you felt nothing for her, you will feel her fear as well."

"Fuck," he muttered as he settled himself behind me. Protecting me.

Marsum was protecting me.

And I was going to let him.

15

The next two days were the same as we rode to the east, farther east than I wanted. There was no choice, though, unless we wanted to stop and have a chat with the ophidians and see if they would mind not driving us. Every time we moved off the hard, flat rock to the softer sand, they appeared within minutes.

Four days, we had four days until the golden moons rose. Just thinking about that time frame made me sweat. Could we make it?

Every step we took, I tried to figure out if what we were doing—where we were going—was right. The Wyvern's Lair was close, and while I knew we'd have to go there at some point, I didn't want it to be now.

But the Emperor's words from the dreamscape stuck with me. He never once said he would bring

Bryce back to life, but free him. The Oracle had said that the Wyvern was part of the answer to bringing Bryce back.

Then there was Ishtar. What would she have told me to do? What was she going to burn away in me, and would it have worked if Marsum hadn't woken me? My nights were restless, with Marsum waking me at least three times each night as I slipped into the dreamscape world. Or was pulled there. That was more likely. Even without those dreams, the rest of my sleep was broken with nightmares I couldn't escape.

Because awake, one of the worst was right in front of me. Marsum holding onto Maks's body, not letting him go. I didn't like how easily he'd slipped into our lives and taken a spot that was not his. Even though I knew it would help me if I led him on, even though I'd started down that path, I didn't like it.

Of course, the thing that was forefront on my mind was a bit more personal than even all that.

I put a hand to my chest and grimaced. A pang wrapped its way around my heart that had nothing to do with emotions and everything to do with the fucking stone I'd exploded against my chest. I needed to get this shit out of me, like digging out a splinter that had driven deep into the muscle. I didn't feel it all the time, but I knew it was there, knew it needed to come out before it turned septic.

"Hurting?" Lila flew around my head like an over-sized bug.

"A little." I nodded ahead at Marsum who rode just to the side of us. He had his hand on his chest too, feeling the pain as it rippled through our bond.

Lila dropped to the saddle. "I still don't like that he's holding you at night. I could wake you."

I laughed. "You sleep too deep, farting and snoring away."

Her eyes bugged open. "I do neither of those things!"

"You do," Marsum called over his shoulder.

Maggi nodded from her camel—*Demon* she named him after he spat at her—"You do."

Lila hunched.

I touched her on the head. "We still love you. Words are easy: like the wind. Faithful friends are hard to find."

She blinked up at me, a wicked gleam in those gemstone eyes. "*The Passionate Pilgrim* and don't distract me. You talk in your sleep."

"You do," Marsum said once more over his shoulder and again Maggi nodded.

I shrugged. "Nobody is perfect."

Laughter from the other two, and I thought about how weird it was to be on this trip with two people who'd previously been mortal enemies of mine. What did that say about my friends that I'd replaced them with the Ice Witch and a Jinn master?

I snorted to myself. A question that was stupid seeing as I hadn't asked either of them to come along for this ride.

"A friend should bear his friend's infirmities." I took the quotes down that same line, my mind caught up with what a friend was. What happened when an enemy became a friend? Or at least, not an enemy any longer?

Lila squinted up at me. I raised my eyebrows and a slow grin slid across my face. "Did I finally stump you?"

"No." But she closed her eyes and tapped her claws on the pommel of the saddle in a steady beat that sounded irritated. "Give me a moment."

Marsum dropped back beside us, arched one brow and shook his head. *"Julius Caesar."*

"Damn it, Toad. I was going to get it!" She launched across at him and landed on his shoulder to smack him in the head. He pushed her away, and she barrel rolled around our heads. He turned to look at me, his eyes way too soft to be Marsum.

"Hey." I smiled back. Thinking it was Maks.

It was not.

He shook his head and urged Batman to hurry forward.

"Well, shit," I muttered.

Lila flew back to me. "I thought it was Maks too."

This was where things were getting sticky between my heart and my head. Marsum was becoming a blend of Maks and the others, making it hard to see where one started and the other took off. What happened when . . .

An idea hit the front of my brain, a horrible, terrible possibility that I hadn't considered until that moment and it stole my breath in one fell swoop. Trying not to panic, I urged Balder into a trot, moving to the side of Maggi and Demon. The camel gave us a serious stink eye as it chewed its cud.

"Don't you fucking dare." I pointed at his droopy face and he turned his head away from me, nose in the air.

"You have something you want to say?" Maggi looked down at me.

Like a bandage, I needed to just rip this question out of me before I was too afraid to ask, before the fear choked me. "Is there a time limit on splitting Maks away from the other Jinn masters?"

She frowned. "What do you mean?"

I tried to get the words straightened out in my head before I spoke again. "He seems to be more and more a blend . . . like he's not always Marsum. He's a mix of Marsum and Maks." Oh shit, what if that was what was happening? How did you split them all apart? I mean, I knew that I was going to try, but what if there was a time limit on it? At least I had a direction where I could go to bring Bryce back. I didn't even have a hint of where to start with Maks.

Maggi looked to her other side, I assumed at

where Marsum rode. "Why wouldn't they become a blend? That is what they do. They assimilate the personality of the new host body, the dominant personality owning the others."

"But Marsum was Marsum, not your Davin, by what you've said. You said Davin was a decent guy, that he wasn't an ass like Marsum," I said.

"Marsum is a very strong personality. And it was his body. The host body is always stronger. Or should be." She squinted into the direction we were headed. "Do you see that?"

I didn't look at what she was looking at because I was too busy trying to get my head wrapped around what she was saying. Maks was strong. I knew he was. So why wasn't it working this way? Or was I missing something? Only one way to find out.

With pressure from my legs, I spun Balder and sent him toward Marsum and Batman, trotting alongside them. "I need you to answer a question."

"Do you see that?" He tipped his head toward the horizon.

"Are you assimilating Maks?" I asked and he slowly turned his head to me.

"What?"

"Answer me. You have to. Are you assimilating Maks? Is that why you are softening toward me? Is that why you're falling in love with me because you are getting his emotions?" The questions poured out of me, and with each one, I could see his face tighten further as if he wanted to not answer me, as if he wanted to tell me to fuck off. But, of course, he couldn't. Those were the rules of the cuffs that bound us together. But maybe, also, I was hitting too close to the mark.

His jaw flexed and tensed. I could see him prepping an answer.

Before he could speak, an arrow landed between us, twanging hard into the ground, and actually sticking to the hard rock. No, not sticking, driving into it. The ground hissed and bubbled as the arrow burrowed in farther, actually wriggling. Not unlike the catch nets that Maggi's goblins had used.

"Maybe we can discuss this when we aren't under attack," he snapped.

I steeled myself. "Nope, I want my answer now. There will always be something in the way."

Lila squeaked and clutched at the front of my shirt. "Zam, Zam, I think you need to look at what's coming this way. Like, right now."

I finally looked and kind of wished I could have just kept my eyes locked on Marsum.

Directly ahead of us was a writhing mass of creatures I didn't at first recognize. To be fair, my first thought was gorc. But they were too light of body, too lean, and their bodies were covered from head to foot in a sand-colored cloth that floated in the wind. I'd heard tales of these things, but never seen them. They moved like the wind, and killed those who crossed their paths, but not before they sucked their souls out. They were known for being in the southernly regions of the desert. I'd just hoped we'd dodge them.

Just what we needed. I kept my eyes on the group of sand wraiths. They didn't have mounts; they just kind of floated on the sand, dust swirling up around them. The stories of people who'd encountered them often said they thought it was just a windstorm they were dealing with, at least, until they were attacked. Again, all stories and rumors said the likelihood of surviving something like this was not good.

"What are they?" Maggi asked.

"Sand wraiths," Marsum growled. "They are second only to the Jinn in power and are fiercely territorial."

"Like every other supernatural creature, you mean?" Lila offered as another arrow snaked toward us in the air, landing with a thunk just ahead of us. They weren't attacking, not yet.

These were warning shots.

"Worse than dragons, and that is not friendly fire." Marsum looked around us.

"They are directly in our path," Maggi said. "If we let them push us, we will be back into the soft sand of the ophidians' turf."

"And we probably can't just run down between them? They look like floating bedsheets." Lila sounded hopeful and doubtful at the same time. I knew how she felt.

"No," Marsum said. "Now that we are in their sights, we will have difficulty throwing them. But they aren't attacking, so we have that much in our favor."

That's what he thought. Already I could feel the oncoming fight, like smelling rain in the wind, knowing it was there just waiting to fall the second you hung your clothes out to dry on the line.

A chorus of war cries lit up the air. Lila's scales shivered and shimmered as she lifted into the air. "That can't be good."

"Those weren't warning shots, those were 'get the fucking trespassers' shots," I said. "Now answer my question, Marsum!"

He let out a snarl. "No!"

Damn him. If he wanted it to be hard, then we'd do hard.

"You wanna play dirty then?" I reached for my flail and pulled it from my back. "I'm tired of running, tired of being pushed in this direction and that, tired of the games." I put my heels to Balder and he shot forward, leaning into the oncoming wind. As if he'd never been bit, as if he'd never walked the line with death.

Lila raced along with me. "We really doing this?"

"What choice is there? I'll offer them an out first." At least, that was what I hoped to do. I spun the flail at my side, almost lazily. The weapon was so light, I could make using it look exceptionally easy.

I slowed Balder and raised my hand. "We want only to pass through. We are not here to fight."

Three arrows shot toward us, wicked fast, and it was only a combination of Lila's speed and Balder's quick response to my aids that we avoided them. Another round of war cries lit up the air.

Just fucking awesome. "Guess that answers that."

I dug into the saddlebag for the sapphire and tossed it up to Lila. She took it, but there was a grimace on her face as though it pained her. "You got this."

"I know. I just hate how it makes me feel." She slipped the harness on and I had no more time to watch her.

The wind around us picked up speed, the bits of sand smacking into us and blurring our vision.

"We gotta end this fast!" I yelled up to Lila.

She bobbed her head and was gone in a streak of blue and silver. I urged Balder forward. Running would do no good here, they were out for blood.

Or souls.

Souls.

They ate souls.

Marsum was a soul. All the Jinn masters were.

"WAIT!" I screamed the word at Lila and she stopped in midair, nearly taking an arrow. Marsum had wanted to run by them, wanted to get away as fast as possible and even now . . . I turned in my saddle to see him sitting far behind us, Batman dancing underneath him, wanting to be with us.

He shook his head. Did I dare?

"What if we offered you a soul to pass by?" I yelled at the sand wraiths. "Payment for passing?"

The wind slowed and the sand wraiths glided closer to me, no arrows flying, no sand spitting. Balder pawed at the ground. I didn't let go of the flail. "We need to pass. What if we give you a soul?"

They moved together as if they were one creature instead of the many that were obviously there. The voice that spoke for them rasped through the air, like sand scratching against rock.

"You would give over a soul for passage?"

"If we fight, I'll kill at least some of you," I held the flail up, "with this. You know it's true. And there is a Jinn master behind me waiting to take you down if you harm me. Sure, we'd probably die too, but this way, we all win."

They flowed in and out of each other as if they weren't quite solid. I wondered where they'd been created and then I realized it could have been Ishtar before her powers had been stolen from her.

Not that it mattered. We had to face them.

"Whose soul would you offer?"

"What about a Jinn master?" I knew I was taking a chance, but this was too good of a chance to pass up.

SHANNON MAYER

Creatures that ate souls? Maks had too many souls that weren't his own in him.

Oh, gods, if only I'd known the trouble I was about to cause myself, I would have swung the flail and fought our way through the wraiths. I would have taken the chance of dying.

16

"Lila, bring Maggi and Marsum close. Tell them we have to make a payment, but we can pass by the sand wraiths," I said. "Do not tell them what the payment is."

"Do you really think he'll fall for it?" Lila's eyebrows dipped low. "I mean, he's not stupid."

I grimaced. "It's a chance to get Maks back. If we eliminate some, or maybe all of the other souls, don't you think?"

She nodded. "It is. To get Toad back, it is worth the chance."

With that, she flew toward the other two, and I was left alone to stand with the sand wraiths. I should have been afraid of them, but curiously, I found myself more intrigued. "Who made you?"

"The one who creates all life."

"No, no, not that. You all haven't been around that

long, and you were created by someone. Does that someone have a name?" I rolled the handle of the flail in my palm. Warm, but it had unstuck itself from me. Maybe it realized it wouldn't be used. That didn't mean I was putting it away.

They hissed and a low chittering rolled out of them before there was an answer.

"We do not speak the name of the one that made us. Sacrilege."

Slow hoofbeats announced Batman's arrival. "Sure, sorry about that."

I looked over my shoulder to where Marsum sat astride Batman. His eyes locked on mine, and whatever he saw there, his own narrowed in response. "What have you done?"

"I've struck a bargain. Get off Batman," I said.

His jaw flexed and I could see him fighting the command. "What have you done?"

"A soul for passage," I said. "You have many of those, do you not? Surely one could be offered up?"

A slow smile crossed his face. "Fine, we give them Maks."

Oh fuck.

"No, you give them you, Marsum. Or one of the others," I said. Damn it, my heart was pounding out of control with just the thought of Marsum handing Maks over. Maks was the only reason I was doing this.

A sharp, dagger-like pain bloomed in my chest

and I put a fist to it, as if I could calm it with some good pressure. Marsum did the same, leaning over his saddle. "You can't disobey me."

"Actually, he can," Maggi said softly, "if you tried to put his life in danger."

I shot a look at her.

"Our patience is fading. We do not play games. We want our soul. We will take yours."

I turned as one of the sand wraiths launched itself at me. Chest still throbbing, I swung the flail, catching it square in the head. The flail's handle shivered against my palm and stuck itself into the creature's skull. Twin balls covered in spikes dug into the sand wraith, a pulse of power sucked away and into the flail.

The scene exploded, sand everywhere, a wind snapping around us and making it hard to see. "Maggi, get out of here!" I yelled. She was useless now with all her power gone, and it was going to be hard enough to protect myself, never mind her too.

I hoped she heard me.

I could barely see through the sand swirling around my face. "Shout out, so I know where you are!"

Lila hollered from way above and there was nothing from Marsum. The bastard had probably run. Then again, I had just tried to feed his soul to a new master.

Without another thought, I swung the flail as I

turned Balder to the side. Hands slid over my arms, and I smashed through them, the bones breaking with resounding cracks. The sand eased around us and I squinted through the swirling pieces. Marsum faced off with four sand wraiths, and Lila was in the air, dropping in and freezing them—or at least she was trying to. They would freeze and then shake the cold off like it was nothing.

"Go with Maggi!" I yelled to her.

She was no good here. Again, I didn't wait to see if she listened. I fought my way to Marsum's side, knocking the sand wraiths down with what felt like ease.

"You're a fool!" he shouted at me.

"Are you assimilating Maks?"

"YES!" he roared the word as he lifted his hand and the black magic of the Jinn poured out of him, wrapped up the sand wraiths and pulled them apart. The wind died down immediately, and the sand at our feet shimmered and shivered.

Anger snapped through him, and without the sand wraiths, I would never have gotten him to this point. To this much emotion.

He glared at me. "They will pull themselves together in a very short time. I suggest we move. If that pleases you, *mistress*."

My jaw ticked. "It would please me to have Maks back."

"He is, you fool. We are all softening because of

him," he roared. "I don't want this emotion. I don't want to care for you. Fuck you, yes. Get a child on you for the next in the line of the Jinn, yes. But love you? No. That's a fucking mess that no amount of magic can fix."

I just stared at him. "Tell me there is a way to—"

"There is no way to bring him back," Marsum yelled. "There is no way to separate us. I took over Davin, and now I've taken Maks, but . . . his love for you is insane! He would die for you, and I can't stop him from wanting that. From making *me* want it. It makes me want to love you and protect you and cherish you in a way that would make us both targets. It would make us both weak and that will kill us both!"

He roared the words at me, and in them, I heard Maks. I heard him trying to stay at the front of his own mind, of his own body. He was fighting for me with all he had, with his most powerful weapon.

With his love for me.

"I am not giving up." I choked on the words. "I refuse to give up on him."

"That's the problem!" he snapped. "Neither is he!"

I urged Balder forward, passing by him. I didn't reach out to touch him. But he flinched like he was afraid I would. Or maybe he was afraid of what his own reaction would be to me.

Following my instincts was something I knew, something I'd always heeded. More than once, they'd saved me. They'd brought me out of situations everyone thought would kill me.

What my instincts were telling me to do, though . . . they went against everything that had brought me here. Maggi was wrong about the cuffs. Merlin was wrong.

Caging the person you loved was not how you kept them near you.

I dismounted Balder. "Get off my horse," I said softly.

He dismounted, snarling. I walked up to him, cupped his face and kissed him. He made as if to pull away, then gave into it, wrapping his arms around me, holding me tightly. I tipped my head back so I could look him in the eyes.

"Maggi was wrong. I love you. I love you completely, even if it damns me to die. Maybe it would be better to give the sand wraiths my soul, but as it is, you have it."

Suspicion was written clearly across his face. "That changes nothing." That's what he said, but he didn't let me go.

"You're wrong, Marsum. Love isn't weak. It's the strongest thing in this world. It's made me better, made me stronger. I fight the way I do for those I love." I touched his cheek. "If you and Maks are assimilating, if you are becoming one, then . . . I guess I love you too. And I can't risk either of you dying on my account. That's not what you do to someone you love."

He went very still but said nothing.

I let him go and stepped back, took a deep breath and spoke as clearly as I could through the sudden wash of tears, because I knew the cost of what I was doing. That doorway inside me to my magic opened and I pulled it through me, finding the handcuffs easily, following the same instincts that had saved me time and time again. "I release you from your bonds."

The metal cuffs appeared over our wrists, then fell off with dual snaps. They fell to the ground and slithered toward one another, clicking as they came together. I scooped them up, mounted back on Balder and rode away from him.

Love didn't bind those you loved forcibly. If there really was *no* way to bring Maks back to himself, then I either would find a way to love the person he'd become, or we would go our separate ways. I wasn't sure I could do the first, and the second was likely to kill me.

More than that, I had hope that there was an answer somewhere in between.

I had to trust that Maks had shown Marsum I was worth saving.

There had been a moment where Maks had tried to bind himself to me, and Marsum had stopped him. I would take the chance that love was enough to save me.

I had to.

I caught up quickly to Lila and Maggi.

Lila shot over to me, tore off the sapphire and shoved it into my hands. "Take it now, take it now, and never give it to me again."

I nodded, my throat too tight to speak. But I knew why she said what she said. The sapphire made her mean, and prone to violence. I could almost feel the anger rolling off her as she thrust the stone back at me. I tucked it into the pouch at my side and kept on walking.

Maggi asked me what was wrong, and I just shook my head. Already the pain and nausea I'd endured before the cuffs went on rose inside me. Flaring in my body, the vertigo rolling up and around me.

I knew that if I died, if this magic took me, there would be no stopping Ishtar, no saving my pride, no keeping the Emperor imprisoned. But there was no saying any of that would happen if I did survive.

I'd have never said I was a gambler before, that I would take a risk with so little obvious ability to come through it, but then again, my middle name was Reckless.

"What have you done?" Maggi whispered, her hands on me, holding me upright.

"I let him go." I blinked up at her. "I had to, Maggi. I had to let him go. It's the only way to make this work. He'll keep fighting, and in the end, that will kill us. So this way . . ."

"Oh, my dear girl." She touched my face and took the cuffs from me. "You have more faith in him than you should."

Lila grabbed at me and I closed my eyes. "I'm sorry, Lila."

"No, no you don't get to decide to die on me! You brought me back from the brink. I was dead and you saved me!" She was yelling at me, and I knew that I was breaking her heart, but this was how it had to be. I had to try. I had to . . . gods, what if I was wrong?

"Go with Maggi. Get to Trick and Ollianna. Go far away," I said. "Go." I tried to push her away and she shoved at me, took off and flew the wrong way.

She flew toward where I'd left Marsum.

"Oh my heart, this is a mess," Maggi said. Surprisingly, she pulled me out of the saddle and onto Demon's back with her, shocking me. "Yes, I am stronger than I look. Don't be so surprised I can lift you."

I might have smiled. I'm not sure. *Dying wasn't so bad.* That was about the only thought going through my head. The magic pooled in my belly, sending out waves of warmth.

My gamble was not working. Maks wasn't taking control of Marsum. He wasn't coming to save me.

"I'm sorry. Can you tell everyone I'm sorry?" I

slurred the words as if I'd been drinking țuică for days.

"Hush now. I'm going to try to get you to the Wyvern. He might be able to help."

That was what she said, but I heard the doubt in her voice. She didn't think I had long left. With Marsum and me holding the magic at bay together, we'd had only a few days left to get to the market and then to the crossroads. That time had been more than cut in half by the way my body felt.

Maggi sighed. "You have hours left, dear girl. Hours."

Well, damn.

17

MERLIN

Merlin had his head against his horse's neck as they raced after Shara, who galloped toward Ishtar. His dreams were haunting him, showing him what was coming for him, for Flora, and for Zam. Just thinking about the visions had him breaking out in a cold sweat that left him wracked with fear.

He knew the difference between a nightmare and a glimpse of the future. There was no point in telling Flora. She wouldn't believe him. Wouldn't believe that he had gained an ability while his father's power had taken hold of his mind. Perhaps his father had unlocked the capability so he could use it for his own benefit. Merlin didn't know, and also knew it didn't matter much except for the fact that it was the truth.

Besides, in the last two days, Flora hadn't said a single word to him, so speaking to her was difficult at best. Never mind a cold shoulder, she was giving him a full-on snowman. Or snowwoman, he supposed. But even that wayward thought didn't do much to soothe his worries and fears. Beside the nightmares was a raging headache that made it hard to focus. He kept wanting to turn south, away from their current path.

The crossroads called to him, and that was a thought, a desire he knew wasn't his own, no matter how he tried to ignore it. Something in him was cracking. Each night, he was losing more and more of himself in the dreams that blurred his mind.

If only he could remember them.

He touched a hand to his head, feeling the weight of something there he couldn't quite put his finger on. A deep throb started in the base of his skull and spread upward, fanning across his skull like a pair of hands gripping, digging in tightly to the meat of his brain. He groaned and leaned farther against his horse. He was out of time.

"Flora." He said her name and then pulled his horse to a sweating, heaving stop. "We need to stop."

"No, we need to catch her if you don't want her to die! Ishtar will kill her, and while I'm not sure that is a bad thing, she is your child." Flora spun her horse around to snap at him.

"Something is wrong, something is in my head." He stared at her in horror as his hand began to lift without any desire on his part. The fingers across his skull tightened farther, and his back arched in response. "Flora!" His magic pooled up just at the tips of his fingers. The spell was there, ready to launch at her, and it would end her. "Flora, strike me!"

For a moment, he thought she wouldn't. He thought maybe she couldn't because she cared for him so much. Those green eyes widened and the wind caught her hair, flinging it around her face. In that moment, she was the girl he'd met all those years ago.

Then her eyes narrowed, and she flicked her hand at him. A bolt of lightning flew from the sky and slammed into him and his horse with a boom of thunder following close behind. He was thrown sideways, his body limp, and his horse fell in the opposite direction. The fingers in his skull eased for just a moment.

"Damn you, Merlin!" Flora's voice sounded far away and tinny as if he were in some sort of metal box.

Hands cupped his face and he pushed her away. "Go. Get away from me. Something is in my head and it wants you dead." He didn't dare open his eyes. That was how his father, the Emperor, had controlled him. By seeing through him, his father had been able to direct him to do his deeds. Was this what was happening again?

"Is it the Emperor?" Her hands were cool against

his flushed skin, her words echoing his own thoughts.

"You don't listen well," he said. "You need to go. I don't know who it is. Like fingers inside my head, digging in."

"I'm not leaving you." Her voice was closer, next to his ear. Lips brushed against his cheek. "You don't leave family behind. Neither do I. Keep your eyes closed."

He squinted his eyes shut tight, his other senses straining. The rustle of her skirts, the tearing of cloth, the smell of her skin so close, he could lean in and kiss it, and then a swath of material covered his eyes. She tied the blindfold, pulling it tight enough that he winced. He couldn't help but touch a hand over it.

"Can you get them out of your head?" she asked.

He blew out a slow breath and focused on the sensation in his mind. The fingers digging in there, the power rolling through him that was not his own. The feeling was strange when it wasn't painful, as if someone were probing through his mind, reading his thoughts, reading his memories. But who could have such control over him?

"Not my father. Someone else." He bowed his head and continued to search himself. He needed to figure out who this was so he could detach them from his mind. He lifted a hand to his head as if he could touch the fingers that dug into his mind. There was sense to them that he could only feel as one thing. "A woman," he said.

"But who?"

He had the same question. "I can't figure out who, only that it is a woman."

Maggi could walk the dreamscape . . . could she have turned on him? His plan did require that she give up her life, but she should be dead by now, and to stop her sister Ishtar, she'd seemed willing. Of course, there was Ishtar herself, though he didn't think she could actively walk the dreamscape. And that was where he was sure he'd picked up this spell.

Like picking up a disease in a foreign country. His nightmares and restless nights, the visions, they all made more sense. But now he wondered if the visions of the future were true, or were they planted by whoever this woman was?

"I think we have a traitor in our midst." He worked his fingers, massaging his own skull, using his magic to untie what was knotted inside him. Slowly the threads came apart and he breathed a sigh of relief. "It is undone. But that I could be taken at all, that is concerning."

"Who though? Because we have not been near anyone," Flora said.

"The dreamscape," he said softly. "Temporarily this will work, but what happens when we face someone? What happens if even with this spell gone, my mind is taken again, and I attack you?" And when they faced Ishtar or Shara? Both were powerful enough that Flora and he would need to be on their best game.

"I don't know. But we've come this far, so we must continue on." Her hands slid to his and she helped him stand. "Good thing I focused on you and not your poor horse."

A muzzle shoved against him, and he fumbled to find the horse's reins. "Beautiful and smart."

"Compliments will get you nowhere." A sigh followed her words. "What are we doing, Merlin? Are we even helping? It's like nothing we do here has had the impact we wanted. I tried to help Zam with her magic, and I couldn't teach her a thing. You tried to help her by sending Marsum back to her so she could find a way to free Maks. You saw the crystal ball this morning, they've separated again.

"The Emperor is nearly free, and Ishtar is growing in power every day as she heals. Even Ford and the other lions are trapped. And now your mind is being attacked. There are too many, on too many sides."

He held a hand out to his side, hoping . . . and she took his fingers and he held on tightly to her. "We keep trying, Flora. We keep trying to help. Even if they are mistakes, I don't want to be known as the Merlin who gave up, the warlock who ran away when the world needed the most help. I will do all I can until there is no breath left in me. Even if that moment is getting closer and closer."

Her fingers squeezed his. "Don't talk like that."

"It's the truth," he said as the horses started forward, slowly. "We might not like it, but we face odds that are very much not in our favor. With little to no allies."

That drew silence from her, but she didn't take her hand out of his. A smile quirked his lips. "Who knew it would take this," he waved at his head, tapping it with one finger, "to get you to hold my hand."

She gave him a little tug. "Don't think I won't push you out of the saddle if you irritate me."

"That was a pull actually," he pointed out. Flora huffed and let go of his hand with a flick of her wrist.

He sighed. "I think you should leave me, Flora. I think you should go—"

"Where, where would I go?" she threw at him. "There is nowhere else, Merlin. Your father, when he is freed, will make sure that we are dealt with. We stop him, put him to sleep again, or whatever we have to do, or this world is done for."

"I know," he said. "I know." But in his head, all he could see were the things those visions had shown him. The same thing over and over.

Of Zamira freeing the Emperor and standing at his side.

He swallowed hard, his heart tearing into pieces

as the obvious decision stood in front of them. They either rode after Shara, saved her, and tried to stop Ishtar, or they rode to Zamira and tried to keep her from freeing the Emperor.

But which was the right path?

He looked at Flora and sighed. "We have a decision to make."

That was what was needed . . . but the world around him blinked out and he was in the dreamscape without meaning to be there.

Ishtar stood in front of him, her face bruised and battered, her body wounded, but she stood there with a wicked gleam in her eyes and the stones she'd gathered glowing from within her body.

"You are mine now, Merlin."

Only one thing to say.

"Shit."

And then his world went dark.

18

ZAMIRA

The clumping along of Maggi's camel, Demon, below me was jarring, jolting, horrific, and more than once, I thought about puking over the side of the beast. But really, there wasn't a lot in my belly, not much left of me at all.

In letting Marsum go and setting him free from the cuffs, I'd condemned myself to death. I was an idiot thinking that whatever conglomeration of Maks was left in there had meshed sufficiently to convince Marsum that he loved me enough to save me. I wanted to believe it too badly, enough that I'd gambled my life on that belief.

Gambled and lost.

"You just had to do it, didn't you? Why, why, when I gave most of my magic to create those cuffs?" Maggi muttered as she whacked Demon with a quirt.

"Yes," I said. "You said it, we need Marsum to make it through this, and if he's here by force then we can never trust him. And we have to be able to trust him. The market—"

"I know. But I thought if he had more time with you, with us, that I would be able to convince him . . ."

She mumbled something, but my head was fuzzy with all the pain rocketing through me and the nausea so close on its heels. I probably should have been more worried, or upset, or afraid, but the thing was I was almost looking forward to dying.

No more pain, no more hurt. No more worrying about anyone else. No more wondering if the world would be saved, or the Emperor freed. Someone else could do the job, someone else could put the lives of those they loved on the line.

I closed my eyes as Maggi pulled Demon to a stop. "Zam, I need you awake, and I need you awake now."

I opened my eyes. "I wasn't asleep."

"You've been out for the last nearly two hours and I don't believe we have much time left in you." She slid off Demon first and then pulled me down.

I could barely stand, but using Demon, I could keep my balance. "What?"

"We have to cross the sand to get to the Wyvern."

I looked around. Ahead was a rolling body of water that could have been the ocean the way the waves crashed over sand. The sound of waves on the sand, the distant smell of salt and fresh air, the call of a sea bird. But between us and that was a hell of a lot of sand.

And ophidians, a hell of a lot of them too.

The sand writhed with the fuckers, their bodies humping up and down, tails flicking out with a burst of sand here and there like the spray of a whale. There was no telling how many of them there were, only that every inch of ground ahead of us moved. "What am I supposed to do?"

"We'll send Demon in one direction. The snakes will chase him down, and then we will cross. Your horse, at least, kept up, and we can double on him." Maggi hefted one of my arms over her much higher shoulders so the tips of my toes dragged in the sand to where Balder stood, breathing hard. Sure, he'd kept up, but barely.

"We won't make it. Not double. Soon as they hear his hoofbeats, a single camel won't save us," I said.

"It is your only chance, so we will take it!" she snapped, shaking me.

"I should have trusted you more," I said. "Sorry about that." My words were slurred as I slumped. "Hard to trust in this world, hard to know who is on your side. I think Merlin is trapped by Ishtar."

She jerked as if I'd slapped her.

A whoosh of wings cut through the air and then Lila was there as if she'd never left, sitting on my shoulder and breathing hard. "Wait, just wait." She grabbed me tightly around my head, squeezing me. "There is a better chance than the Wyvern."

Maggi gasped and turned to look behind us. I wobbled and turned my head, not sure that what I was seeing was correct.

Batman raced toward me, his coat slick with sweat and foam from trying to keep up with the damn camel. His rider pulled him to a stop, slid off, and stalked toward me. Lightning danced in those pretty blue eyes. The closer he got, the more the air charged around us, his magic swirling up and around his lower limbs in a black mist I knew too damn well.

"Damn us both," he snapped as he grabbed me and pulled me away from Maggi. She gasped again but let me go.

His fingers burrowed into my hair, and that was all that held me up as he kissed me. I caught some of my weight, hanging onto his biceps, digging my fingers in for traction. His mouth was hot and demanding and the magic that shot through me felt like I was being swallowed whole by the desert sand, the individual grains branding me as theirs, calling me home.

Desert born, desert cursed, desert loved.

No matter what else happened in my life, this was who I was, and who I would always be—a queen of a lion pride, an alpha, a fighter for justice. The fire in me burned, hot, hotter, till the power of the stone was pushed down and away, pinned beneath the magic that was the Jinn and their jewel.

My mind swirled with magic that was not my own, and he was there, holding me together, taking my pain into himself, spreading out the power of the gemstone so I could function—again. Only this time there were no cuffs, no one was forcing him. He did this on his own.

Maks had done this. Maks was still fighting for me. And maybe Marsum was fighting for me too.

I wrapped my arms around him and held onto him as though he were the life raft in a boiling ocean storm. My own magic opened and I let it flood me, let it go where it wanted. And it wanted him.

The two magics twined about one another, and I saw them in my mind's eye, wrapping the tendrils tighter and tighter until they were totally merged. The black mist of the Jinn, and my magic that glittered silver and gold. The tighter the magic wove, the tighter his arms locked around me, until he was crushing me to his chest. Mind you, my arms were around him too, and I was not about to let go. Maks had done this, and I would hold onto him as long as I could.

Slowly, ever so slowly the world came back into focus, though not that well, I'll admit. I was still a bit wobbly, but that could be because of the raging lust rushing through my veins. Marsum pulled back enough that we weren't kissing, but our lips touched as he spoke. "We are tied. You can't die."

"Um, thanks?" I tipped my head back so I could look at him. "I mean, I could still die."

His lips twitched. "Fair enough. But I will do what I can to keep you alive."

"Very sweet," Maggi drawled, breaking the moment into tiny pieces. "But we have an ocean of ophidians to cross. Regardless of how we look at this, we cannot move farther south without dealing with them."

Marsum let me go, but there was reluctance in every movement of his body, in every flick of his muscles. To be fair, I was not in a hurry to release him either. The feel of him in my arms and his mouth on mine were too good, too right to just let it go without any lingering.

I turned back to the ophidians and cleared my throat. That much magic, that much lust and under-current of my heart and Maks's was no small thing to just act like it hadn't happened. But I was going to try. I cleared my throat again. "Are you sure the Wyvern is there, on the other side? In the water?" It looked like what I'd seen in the dreamscape, but I saw no eyes peering out of the water at me.

"Yes." Maggi and Marsum spoke in tandem.

"Maybe we can just use the edge of his territory to keep the ophidians at bay?" I said, because there was no energy left in me for another fight. Almost dying did that to a girl.

"We can try," Marsum said. "But remember the territorial part? He makes dragons look like pussy cats."

"Shit," Lila and I whispered together.

I didn't want to sacrifice any of us to get across the sand to the water, but the water was our only hope. In large part because there was no guarantee that once near the water the ophidians would fuck off. I mean, I hoped because the sand would be wet, thick, and full of water that they would, but there was no way of knowing.

On my back, the flail pulsed, sending a flush of warmth through me. I reached for it before I could stop myself. My fingers brushed the handle, and I paused there, my mind clicking into overdrive, working to find a way through this obstacle. Sure, the flail was a powerful weapon, but only if I was alive. Only if I was still able to stand and not being flooded with poison.

If only we could fight our way through this, hell, even gorcs would be more acceptable than this clusterfuck. I blinked a few times and drummed my fingers on the handle as an idea took root and grew at a rapid rate. Maybe there was a way through this. What were the chances, though, that my idea would work?

"You got a pull on any gorcs around here?" I turned my head to Marsum.

His eyes narrowed and he turned his head from me to look to the north. "There's a band not far from here. They aren't mine, though. Wild gorcs are not easily tamed."

I let go of the flail. "Well, don't you worry about it. I just need to piss them off and they'll come a-running." I grinned. Tried not to think about ripping his clothes off and—

Lila tapped me on the head, and it was only then I realized she had been there the whole time, even when I'd kissed him and all that power had run through the two of us. "You piss off gorcs? There is no way sweet, soft little you could do that."

Marsum snorted. "They do like her, don't they?"

"Oh, I think they'd like to roast her on a spit." Lila shook her head. "But of course, they have to catch her first."

Marsum went to Batman and mounted. "Let's go find them then. I assume you want them for bait?"

I nodded and pulled myself onto Balder. My arms and legs were still wobbly, but I wasn't falling over so that was a massive improvement. Marsum led the way, and I followed on Balder, Lila clinging to me.

"You convinced him?" I asked her.

"Those friends thou hast, and their adoption tried, grapple them unto thy soul with hoops of steel," she said softly. "*Hamlet.*" She smiled. "You are my family,

Zam. That was a risk what you did, and I was not about to let you go without a fight. And he isn't either."

"I didn't mean to scare you." I grimaced. "I thought he'd—"

"Make a grand gesture? Maks would throw him off and come to the front of his head and you'd be together again?" Her words were not sharp, but I felt them like blows, whether she meant them to be or not. "I'm not sure how much of Maks is in there. It was Marsum I appealed to."

She hunched her back and tucked her head down. "Maybe Maks is gone. I hate that I am even saying it, but it is a possibility and I would be a shit friend if I just let you keep on believing in him when maybe you shouldn't. Marsum was the one who agreed to come back and save you."

I wondered what she'd said, but then realized I already knew.

A child.

Marsum wanted a child from me.

I gritted my teeth and leaned over Balder as he loped after Marsum and Batman. "I won't give up." Not yet, I wasn't done. There were the crossroads and a curse to be broken there. Maybe the curse would be the curse of the Jinn.

"I know. I wouldn't give up on Trick either if something happened to him like this." She butted me with her head. "Then again, if he turned into my father, I might not say that. I might kill him myself to put him out of his misery." I blew out a breath and she grabbed at me. "Sorry, I didn't think before I said that. I know you would have taken Marsum's head yourself if you could have."

Ahead of us, Marsum and Batman disappeared over a hill. A throaty rumble and the stomp of big flat feet reached me, a sound I knew all too well. "What do you want to bet that he found more than a single band of gorcs?"

"Well, more are better, right? They'll keep the snake things busy. Right?" Lila didn't sound any more convinced than I felt.

I urged Balder up the hill and he took it in a few strides. At the top, looking down, the scene that spread out wasn't as bad as it could have been. Three bands of gorcs looked up at me. I waved at them.

Marsum stood in the middle of them, his magic reaching out like the tendrils of a fabled sea monster, each one touching a gorc. Within minutes, they all stood quietly with their heads down and their breathing slow as if they were sleeping. Marsum stood there, snapped his fingers and barked at them in gorc.

"*Fravorsh. Grlort blashk.*"

"Say that ten times fast," Lila said.

I watched carefully, waiting for the gorcs to break rank, waiting for them to turn and attack me. But they didn't, they just marched up the stone hill, past me, and toward the sand of the ophidians.

Marsum and Batman were the last ones up the hill. "A number of the gorcs were mine, so easy enough to turn them and convince the others," he said casually, but he was sweating and his mouth was tight.

"You okay?"

"Fine."

I didn't like the way he wouldn't look at me. What was his game? Was he going to turn on me in the middle of all this? I couldn't help but tense my hands on the reins. As long as Marsum was there, in Maks's body, and as much as it killed a part of me, I would never fully trust him.

The only problem with that was I needed to trust him to get us through this. Crap on a camel's ass, this was a sticky situation if there ever was one.

Lila snickered. "I'm stealing that. Also, you know you mutter a lot when you're all wound up?"

"Yeah, thanks," I said.

We were drawing close to the sand, and Marsum had the gorcs lined up along the edge between stone and loose ground. The ophidians were quiet and the sand was still, but I had no doubt they were there waiting for us to take a single step onto the soft sand.

"When you get to the water, ride in," Marsum said. "The ophidians can't handle the water through the ground so we should be okay. Hang a hard right, keep the water on your left."

I twisted in my saddle to look at him. "Should be?"

He shrugged. "I've never faced them before in these numbers." He winked at me. "But just think, at least you and your precious Maks would die together then."

That was a new jab.

He barked a sudden order at the gorcs and they launched into action, running onto the sand right along the edge of the stone. Their big flat fleet made a thunderous staccato, enough that it should pull the ophidians away and mask our own footsteps. They were a quarter mile away and running hard when the first of them went down onto the sand. The other gorcs didn't notice they'd lost someone. That was the power of Marsum and the Jinn riding them, making them do as he wanted. I shuddered.

We watched as the plan began to unfold, and just as we'd hoped, the ophidians went for the bait. The gorcs went down, one after another, and then they began to fight back, making even more noise.

"Now!" Marsum yelled as the gorcs and ophidians tangled up a half a mile away from us. It had to be enough.

I hissed at Balder and he leapt forward, plunging across the line between solid ground and soft, and I held my breath, waiting for a strike to happen. But it didn't come, and I urged him even more.

A quick glance to my right, though, showed me what I feared. Not all of the ophidians had been fooled.

A swarm of them swept through the sand, straight for us. Ten, I could see ten of them in the waving lines of their bodies. "Faster!" I yelled.

Demon stumbled and threw Maggi off his back. She hit hard, her head bouncing against the ground. She didn't get back up. Shit.

She'd tried to save me from myself.

Tried to help me bring Maks back.

Fought to keep Ishtar away from me.

She was not my enemy.

I did the only thing I could.

I leapt off Balder, pulled my flail, and put myself between Maggi and the ophidians.

19

The ophidians didn't slow now that I was on the ground; their armored bodies whipped through the sand faster, if I were to guess. "Lila, take the high ground, call it out for me!"

"Zam, don't you dare get bit!" she yelled as she shot into the air, spun and stared down at me. "Three in the lead, the one to your right is going to circle you."

I took off to the right, spinning the flail as fast as I could. The armor on the ophidians was thick and I had no idea just how big of a hit it would take to do damage.

The sand gave under my feet, pulling me down and I dove sideways as it gave way completely. Rolling, I came up to my feet and spun, twisting so that I brought the flail down on the ophidian I'd been

236

going for. The creature's body was barely above the sand but it had to be enough.

The twin spiked balls slammed into the sand snake's body, and dug in hard, flexing and pulsing as it drew down the ophidian's life force in a matter of seconds. I yanked it free.

"Left, left!" Lila yelled.

I spun, and brought the flail down, hitting what looked like just sand, but trusting Lila. Blood burbled up through the desert ground, and then it was gone, sucked down by the flail.

"The last one is going for Maggi!" Lila yelled and I was off and running, the flail held out from my side. "Straight ahead!"

I fought to pick up speed, the ground moving wickedly fast ahead of me. "Come on, you worm! I'm back here!" I yelled at the ophidian, wishing, hoping, they could understand me.

Of course, the creature didn't so much as slow for a second.

"Behind you!" Lila shrieked.

Everything seemed to slow. I leapt up into the air, spun and shifted forms as I came back down, landing on top of the ophidian's head. I dug my claws in, driving them through his skull as if I were the jungle cat I was meant to be and not a house cat with delusions of grandeur. The ophidian lashed its head side to side as if to dislodge me.

"Lila, get to Maggi!" I yelled as I fought to hang

onto the ophidian. It wouldn't take long before the big bastard would figure out that if it went underground it would lose me. I had to kill it now.

It let out a long low hiss at me, and I hissed right back, letting the growl rumble through me. The ophidian exploded out of the ground, writhing and twisting. I dug in with all four feet, my claws strengthened by shifting while carrying the flail. I clawed at the top of its head, peeling back scales in chunks.

Blood flew, sticking into my fur, stinking like raw sewage. Why did everything have to stink so fucking bad? There wasn't a lot of time to consider the question as the ophidian snapped its head hard to the side and I lost my grip. Once more I flew through the air, shifting forms and landing on two feet in a crouch, the flail in my right hand. I stood and swung the weapon in an uppercut that caught the lower jaw of the ophidian.

The flail drove through, pulsing and vibrating, the handle warming and sticking even more to my fingers. Happy, the weapon was fucking happy to be eating down the ophidian. I yanked the flail back, and the ophidian fell to the ground, dead.

Before I could even think, I was off and running toward Maggi. Behind her were Balder, Batman, and Demon.

And Marsum. Only he stood in front of her, his magic swirling around him, driving the ophidians back, keeping them at bay. "My magic can't get through their hide!" he yelled.

I gave him a nod. "Lila, eyes!"

Once more she flew into the air, circling around me. She called out where they were, and I slammed the flail into them. Four more fell in half that many minutes and then we were scrambling to run once more.

"Get Maggi." I grabbed Demon and directed him to lie down. Marsum and I shoved her onto the camel's back and then we mounted the horses. Balder's eyes were rolling hard and his body frothed with a nervous sweat. I didn't blame him. We'd been here before and the outcome for him had been rough. "Easy, buddy, no bites this time."

Lila flew ahead of us, circling around and then checking on the ophidians as we raced toward the water's edge. I held Demon's lead and prayed that we would make it, prayed to whoever would listen, whatever gods were watching over us, to buy us a little more time.

"Right into the water," Maggi groaned, finally sitting up. "Right into the water if you want to find the Wyvern."

"I don't want to fucking find him! Not yet!" I yelled at her. That was the last thing we needed.

The waves crashed toward us, booming as they hammered the sand as if driven by the motion of the sea. I wondered in a flash of curiosity that overcame the fear of running from the ophidians, where the hell all that water had come from. Because there were no oceans out this way, no lakes or rivers even the size of what we were seeing.

Like the witch's swamp out in the middle of the desert, this body of water had no reason for being here other than existing on the whim of the Wyvern. Marsum and Batman rode into the water first, legs splashing through, and a moment later, Balder and I hit it, slowed to a trot and looked around. Maggi was fully sitting up, the side of her face purpling all across her cheekbone and jawline.

"You okay?"

"I believe so." She put a hand to her head. "But we have other concerns, I think."

She lifted a hand and pointed out into the water. Something swam toward us, undulating through the waves, sending more waves our way. There was a flip of a scaled tail and a burst of air as the Wyvern cleared its lungs. An enormous head shaped like a bullet turned our way, and its eyes, jeweled like Lila's, only blue, locked onto us. No, locked onto me before he dove into the water and headed our way.

Lila was still high above us and she dive-bombed to me, pulling up at the last second. "Um, he's bigger than my father."

"Goddess on a crippled cow, are you serious?"

"Ride!" Marsum yelled.

I booted Balder to the right, Maggi turning Demon at the same time.

We raced along the edge of the water as fast as the horses could go.

The thing was, we could see the end of the water, it looked to be about a mile away from us.

Only it kept stretching, kept spreading farther across the sand. Good for us in keeping the ophidians away.

Bad in that it kept the Wyvern close.

I looked across at Marsum as he turned his face to me.

"What are we going to do?" Lila clung to the front of my saddle, her body vibrating.

"Marsum, any ideas?"

He shot me a withering look. "I have not dealt with the Wyvern in a very long time and we did not part on good terms."

"Davin dealt with him," Maggi said. "Maybe he could help."

Before Marsum could answer, a wave crashed around us, spreading out and disappearing into the sand behind us. The water stilled and the Wyvern rose out of the waves ahead of us. The horses slid to dual stops and backed up rapidly. Demon stopped but just stood there, chewing his cud like the ass he was. Okay, camel he was.

"Bad, this is going to go bad," Lila whispered. "He's very angry."

Indeed.

I stared up at the Wyvern, taking him in. That was an understatement. The Wyvern was built like a whip-thin dragon with longer legs and what looked like webbed toes. Scales of darkest blue and green, he would blend in well with the water, especially with the silvery scales along his belly. A row of spikes ran from the tip of his nose up between his eyes and down his back, following a pair of ivory horns that swept over his head. Smallish eyes locked onto us.

"You are either very brave, or very stupid to come here." His voice rumbled around us and the horses whinnied, prancing nervously, splashing water up in sprays.

"Likely the second," I said. "I wouldn't say I'm particularly brave."

The Wyvern snapped his long jaw into the air and a booming laugh rolled out of him. "Funny, cat. What do you want?" His head shot forward and I found myself staring into his maw. I swallowed hard, understanding clearly what he was saying without uttering a word. He could kill us in an instant and we wouldn't even see it coming. As big as a dragon and faster than the ophidians we'd run from, there would be no facing the Wyvern.

"Are the ophidians yours to control?" The question popped out of me. I needed to buy myself time to figure out how to get the stone from him. Hell, I didn't even know where it was . . .

The Wyvern shook his head, still far closer than I would like. "No, they have a new queen, and she has been pushing on my boundaries for the last week. Irritating fleas." He blew out a slow breath. "But that is not why you are here."

Lila hunched herself down farther on Balder's neck and I tried not to do the same. I was looking straight into his mouth, eyeing up his teeth that were easily the length of my left arm. The right being a smidge shorter.

"Well, there is a problem that you might be able to help with," I said.

The Wyvern pulled back. "A puzzle? I do like puzzles."

I glanced at Marsum and he just shrugged. I realized then that he'd been very quiet this whole time. Both he and Maggi had said nothing.

"Yes, I guess you could call it a puzzle." I cleared my throat and composed my thoughts. "The Emperor is trying to free himself. Ishtar is gathering the stones, and the Falak could be freed."

There, that about summed it up.

The Wyvern pulled his head back. "Truly, all of that? And what of these two with you?" That big head slid toward Marsum and Maggi, eyeing them up, his posture shifting each second. What would he do if he knew that one was the Ice Witch, and the other a Jinn master? Nothing good.

"That's Maks, he's my mate and a caracal shifter," I

said, pointing at Marsum. "And that's my aunt. She has no power, so to speak, but has great wisdom."

A low rumbling chitter slid through the Wyvern. "Your problem is you do not think I can smell a lie, cat. That I cannot see who these two are, or what they have done. You are right about the world falling to pieces, but that is of no concern to me." His head turned to *my aunt*. "I hold the stone, Maggi, and you won't be getting it."

"She doesn't want it—"

The Wyvern's tail slammed down in the water between me and the others. "They show you what you want to see: That this one is your friend," he motioned at Maggi, "and that this one loves you." He motioned to Marsum. "Creatures who desire power cannot be trusted, cat. You should know that by now. Have you not realized that the Emperor wants the power you hold? That you are the key to his freedom?"

"I can't free him," I said.

"You already started down that path, and you will free him willingly before this is done, which means perhaps you are better off dead now." He circled Marsum and Maggi, his body big enough to coil more than once. I stared in horror as my two traveling companions disappeared from sight.

"Please, don't hurt them!" I yelled. "Wyvern, if you are as reasonable as you seem, then you have to know that sometimes things are not what they seem."

That slowed him and he looked over the rounded edge of his body. "You have traitors all around you, and yet you trust them. Why? Are you so starved for love?"

I held up both hands, palms out in a sign of surrender. "What will you do when Ishtar comes for the stone? What will you do when she *cuts it out of you*?" I was taking a gamble that the stone he held was within him.

"She cannot." He snorted.

"You are either very brave, or very stupid." I parroted his words back at him. "She is not the Ishtar you knew when you worked with her to put the Emperor to sleep. She raised me as her daughter, as the child she never had, and she tried to kill me when I did not give her what she wanted. And she has been working with the Emperor all along, playing us all. She has Merlin now too, I think." Again, that was a lot of info, but for some reason I knew I had to tell him.

His eyes narrowed to glowing slits. "Brave or stupid, perhaps I am stupid then too."

"I can carry the stone for you," Maggi called out. "I have the strength she does not, Wyvern. You know this."

"What the fuck?" I growled. "Maggi, are you insane?" Even as I looked at her, the madness that had been there before flickered in her eyes. The need to be strong, to not be the weak link. I understood it, painfully so. "This is not the way!"

The water lashed at the horses' legs and they danced sideways. The tail of the Wyvern appeared and flipped between us, Maggi and Demon on one side, Marsum, me and the horses on the other. "None of you will have my power!" he bellowed, whipping his head toward Maggi. So much for being reasonable.

She let out a shriek.

"Time to run!" Marsum yelled as he threw a ball of energy at the Wyvern, slamming him in the side of the head, knocking him down, a splash of water rising up over him as he sank. Maggi got Demon going, and only had that chance because of Marsum. But I suspected him helping her was going to bite us all in the ass.

"Go!" Marsum shouted, and I wanted to grab him and shake him and Maggi. The Wyvern turned and roared at us, showing off every row of teeth and then some. "None of you will escape death."

I leaned over Balder's neck. "Faster, my boy." He dug in hard, and we galloped through the water, the Wyvern pacing us out in the depths of his ocean.

We were royally screwed. The water would go as far as the Wyvern wanted it to.

Maggi was catching up to us, her face twisted with shame. "I'm sorry! I couldn't help myself."

"Later!" I said. We would discuss her issues later. If we all made it out of this alive.

Another wave pulsed toward us, hitting the horses and Demon hard enough to make them stumble but still they managed to keep going. Another roar from the Wyvern, a bellow that rattled the air around us. "Death to you all."

"Yeah, fuck you too!" I hollered back, giving him a standard one-fingered salute.

"Like that will help?" Marsum snapped.

I looked at him. "How in the hell will it hurt at this point?"

Oh, being wrong sucked so badly, and I really had to stop asking questions like that.

Lila tugged at my shirt. "The water! He's going to leave!"

I took a quick look at the water below us as we galloped, watched as it pulled back from us out to the depths. I blinked and lifted my head as the water slid farther down Balder's legs. "You're right. The water is receding." That was good, wasn't it?

Maggi twisted in her seat. "Oh, he is a crafty one and won't even bother to kill us himself."

The water continued to drop, now just to Balder's hooves. The sand to the right of me was drying rapidly with the heat of the desert.

"Crap, the ophidians," Lila yelped.

Now it was my turn to twist in my saddle, looking out the way we'd come to the dry sands of the desert.

There were no gorcs left, only a few bits of armor that could be seen dotting the landscape. A puff of sand went up as an ophidian rose to the surface and slithered across. I could almost feel its beady damn eyes lock on us, and the forked tongue slid in and out, tasting the air. Tasting us.

"Shit fuck damn." I cursed through gritted teeth. "Keep moving, we have to use what time we have of the water still around us." Even as I spoke, the "ocean" slid farther away, toward the east as the Wyvern laughed. Fucking laughed at us. How was I ever going to convince him to help me find my brother?

"Go, as fast as you can." I leaned into Balder, hissing softly at him. Behind us, Batman didn't hesitate, leaping after us. Demon was the slow one to start, but a few whacks from Maggi's quirt and he passed both horses.

The water had soaked the sand thoroughly, which would buy us a little time, but not enough. And surely not enough to get all the way south. "I don't know the terrain, Lila. Can you scout ahead?"

She launched into the air, and shot ahead of us, her wings a blur like a hummingbird. "I'm on it!"

I blew out a breath and looked at Marsum. His hands were black with the Jinn's magic, but he did nothing with it. "I can't kill them; they are immune to my magic. The best I can do is slow them down. Maybe."

Between one hoofbeat and the next, we went from wet to dry sand and the horses slowed, their hooves sucked down into the looser material. Going slower was not going to help us.

"Can you firm up the ground?"

"I'm not a fucking elemental!" Marsum snapped. "I kill things."

Elements. I had a stone that froze the shit out of things. I reached up and touched the stone under my shirt. "I'm going to try something."

Maggi's eyes were hard on me. "I could freeze the sand with that stone. I could stop the ophidians in their slithering tracks. Give it to me." Again, that madness was there, creeping back in around the edges of her eyes.

I stared straight back at her. "You'd kill me once you had it back in your hands."

I let go of Balder's reins and he took off. Wrapping both hands around the stone, I tried to open myself to that part of me that was magic. The doorway in my mind was there. I could see it. "Come on, come on." I squinted my eyes closed. Open. Open. Open.

Nothing happened. There was no pulse of magic, no flood of power. I squeezed the stone harder, but then backed off. What if I broke this one too?

"Whatever you're going to do, hurry!" Marsum yelled.

Please. That was my only thought, just please. We

couldn't come this far to die now at the mouth of a bunch of oversized sand worms.

Please. The doorway opened a crack. Just a little, enough that the magic in me began to spill out.

My muscles quivered as a blast of cold air hit me in the face. I gasped, clutched the stone hard enough to dig my nails into it, and the doorway in my mind flung open. My fingers holding the stone iced over, and the stone stuck to my chest . . . I couldn't breathe. I opened my eyes and mouth, forced a lungful of air down though it tasted like cold fire, scorching my insides with an arctic blast.

I had to move. I had to finish this.

I took my feet from the stirrups and slid to the right, hanging from the saddle, dangling like a stunt rider, one knee hooked over the pommel. With a wrench, I pulled the stone free of where it stuck to my chest and held it in my hand. Each beat of Balder's stride rocked me, threatening to toss me the rest of the way from the saddle.

I reached out and tipped the stone into the sand. Ice shot outward from it, freezing the desert in a line that ran straight south and north, blocking the ophidians. I hoped it would, anyway. Even if it blocked the majority of them, that would have to be good enough.

I counted Balder's strides as a point of focus, as I pushed the stone in as far as I could, opening myself to that doorway inside me. The magic pulsed and danced, and I stared as my hand turned blue, as the world around me cooled, my breath leaving me in puffs of condensation.

And the magic trapped in me from the stone I'd destroyed woke up, tingling across my chest and through the bones in my torso. "No, no," I whispered, trying to grab hold of the magic, but it slid through me like wet reins in my hands as it ripped through both me and the sapphire.

The ground erupted with ice, shooting outward in long spikes like lances from an enemy.

"Watch it!" Maggi shrieked. Only I couldn't watch it. I could barely move from where I flopped half in and half out of the saddle. There was too much power and no control.

"I got you!" Lila was suddenly there, her claws digging into my scalp as she took hold of my hair and yanked me upward. The magic shifted, sliding through me faster and faster, through that open doorway as I tried futilely to gain some sort of control of it.

"Help." I'm not sure if I yelled the word or whispered it, but Lila gripped me hard, and Balder slowed. Hands caught hold of me and then Marsum was there. The heat of a desert fire to battle the ice burning through me.

"Let me control it," he said. "You don't know what you're doing."

"Don't trust him!" Maggi said, her voice from a

distance. Only I had no choice. I'd opened up too much magic, too much of everything and now I couldn't stop it. And if I had to pick which one of them to trust, two guardians of the stones, it was Marsum. It was Maks.

His fingers dug into my arms and the amber stone flared to life under his shirt. His magic warmed the frozen parts of my hands long enough to pry the sapphire from my fingers. He took it and dropped it into the leather pouch at my side next to the emerald stone that had lain quietly through the whole episode.

But the power wasn't done with me. It spiraled out and into the sand, sending one last pulse through the desert.

Still held by Marsum's hands, I turned my head to watch the magic that was technically mine freeze mile upon mile of sand in a swath a quarter mile wide.

"Is that really what I'm seeing?" Maggi shook her head. "Even I could not do that with—"

"She is not you," Marsum growled. "She has more inherent magic in her pinky finger than you have in your whole body."

I just stared at the block between us and the ophidians. I twisted around to see that the cold had circled behind us, cutting off those that had been on our tails. This would give us a good head start on the ophidians, maybe even take us all the way to the

Blackened Market. The ground cracked and heaved, white frost rimming the ground. "That'll help." My lips struggled to make the words.

"Yes, but at what cost? Did you break the other stone?" Lila tapped on my head from her perch up there. The magic in me receded and as it left, it felt as though my strings had been cut and I slumped, sore and tired. So damn exhausted.

"Damn it, I hate feeling weak. And the cost is not too much. I'm just tired." I reached up and patted her, my fingers still numb, but already feeling was coming back to them.

Maggi stood apart from us, her eyes wide. "That is not . . . you shouldn't have survived that."

Marsum pulled me from Balder's back and held me in his arms. "You need to shift. Your core temperature is still dropping. That was too much magic, even for your bloodline."

I didn't hesitate, and I should have. I really should have thought what he would do and how it would make me feel once I was a house cat. But I didn't and that was a mistake I'd regret.

20

I shifted to my house cat form while my body continued to refuse to shiver. I was so cold, my body didn't even have it in it to make the effort to warm up. "Too much magic?" I mumbled the question to Marsum as he scooped me up and stuck me inside his shirt. Inside against skin I knew so well, wrapped in the smell of Maks. It curled around and sunk into me, the scent of the hot desert sand and a wisp of magic that made my skin tingle in all the right places as I breathed it in, taking it deep into my lungs.

Oh, this was dangerous. I had to fight to keep the purr from rumbling through me.

"Too much magic that is not inherently your own. Not unlike that of the stone you shattered, and unintentionally drew into yourself," he said, and there was a deeper tone, a new tone to his voice, one as though he were lecturing me. Teaching me. I blinked up at his face, the lines of his jaws so close I could kiss him, yet I didn't think that was a good idea. Because this wasn't Marsum or Maks. This was another of the Jinn masters talking; I was sure of it. This was back to Davin.

He clicked his tongue at Batman and led Balder. "Maggi, it has been a long time," he said as we caught up to her.

"Davin?" She gasped his name. "I thought you were not strong enough to come forward."

"For the moment, I am, old friend. This is quite the mess you all have found yourselves in. Three stones and three curses. I am shocked any of you have survived this far. Though the Emperor's grand-daughter has managed to buy you time with that neat little trick." He tipped his head toward the ground and the thick band of ice that I'd made.

Lila landed and tugged at his shirt. "Let her out, or let me in, Toad."

Marsum—or Davin, I suppose—brushed her aside. "Let her be. I'll keep her warm."

I closed my eyes, thinking about Ford. That was what he'd said to me only a few days before and I'd taken him at his word, and then sent him away. I missed him in that moment, missed his quiet strength and solid personality. I checked in on my bond with him and the others of my pride and found nothing.

SHANNON MAYER

On a whim, I reached for Steve.

And that fucker showed up loud and clear. There was a moment where I could see him lounging in bed, Darcy beside him, and I wondered if I was really seeing it, or just imagining it.

"We need to keep close to Ish. She is going to rule the world," Steve said, sliding a hand over Darcy's hip. *"The pride is mine now as it should have always been and we will rule at Ish's side."*

"What about Kiara? And Ford? They are loyal to Zam and won't take this lying down." Darcy traced his body with her mouth.

"Kiara will fall into line. I'll kill Ford when the time comes." Steve yawned. *"I'm surprised you didn't ask about Zam."*

"She . . . has never really been one of us," Darcy said. *"I was her friend because she was the only one to be a friend with that wasn't human. I'm sad for her, to be all alone, but I don't want her in our pride. I'm glad she's gone."*

I jerked hard as if the bitch had slapped me herself.

A shiver went through me and then I began to shake hard, violently—though with the cold or what I'd seen, I wasn't sure. The thing was, I wouldn't have thought Darcy would have the power to hurt me. But to hear her speak so casually of me not ever really fitting in stung more than it should have. I closed my eyes as the horses picked up their speed, the sound of their hooves lulling me even as I fought to stay awake. Davin glanced down at me. "You are a curious one, little shifter. Curious indeed."

"Thaaaannnnks?" I stuttered out between chattering teeth.

He grunted a sharp laugh that sounded strange coming out of his mouth. "The Jinn do not produce females with power. That has been bred out of them, did you know that?"

I shook my head and he went on.

"The reason, if you are wondering, is simple. Jinn females could manipulate all kinds of magic. Just like you are showing signs of. They were creatures of great talent, and the men were, in a way, slaves to them."

"Hot damn," Lila said. I peeked out of the shirt to see her perched on the horn of Batman's saddle, watching us closely. Guarding me. I was sure of it. "You mean—"

"Well, perhaps slave is a strong word. But we did not have their power. The first of the Jinn masters was the one to put the new hierarchy into play. He poisoned all the women at a yearly solstice orgy."

"Wait, did I hear that right? An orgy?" Lila asked exactly what I wanted to know.

He waved a hand, quieting her. "Yes, we were far more liberal with our ways then. He poisoned them, and all but the weakest were killed. Those weak females were used as breeders, and we culled any women with power. A dark time, a time of great change for all the Jinn."

A shiver ran through me that I wasn't sure had anything to do with the cold that still clung to my fur. "How old were the females when they were culled?" I asked.

"A female Jinn rarely shows any ability before thirty." He glanced down at me, a brow arching. "So you see why you've become rather popular these last few months. Though even that was no reason for Marsum to tie his life to yours. There *are* other possibilities when it comes to finding a mate."

Lila snorted. "Popular is not the word I'd use."

"Is that why Marsum wanted to kill me?" Horror flicked through me. How long had I been hunted by the Jinn? Was it because I was part of the Bright Lion Pride, or because I had Jinn blood running in my veins? Had he known all along?

"Initially, yes. He saw you as a potential threat. It's why he killed your mother. She was beginning to show signs of real power, enough to overthrow him had she decided. If you'd been weak, you'd make a perfect mate—powerful lines but no power to speak of—but he wouldn't know that until much later. It's why—"

I cut him off. "Why he didn't kill me at the Oasis as a child? Why he drew me to him across the desert? Why he let Maks kill him? All because he wanted to see what I was made of? To make sure I was weak enough?"

"Yes."

That one word shattered me. Because that meant this mess, all of what had happened in my life, in Maks's life, was my fault. My fault for existing, my fault for not just being weak but for having Jinn blood. I shook my head and buried my nose in the cup of my paws as I tried to push the negative thoughts away. That was stupid. I was being stupid.

"This is not my fault." I lifted my head, my jaw tightening. "Don't you dare try to blame me for this."

"No, it's not your fault," Davin agreed. "But I felt you should understand him. He does not love you for you, little cat. He loves you for what you could give him, a child of great power. But he will kill you the second you give him what he wants."

I blinked up at him, feeling the need to misdirect him, at least about Marsum. "I never thought Marsum loved me. Maks loves me."

Davin's eyes were sad with a depth of sorrow I did not like. "Does he? Or did he help bring you to this point? You do not know how deep a game either of them play." His face twisted and a snarl ripped out of him, guttural and pain-filled. "You fucking liar!" He roared the words, clawing at his own throat with one hand.

I cringed as his arm came around me, trapping me against his chest. I mean, I could have dug my claws

259

in and opened him up like a fillet, but I didn't want to hurt Maks. Squirming, I managed to push off and out the bottom of his shirt while he reached for me.

He breathed heavily as if he'd been drowning and barely managed to come up for air. "Zam. Davin is a damn liar." Marsum spoke now and shook his head, a grimace on his face. "That was always his strong suit, being able to convince people of a version of the world that wasn't true."

I bounded off Batman, landing on Balder's saddle. My limbs still ached with cold, but I could move, and that had to be enough. Because I couldn't stay there, close to him, breathing in his smell and thinking that he'd loved me once.

Davin's words cut too close to truths I'd found myself circling since I'd found out Maks was Jinn. What if, what if, what if.

Lila flew over to me and I forced myself to shift back to two legs. My body molded to the saddle and with shaking hands, I reached for the reins. Far from warm I might have been, but right then I didn't care, and the sun was still high and beating down on us. That would have to be enough.

I couldn't look at him, not with the way the doubts snuck through me, like ghosts on the wind.

I shook my head. "We have a job to do. We're going to the Blackened Market, then to the cross-roads. Marsum, you're still with us?" I shot him a quick look and he nodded.

Those blue eyes filled my vision and he gave me a bow at the waist as he spoke. "I tied my life to yours, Zam. I am with you. Your pain is mine still, as mine is yours."

I swallowed hard, a tight knot in my throat making me want to hurl. No, I'd done enough of that, enough of all the hurt and pain. Time to suck it up and get this done. Then, and only then could I figure out what to do with Marsum, with Maks. "We ride hard because we have an opening. We need to take it."

Maggi didn't protest, and neither did he, as I urged Balder into a gallop. They and their mounts followed, the sound of drumming hooves and pads heavy on the sand, like distant drums.

On the far side of the ice barrier, the ophidians kept pace for some time, and then slowly dropped away, disappearing into the sand. I kept waiting for the ice to melt, but it didn't. Or at least it didn't that I could see. All I knew was that we had to move. We had to keep ahead of the ophidians.

"The market is on solid ground. We should be safe there," Marsum said.

Safe, I wasn't sure that word meant what it used to, at least not to me. "Ophidian-free works," I said. "You think it will be safer than that?"

He opened his mouth, paused and then shrugged. "No idea."

That was the problem. There was no real idea as to how this was going to work. How we were going to get a new stone, how we were going to draw magic out of me, stick it in said stone, and then *still* get to the crossroads in time. I did a quick calculation that made my guts tighten and my stress levels soar. We had two days before the golden moon. Give or take a few hours.

The pace of Balder's feet lulled me, and the sun did indeed slowly melt away the worst of the cold that had sunk into my body.

"We need to slow," Maggi said as Demon drew close to me and Balder. "The animals need a break and we do too."

"There is no place to camp," I pointed out with a sweeping gesture. "Do you see any rock to camp on?"

She frowned. "You don't think the ophidians would still be here?"

"Whoever their new queen is seems to have a serious hate on for us," I said. "I don't trust that they aren't here now. You want to wake up with one of those fuckers on top of you? I sure as shit don't. I've had enough to deal with lately, don't you think?" A pang slid through my chest that had nothing to do with the cold, and everything to do with the magic from the clear stone. I sucked in a labored breath, leaning over the saddle horn as I fought to push the pain aside. A hand slid over my arm, Marsum's hand, and the pain eased. I looked at him.

"Stronger together," he said, his face also twisted up as he fought off the waves of pain. But he was right, touching him made it go faster, made it hurt less.

I pushed myself upright in the saddle. "Always fun, let's not do it again, shall we?"

Marsum barked a laugh. "Oh, if it were that easy."

Maggi's frown deepened and she shook her head. "We could protect ourselves better." More telling, though, was the way her eyes slid to my shirt, where it hung over the pouch at my side, a hunger dancing through them as though she could taste what it was she desired. If she'd been a man, I'd have said she was checking me out, but it was what I carried under the cloth that I knew she wanted.

The sapphire stone.

I snapped the fingers of one hand in her face. "Knock that shit off."

"Yeah," Lila flicked her tiny claws at Maggi as if shooing her away. "Knock that off!"

"There is a place up ahead that will work," Marsum said. "Two miles, maybe a little less. We can camp there."

I turned to him, slowing Balder. "How do you know that?"

He pointed to a rock jammed into the ground, words scrawled across it in pictographs I could almost understand. "That is a marker. The Blackened Market awaits. We have arrived."

21

P art of me wanted to hurry ahead to get to the Blackened Market, and part of me was terrified. Because the thing I'd been pushing aside this whole journey was now right in front of me.

What if there was no way to get the magic that had once been Ishtar's out of me? What if I was about to find out I had a death sentence, a true death sentence?

"Goddess damn it to the seventh level of hell and back," I muttered to myself, "pull your shit together."

Lila crawled up to my shoulder and grabbed my earlobe for balance. "It's going to be fine. Stop freaking out. This isn't like you. We've got this; we're a team."

She was right. We were a team. I looked at

Marsum, at Maks, feeling the ties to him that wove between the three of us.

Three. Three. Three. The Oracle's words resounded through my head.

"Maggi, you need to stay out of the market." The words popped out of me as if someone else were saying them.

She blinked at me. "But I am here to help."

"I know, but . . ." I rubbed a hand over my face, trying to hide the fact that she was making me nervous, that I knew as long as I had the sapphire, she would want it. "The Oracle spoke about three being the number. Three. And Marsum has to go in with me, and Lila. So that means you have to stay out." And I didn't trust Maggi, not after what happened with the Wyvern. Not after what happened when I'd used the sapphire stone. If given the chance, she'd double cross me now, I was sure of it.

Maggi's eyes narrowed. "The Oracle does not always give the information you need. Occasionally she even lies."

"Well, it's what I've got and I'm running this show," I said with a wave of a hand. "We will meet up with you on the southern side as soon as we can. If we aren't there by tomorrow morning it's because . . ." Because we failed. I was dead, and Marsum was free. Maks trapped forever.

With a huff and a swing of her quirt, Maggi

hurried Demon and the two of them galloped out to the southeast. Away from us.

Three. Three. Three. I might not know anything of what the rest of the Oracle's riddle meant, but that much I understood and could do.

As soon as Maggi was out of earshot, Marsum burst out laughing. "You think that we'll be able to get a stone and draw the magic out of you in under twelve hours? You have no idea how difficult this is! It took Merlin and the others months to do it the first time."

"You mean with Ishtar?" I arched a brow. "Let me guess, she fought you on taking her magic?"

"No, she didn't. She wanted the Emperor caged," he said, his eyes thoughtful. "He'd been—amongst other things—unfaithful and cruel to her."

"Did she? Was he? Or was that what she told you?" I wasn't sure I wanted to tell him what I'd seen in my dreams, of Ishtar working to free her husband. Why, I'm not sure, only it felt like the wrong time.

"What do you know?" His question was sharp and I held the answer in. Not the time.

I turned my back to him so he wouldn't see the doubt in my face. "We have to do this, and quickly, or we'll miss our chances at the crossroads. I don't think we can trust what Ishtar told you any more than we can trust what Maggi has been telling me."

The crossroads were where I would find a way to break a curse or curses. Maybe the place to deal with

Marsum, freeing Maks. A place where we would displace the Emperor. Of course, that was assuming everything the Oracle had said was true.

My throat tightened and tears wobbled at the edges of my eyes. Lila tapped on my thigh and whispered, "What is it?"

"I'm feeling all jittery, like too much coffee and not enough food," I said. My arms tingled and every part of me was on super high alert.

Marsum rode Batman closer to me, Balder, and Lila. "That is the inherent danger you are picking up on. This place is not for the faint or weak of heart. Nor for the weak of body."

Lila shook a fist at him. "She is none of those things, you shit."

He flicked a blast of a spell at her with one finger, and I shot a hand out, catching it in my palm without a thought. The black mist crawled over my arm, giving me a bit of a tingle, like a mild electric shock. I held it and then flipped it back at him. "Don't you so much as think about hurting her."

Marsum eyed me as the black mist danced across his fingers. "You felt it. Would it have hurt her?"

"Maybe it didn't hurt me because of who I am." I pointed a finger at him. "Knock that garbage off."

"Davin's words got to you, didn't they?" He snorted. "Damn him, he always was a shit disturber."

I moved Balder into a trot. Marsum and Batman

caught up easily. "You can't go in like this, ahead of me on your own horse."

Slowing Balder a second time, I found myself staring at Marsum and what he'd materialized in his hands.

I glared at him. "You are crazy if you think I'm putting that on."

"Women are property here. And if you aren't my property, you can be taken. This is not a nice place, Zam." He held the end of the thin chain to me, the collar from it hanging loosely.

"No, no, that's a whole lot of nope." Lila shot into the air. "She's not putting on a freaking leash!"

He glared at her. "Then we aren't going in there. You don't understand, Lila. There is no other way to get in there with as little notice as possible. This is a place of monsters, and people who will slit your throat for looking at them wrong. They don't respect women, even women of power."

"There is a better way." I drew a breath and shifted down to my cat form. I hopped across to him and climbed up to his shoulder. "You see? In the saddlebags is a long cloak. We'll use that."

"And what about me?" Lila all but paced the air in front of us. "I need to come too."

"I know," he said and then crooked his finger. "Promise you won't throw up on me."

"Promise you'll give us back our Toad?" she said as she landed on the front of the saddle.

His eyes closed and a shiver went through him. From his saddlebag, he pulled out a long tan-colored cloak and slid it over his shoulders. "Get under the back of it."

Lila and I pinned ourselves to his back and clutched at the saddle, and he took Balder by the reins, leading him along. His magic whispered down the leather lines and turned the bridle into a halter. Better for leading, but not so good for a quick escape.

Lila and I shared a look. We'd been in worse situations before. At least, that was what I thought in that moment.

Fewer than twenty minutes later, we rode into the outskirts of the market. The noise had been steadily growing, the sound of a multitude of male voices, drums, shouts, catcalls, a woman shrieking, the clang of metal on metal, the bellow of a blacksmith's furnace, the distant boom of a gun. I peeked out from under the cloak, grateful for my small form and dark fur that helped me stay unseen.

How long since I'd been in any sort of a city or town other than the Stockyards? I could barely remember the last time. It had easily been years, and I found myself unable to look away despite the danger that sneaking a peek represented.

"Wow," I whispered as the merchants came into view.

A row of wooden, three-sided roofed stalls were set up on either side of what had to be the main street with tiny side roads here and there. Houses were crammed against one another, mostly near the merchant street, their rooftop edges touching as they leaned precariously every which way. The stones below the horses' hooves clanked sharply on their iron shoes and the smell of unwashed bodies cut through it all. I crinkled my nose.

None of these goods in front of us were taken honorably. More than that, though, I found myself staring at the people. Each merchant was dressed sharply, clean, as if they were upstanding businessmen and not the thugs and thieves that we all knew them to be. There wasn't a hair out of place, or a smudge of dirt anywhere I could see. And yet they still stunk.

It took us a few more feet for me to put two and two together.

"Slaves," Marsum said softly as we passed by the first section of stalls. That was who I was smelling. Women and children mostly, and a few younger men —primarily humans, but a few that had some magic too, though they were weak if the way they stood waiting was any indication. No older people were held as slaves. My heart sank as I saw the resignation on their faces. There wasn't even any fear, nothing. They'd given up, and the smell of defeat rolled off them.

My jaw ticked side to side as I ground my teeth. I hated walking by, doing nothing—just seeing the pain in their eyes, smelling their loss of hope as if it were a wound on their bodies.

"Animals," Marsum said. It took me a second to realize he was looking for a specific vendor, and we had to pass by these others first. He wasn't speaking to tell us; he was talking to himself, ticking off each merchant as we passed.

The animals consisted of birds, hunting hyenas, and . . . shifters. I tensed, staring into the golden eyes of a lion. He stared back at me, not an ounce of humanity in him. Who was he? The cage around him was small enough that he couldn't even stand up. My magic in me rose a little and I could see that the cage was not just a cage but magical in nature. His eyes locked on mine, following us as we passed him by. A shifter for sure, I could smell that much on him, but nothing else. I should have been able to peg which pride he was from, but it was as if he were a normal lion.

Lila choked on a cry, and I twisted to see the other side of the street.

"No." I couldn't believe what I was seeing, and yet I knew I couldn't let Lila go.

The vendor held up an oval, pale white, blue-speckled egg in both arms, filling them. "Fresh off the nests! Fertilized, ready to be chained and trained!"

I grabbed Lila as she moved to lunge out at him. "Not now, not yet!" I hissed the words at her, dragging her under the cover of Marsum's cloak. He swept an arm back, helping me block her.

"Quiet," he growled.

Lila sobbed. "The babies."

"I know. I know." I wrapped her in my front legs as best I could and found myself still staring out at the vendors. I had not forgotten my promise to find the dragons' babies, to return those I could to their mothers. Not in the least. But I knew that now was not the time. We had more on our plate.

And the eggs here, this was not where they were remaining. We'd have to find where they went to next. "We will deal with this, not now, but we will come back," I whispered the words with an urgency I knew she would hear and feel. Slowly, Lila relaxed, nodding and wiping away tears.

The next few merchants and their items were less horrible. Kind of. Jewelry. Food. Whores. Weapons. That one, I tugged on Marsum's shirt.

"No" was his only reply. I tugged again.

"You don't have a weapon," I pointed out.

"I don't need one," he said, keeping his voice low. I snorted.

"Too much ego. Get one, just in case."

Lila sniffed and lifted her head. "That could be the Toad. He was always full of himself."

"I was not," he grumped. But he did slow, and the vendor smiled up at him. Lean as a whip, with corded muscles in his arms. I had no doubt he'd made most of the weapons himself, if the smell of coal fire lingering around him was any indication. A shimmer to his eyes whispered of magic and I wondered . . . "See if he has anything special. Magical like the flail."

Marsum grunted, but otherwise couldn't acknowledge me.

The vendor gave a partial bow at the waist. "Hello, hello! I have all the weapons you could ever desire for killing, mayhem, thievery and general destruction."

"One imbued for absorbing magic?" Marsum asked. "I have heard of some like that."

"Costly, very costly," the vendor purred as he held up a finger. "Wait here, I have just the thing."

"I don't need this," Marsum said, but he held still.

"Trust me. I have good instincts," I replied as quietly as I could.

The merchant came back with a staff, the end of it curved with a wicked blade that had been inset with gold and silver swirls reminiscent of flames. "A beauty, a true beauty and has a few tricks up its sleeve. I made it myself, of course."

I couldn't see him, but I imagined him winking at Marsum, which made me smile. Marsum shifted in the saddle and held out an arm. Lila and I edged closer to him as he hefted the spear.

"Light, well balanced. How much?"

"Three thousand."

"Bullshit." Marsum threw the weapon back at the merchant and rode away.

I let out a low hiss and he hushed me. "That's how it works here. Trust me, Zam, we know what we are doing."

We. As in him and Marsum? I had to still the intake of breath that would have given my surprise away. The last thing I wanted was for Marsum to realize how often Maks was slipping through. Maybe slipping through enough to take over control of his body?

"Stones. This is what we are here for," Marsum said and adjusted in his seat. Lila and I slid down tight against his ass, pinned between him and the back of the saddle.

"Gross. You might like his butt, I do not," she grumbled.

I pulled myself around the side of his hip to look out once more. This was the one we were waiting for.

The stall all but glittered with stones of varying colors, catching the light of the desert sun. They hung from strings I couldn't see so they looked as though they were floating in midair. So many stones, all shapes, and yet I couldn't pick out one resembling the one I'd broken.

The vendor approached Marsum, bowing repeatedly. He was rotund, dressed in traditional loose tan-and-white-colored desert clothing to fend off the heat. But no hat. That seemed stupid, especially with that bald spot he had showing on the top. His eyes were narrow and close-set over a too-large nose that had a bulging mass on the tip.

"Good master, what kind of stone do you have an interest in? Let Jiango help you find exactly what—"

"Clear-cut, black-lightning-kissed," Marsum said without any preamble.

The vendor froze in mid bow, straightened and shook his head. "I have nothing for you like that."

With no more than that, he turned and walked back to his stall.

"You do not wish to try to ply me with another stone?" Marsum asked.

"I have nothing for you." Jiango shook his head and dropped the cover on his stall, hiding all the stones that dangled there only a moment before.

"That can't be good," I said.

"No, it can't be. It likely means there is another buyer. Or at least someone else has been asking after the stone." Marsum turned Batman away from the stall.

"Wait!"

He shushed me again and I bit at my lips to keep them from opening and asking the flood of questions that ran through my head.

All the way to the center of the Blackened Market, I was quiet, all the way to the stable where he waved away the young stable hand. He dismounted, then motioned for Lila and me to get down. I leapt across to his shoulder and slid my ass into the hood of the cloak. He snapped his fingers and Balder's halter turned back into a bridle. Handy indeed.

Lila did the same and he grunted. "I should have known there would be another buyer for a stone like that."

He bent and picked up a handful of pebbles, tossed them once in the air and ended up catching coins instead of stones. "Nifty," Lila said.

Marsum flipped one solid gold coin at the stable boy. "Feed and water them well, rub them down and there's a silver mark in it for you when I come back."

"Yes, sir!" The boy ran to do as he was told, his eyes aglow with the thought of the coin, no doubt.

Marsum strode out of the stable and to the connecting building. It took all I had to remain quiet. Inside, he used another gold coin to procure a room, two platters of food and a jug of some sort of ale.

I kept low in the hood, hanging from my front claws and working hard to keep my back end from drooping too far in the hood of the cloak to give us away.

"Eh, you do be looking kinda like you is sort in the familiar way," a gruff voice said, and then Marsum spun around, grabbed by the speaker. His hands were full of the food and he snarled as he turned.

"Take your hands off me unless you'd like me to

rearrange where your limbs are attached to your body."

There was a tingle under my claws as Marsum's magic rose up. A collective gasp went through the room as the black mist whipped out around us.

"Sorry, I so sorry, master Jinn. My apologies." That gruff voice shook with a fear so thick, it was evident that he was barely able to spit the words out.

Marsum moved with speed up a set of stairs, down a hall, and then a doorway clicked and he put the food down on a low table. With a quick move, he whipped the cloak off. Lila went to the food first, flying across the room. I leapt to the ground, shifting once I'd landed back to two feet.

"How bad is it that they know you're a Jinn?" I asked, moving toward the stack of meat and pile of desert root vegetables that had been smothered in butter and cream. My mouth watered and I didn't even think to ask him. I just took a platter and dug in.

"Not as bad as you being here. If they learn that you are a shifter, you will be tossed to the slave market. Worse for Lila too. She'd be a prize." He ran his hands over his head, scrubbing at his scalp. "But that is not as bad as someone else wanting the same damn stone as us."

I kept on shoveling food in as if it were to be my last meal, and maybe it was. I slowed enough to motion that I would share with him. He shook me off with a wave of his hand as he paced the room.

277

Damn, he cut a fine figure. I sighed and wiped my mouth on my sleeve. "You're worrying about nothing. He has a stone like what we need, right?"

Marsum stopped in the middle of the room. "I'm sure of it. I don't know who else would want it, though."

"Then I'll get the stone." I found myself grinning. "I've been stealing stones for years from much harder places, with far more dangerous guardians than a small desert-bred man with a large bald spot."

Lila snickered. "Bald isn't bad. But he was just—"

"He's pieced together, an animation of another mage's creation. He's not even real. The mage looks through his eyes," Marsum said. "But you are right. You have the best chance at getting in and out of there with the stone. And for now, they know me as a Jinn, but not which one. If they knew who I was, we would be in danger. Someone here would try to take my head to inherit my power."

Interesting that Marsum was not well loved by anyone, even the bad guys. Though really, was it any surprise with how he'd massacred the other creatures around the desert? "All good, he won't even see me; neither will the mage looking through his eyes. I'll be in and out in a flash." I stuffed another chunk of meat into my mouth, camel by the taste of it, and I smiled happily, thinking of Demon's sour face. This was going to work. We were going to get the stone and then . . . well, then we would figure out the rest.

Marsum, Maks, the Emperor. I had to believe this would work out.

The chunk of meat seemed to lose all taste, and I had to force myself to swallow it.

We finished eating—really, Lila finished because I was done, my last thought drying up my hunger. She chirped away happily as she filled her belly, licking up the last of the sauce. "Gods, I could sleep for a week." She groaned and rolled to the side, her gut protruding, a perfect beer barrel in miniature.

I glanced at the window. "We wait until dark, and we'll have the perfect cover."

Lila yawned, and Marsum lifted a brow. "Tired?"

"Exhausted." Lila rolled onto the table and promptly started snoring.

I glanced at her, stood and went to the window, standing to one side of it so I could peer out.

"The roofline will work in my favor with the buildings so close together. I can be to the merchant's stall in no time." I kept looking, not because there was anything else to see but because I didn't want to look at Marsum. At Maks.

He walked over and stood next to me. "You're nervous about getting the stone?" His voice was so close, right against my ear. There were a lot of things I could have said. There were a lot of things I shouldn't have said, and some things that terrified me to say. His hand slid around my waist, flat on my belly, and he slowly pulled me back against him.

Solid, strong, warm, he was the one who matched me in every way, and I couldn't have him. With no way I could see to save him.

"Talk to me, Zam."

Maks.

I closed my eyes. "I should go."

I pushed his hands away and moved to shift. But he caught me and pulled me back to him, eyes full of a fire I knew too well as it burned me every time he touched me.

"Not without a kiss."

22

The kiss of your soul mate is no small thing, especially when they are trying to impress something upon you. Maks's lips covered mine and his arms pinned me to him, one hand behind my head and the other in the small of my back. Gentle and demanding at the same time. I knew I should be pushing him away, telling him to fuck off or at least protesting.

Not me.

Nope, I all but wrapped my legs around his waist and arms around his neck while Lila snored on the table, full of food and totally oblivious to the makeout fest happening. Frantic movements, there was no real thought involved like *hey, we're in the Blackened Market. Maybe we should have our game faces on.* Or maybe, *if we don't get that stone, we'll both die.* Or even better, *if you get that stone and free Marsum from the bonds tying him to you, he may still try to kill you,* because all of those things were valid, strong, important points.

None of them even touched on the need raging through me.

"Zam, I don't have long," Maks whispered in between kissing my face, lips, neck, any part of my skin he could reach.

"Maks, you have to keep fighting, I'm trying—"

"Listen to me." He stopped kissing me long enough to hold my face in his hands. "I don't know if Marsum is the danger to you."

I blinked a few times. "What?"

"Davin has been helpful, I know. He's been coming through, and I think . . . I think he wants to kill you, Zam. He was the one who poisoned all the females, not some other Jinn." His jaw flicked and those blue eyes darkened. For a moment I was sure I was looking at Marsum, and then he receded.

"Was that him?" I asked.

Maks blew out a sharp breath. "Marsum knows you'll listen to me. He's . . . working with me. We are working together to keep Davin in place, but he's stronger than either of us knew and he's taking more and more of us." He kissed me again, pulled back and swallowed hard. "Zam, trust Marsum. I know that's a horrible thing to ask, believe me I know it. But I can't make him give up first position, and I am holding Davin back. He can't. So trust him. Please."

My turn to swallow hard. "I have to get the stone."

"I know." He pulled me into a hard hug and kissed the top of my head. "I love you, Zam. I should never have tried to run away from you, to try to protect you. I should have believed we could find a way through this."

Hope flared inside of me. "You think there's a way?"

I felt him nod. "Marsum thinks there's a way, but he won't tell me. I'll try to get it out of him."

I squeezed him tightly and lifted my face for one last kiss. Only it wasn't Maks there any longer.

And it wasn't Marsum either.

"So, the two boys have decided to work together, have they? I wondered at how they were keeping me in the dark so much."

His lips quirked into a cruel sneer and he took my offering, his mouth cutting across mine, hard as iron as one hand lifted, black mist curling around it.

A death spell, one that would steal my power. It shaped itself like the glyphs from my mother's papers, the ones that had burned up. The snake with the spear through it, the one that meant death.

And I could see it within the mist.

I drove my fist into his chest, knocking him back more than a few steps, and followed up with a kick to his left knee. He went down with a bellow as the kneecap popped out. Mortal, Jinn, two-legged or four, a kneecap still fucking hurt when you blew it out.

"I'm sorry." I took a stumbling step back, feeling the moment stretch as the pain hit me too. His hand went to where I landed the blow. "Run," he whispered. "He knows we're onto him. Run!"

Sweet baby goddess. I was going to lose him after all this.

With a cry, I scooped up Lila in one arm, turned and leapt for the window. Through the curtains we went, and I landed in a crouch on the slope of the roof. The metal and tiles with the dust of the desert coating them made the metal slick, and we slid more than a few feet before I caught us with one hand.

I didn't dare look back to the window. The blow to the knee would give us a head start. There was only one chance I had now and that was to get the stone and get to the crossroads. Without him. We were close enough, we had to be.

Maybe Ollianna could help us undo this spell, or combined with Maggi's knowledge and the power of the golden moons. Yes, I had to believe she could, or what was the point in even trying? I scooted across a couple rooftops before finding an alcove away from prying eyes. Night had fallen, but only just, and I was not all that inconspicuous in my long cloak and on two legs.

For once, I was wishing to be small, but I couldn't

do that until Lila woke. I lifted her up to my face and gave her a light shake. "Lila, wake up!"

"Sleeping, you leave me—"

"He just tried to kill me." The words broke me, and I couldn't stop the tears. Stupid, but it hurt me more now than it had before. Because I knew what it meant. I knew I was going to lose him fully.

"What, what?" She pulled herself out of her stupor. I filled her in between hiccups, about how Maks asked me to trust Marsum and how Davin had taken over Maks's body at the end. About the glyph inside the mist, and what it had meant. "Davin was the one to kill all the female Jinn. And now he wants to kill me."

Suddenly it made sense as to why the Jinn masters were such miserable bastards. "What if that's why . . ." No, I didn't want to think about the possibility of Marsum not being a right bastard, a piece of shit, or of him setting Maks and me up. What if it had been Davin all along?

"What?" Lila tugged at me. "What are you thinking?"

I shook my head. "Not now. We have to get the stone, then we have to get the hell out of here."

That made me pause. The horses were in the stable behind us, fully untacked and locked in stalls.

"Lila, can you get into the stable? Get Balder and Batman out while I get the stone? If Marsum is there

. . . leave them." Oh, gods that hurt. But we couldn't get them back if we were caught, or worse, dead.

"I can unlatch things, but I can't get their gear on," Lila said. I nodded—riding bareback was fine by me —and she flew off, back the way we came, using the buildings for cover. And now it was my turn to do the same. I shifted, walking through the doorway in my mind between two legs and four, ignoring the doorway coated in magic and beckoning me to use it.

"Not tonight," I muttered as I scooted across the rooftops, leaping between them, landing lightly on the pads of my paws as I raced toward the merchant stalls. Only a few minutes and I was there, looking down on the roof of the stone merchant. Or an animated crony, however you wanted to look at him. I leaned over the edge. There was an open window on the top of the roof to allow for ventilation. A perfect entry for a thief.

I leapt across and crouched down at the entrance to the window. The merchant Jiango sat on a stool, unmoving. "Yes, master, I sent him away. Yes, master, I will do as you say. Kill the Jinn. Bring the flail to you."

I shook my head. Indiana Jones surely never had this many issues on one of his adventures. The merchant was being used by the *Emperor*? Of course he was, because my life was a game of just how bad could things get. The answer?

Worse, they could always get worse.

The sound of horse hooves on the cobblestone turned my head ever so slightly.

"No, no, no." I mouthed the words as *he* came into view, riding Batman, leading Balder behind. Not Maks, not Marsum, but the other one.

"One way or another, I will have that stone and the magic out of you, Zamira," Davin's voice cut through the night. He reached behind him and pulled Lila out, her wings and mouth strapped by magic. "You *women* are not meant to wield the power of the Jinn. It makes you crazy. It makes you stupid. Almost as stupid as so-called love makes you." He smiled and his eyes searched the roofline shadows. I slid back farther.

A plan began to form, quickly, with the reckless abandon I could be known for—I just had to make it happen. For Lila, for me, for Maks, I had to do this even though it was the last thing I wanted to do.

I slid through the window and dropped to the ground at the animated man's feet. He startled and then fell backward as I shifted to two feet. I grabbed him by the shoulders and drew him close enough to smell the garlic on his breath. Time to lay all the cards on the table.

"Grandfather, I'll bring you the flail, but I need two things from you."

Goddess, was I really going to do this?

I was. I was going to make a deal with the devil to make things right, to give us all a chance at life.

Jiango stood a little straighter and his voice changed. "What is it that you want?"

"The black lightning-kissed stone, and you will release my brother. Give me those two things and I'll deliver the flail to you in person." Two lives, for one deal. That had to be enough. Three lives if I counted Maks not going down with me and the power of the stone.

Jiango tipped his head to one side, dropped to his knees and pulled a knife from his belt. "What are you doing?" I moved to grab the knife but missed it, cutting my fingers on the edge just before he plunged it into his own belly. I hissed and clutched my fingers; he groaned as he dug the knife around, slicing through layers of fat, muscle and viscera before he finally stopped.

"Like a kid playing in the sand, digging for treasure," I whispered.

Well, stopped isn't quite the right word. He dropped the knife and drove his hand into his belly next, scrounging around before he came out clutching something that looked terrifyingly familiar.

The stone in his hand was the exact replica of the one that had shattered and released all that magic into me.

"Wait!" I grabbed at Jiango as he slumped in front of me, bleeding out. "How do I put the magic into the stone from the one that shattered against me?"

Jiango blinked and then laughed, burbling. "You

can't. Only I can do that. What will you give me to save you now?"

He'd known that I would die without his help, and he made the deal anyway—to take my moment of hope from me.

He fell to the side, laughing as he died, laughing as my death sentence was sealed.

23

Jiango, minion of the Emperor, and purveyor of stones, lay dead at my feet. The stone I needed was in my hands, and Davin the Jinn, slayer of female Jinn, waited to introduce me to the same fate—and he held Lila as a prisoner to make sure I did as he wanted. Which at the moment was die.

Only if I died, he died. Or did he? The cuffs had tied my life to his, but did the bond he'd placed on me work the same? I had a feeling it would. That would explain why Davin had fought Marsum on connecting to me.

I'd just agreed to give the flail to the Emperor for this stone, so I better damn well make the bargain worth the cost.

I rubbed my thumb over the stone and it lit up inside as though I'd turned something on. "I don't want this power," I whispered and closed my eyes. The only thing I could do was try to push the power in me out, using my own magic.

What had Davin said? That Jinn women were too adaptable, too good at using too many kinds of magic. I was a Jinn woman, apparently adaptable in ways other magic users weren't, so maybe I could do this.

I went to my knees, lifted my shirt, and pressed the point of the crystal against the spot where the other one had exploded, following my instincts once more. The glyphs that had been written in my mother's journal swelled in my head, images with meanings that pulsed with knowledge.

Droplets of blood.

The stone.

Jinn.

Marsum.

Lila.

Pushing hard enough to feel blood well up under the tip of the stone, I opened the doorway in my mind between me and the magic that was my own and hoped that the other pieces would fall into place.

The door broke open and Davin stood over me, glaring. "What are you doing?"

"Getting the magic out of me. And if you want it so badly, you can fucking help!" I snapped. My anger was fueled by fear and desperation, and the power in me swirled up and around, drawn into the stone as if it were a magnet.

He dropped to his knees beside me and the black mist rose up around us as he raised his power. "You are a granddaughter of the Emperor. You have it in you to make this happen. I will guide you."

"Bullshit." I snarled the word. "You can't guide me, and I don't trust you." A thought hit me, and I embraced it. "Let Marsum guide me."

"You'd trust him? How would you even know the difference?" He frowned and I glared at him as sweat rolled down my body.

"Just like I knew when it was Maks and not Marsum."

He blinked and there was a moment that I thought he would just kill me outright. But that wouldn't trap the power for him, and that was what he wanted more than anything, I could see it now. The stones. He wanted to take the stones from me.

"You want to be the next Emperor, don't you?" I whispered the question as Marsum put his hands over mine.

"Not me, but Davin, yes." His jaw flicked as the magic swelled around us. He stood and went outside, then came back with Lila. She was spitting mad and he shushed her. "We need to help Zam. It will take all three of us, a true triad of power to push Ishtar's magic into the stone and save Zam."

Three. Three. Three.

"Well, why didn't you say so?" she growled, and then turned to me. "He caught me."

"I saw that. Too much food?" The smile hurt but I did it anyway. I turned to Marsum. "Marsum, Maks said there is a way to stop all this, a way to free him." I clutched at his fingers and then grimaced as the air in my lungs began to burn. Lila grabbed hold of my face and Marsum spread one hand on my neck, holding me upright, the other wrapped around my fingers and helped hang onto the lightning-kissed crystal.

"There is," he said as he held me tightly. "But you have to survive this first." The black mist of the Jinn swirled around us and two of the stones we had in our possession lit up. Blue and amber. Ice Witch and Jinn. I didn't have any time to wonder why the emerald stone, the dragon's stone, lay dormant.

His magic drove into the stone and my own magic rose once more to meet it.

A soundless scream ripped out of me as the air in my lungs went from burning to turning into a ball of fire so hot, it could have fallen from the sun.

"Stop! She's going to die!" Lila shrieked as the magic ran hotter and hotter, more than any desert sun, more than any heat I'd ever known.

"She'll die if we stop!" he roared back at her, and I knew he was right. Of course he was right.

But I had to slow this heat down.

My free hand brushed against the sapphire stone

and I picked it out of the bag. A sudden cold washed through me, dousing the flames and allowing me to breathe again.

The colors spun like a storm around us and seemed to go *through* me. Damn well straight through me.

I couldn't breathe again, but this time, I didn't mind. There was no pain with the lack of breath, just a concern that at some point, this would be bad and there would be no intake of breath for me again.

You can leave me, I thought, seeing the magic that was Ishtar's in the storm of color. *Go into the stone.*

It writhed around inside of me and I shook my head. I would die and the magic would die with me if it didn't go.

That thought was all I could see as the world began to fade, and I clung to it. At least the magic would not be used for evil again, for hurting anyone, because it would be dead too. I would take it with me. There would be no more of this part of Ishtar's power. I held my breath and wrapped my own magic around Ishtar's, holding it to me. If it wouldn't go into the stone, I'd kill it.

Dead magic. Was that even a possibility? Maybe, because I carried the blood of the Jinn. I could kill it when others couldn't.

A growl slid through me, one that was not my own.

There was a pulse of power around my middle,

294

and then a sudden snap of my ribs breaking. My breath came out in a whoosh, skin tingling and eyes watering, Ishtar's power fleeing me, streaking into the stone still pressed into my chest. The piercing point of the stone tingled against my skin and I could *see* the magic inside of it now, writhing and angry. But alive.

There was a set of arms around me and I blinked up into Marsum's face. "What happened?"

He stared down at me, brows furrowed with confusion. "Ishtar's power . . . it just left. The magic was fighting us, all three of us, draining us down. I couldn't stop it—"

"Like it did when you used the stone before." Lila butted her head against my face. "Just like that and like he said, we couldn't stop it, we were all going to die. I was yelling for you, but you didn't hear me."

Marsum held me on his lap. "What did you do?"

I blinked a few times, knowing that there were only a few moments left to this, only a few moments before Davin came back and tried to take the stones from me. "Who killed my father, Marsum? Who attacked the lions of the desert?"

He gave a quick nod. "Davin. He's been ruling the Jinn for centuries. We keep trying to fight him, by killing off our leader with the strongest males we have so that we have the best chance at bringing him to heel, and it's never enough." He bowed his head. "Never enough until you."

295

"How do I save Maks?" I touched a hand to his face. "He said you knew a way."

Marsum's jaw flexed. "I told him that to keep him helping me. We've never held Davin off this long before when a transition happened between souls and bodies. It's Maks's love for you that is strengthening us. The only way to stop Davin now is to kill him."

"How? Then she'll be the leader of the Jinn, and he'll be in her body, idiot!" Lila snapped. "That is not going to happen."

He brushed his hand over my cheek and then he pulled me into a careful hug, holding me close to his chest, his words rumbling through my ear as if by whispering. "Trickery, that is all I can tell you. The answer lies in trickery."

My throat squeezed in on itself. Trickery was not much to go on. "How long before he's back?"

Those arms tightened further and I knew the answer, he didn't have to tell me.

"Oh, little Zam, thank you for these." He plucked the three gemstones he could see out of my hands with ease. I let him. I let him take them. Lila scrambled, hissing, her wings outstretched as she snaked her neck around, snapping her teeth at him.

"By the pricking of my thumbs, something wicked this way comes. What a shithead. I'm going to puke acid all over his stupid face," Lila snarled, her words gurgling with said acid.

"No. Don't." I grabbed her before she could do just that.

I pushed away from him as he stood, his hands full of the stones.

My fingers brushed against the handle of the flail, my heart breaking with what I knew I had to do.

It was time.

D avin strode out of the small stone merchant's stall into the street. "And the power is mine, and my name is *Death*." The starlight above gave a nice glow to the Blackened Market and highlighted his figure as he did a slow circle in the middle of the main street. Strutting.

Death. I had to *embrace death*.

"Lila, we need to take him down the road, away from this place, make him think he's chasing us," I whispered, wincing as I slowly pulled the flail, my heart breaking, the pain in my body barely competing with the pain in my heart. For the moment, he was basking in having the stones, and had forgotten me. But that wouldn't last.

"Oh no." She whimpered the words and then flew from my hand. I didn't tell her what I hoped to do. Didn't tell her that maybe there was a chance, that

Marsum's words had given me one last drop of hope to drink in.

Lila shot around Davin's head, only it wasn't just Davin any longer that we would face.

Maggi strode down the center of the lane of the market, all but glowing in the dark, her gauzy skirts flaring around her. "What did I say, my love? That one day you'd come back to me." She smiled and he *threw her the sapphire stone*.

A traitor in the midst . . . and I'd been looking at her the whole time like an idiot thinking she was helping me. Even when she'd proven herself back at the Wyvern's Lair, demanding the stone, I'd still believed she was on my side. As long as I kept the stone from her. And now she had it once more.

"Well, you did say that." He grinned at her, took her by the hand and pulled her against him for a kiss. I could have stood there, stunned into not moving, but I had no time. I had to change my plan and fast. There were moments to let your jaw hang slack, and this was not one of them.

I shifted to four legs, the transformation forcing my body to heal my broken ribs in that split second, to push through the pain as my bones locked back together, and then I was racing across the road, drawing them down the street.

"We still need her!" Davin yelled.

At least that much could stay the same.

A blast of power erupted in the ground beside me,

ice blue and frozen through. "I'll kill you now, cat!" Maggi screeched. "You took my stone, you took my magic, and Merlin forced me to help you!"

Just like that, the Ice Witch was back to how she'd been when I'd first met her.

I didn't look back, just kept on weaving down the road, drawing them closer to the shifter section of the market.

I dove through the bars on the first cage I came to, crouching in the shadows. A large presence behind me made me flatten myself farther. The smell of lion was everywhere, familiar, and while I wasn't afraid, I wasn't exactly comfortable. "You keep your distance," I growled.

A nose lowered and brushed against my side. "You sure about that?"

I whipped around and his scent slapped me in the face. "Bryce?"

"You shouldn't have agreed to give him the flail. I was here all along. This is where he stuck me. In a cage. I couldn't shift, he blocked my scent, and I couldn't say anything, but we could have figured it out." His golden eyes glittered in the dark and I wanted nothing more than to grab him and hold him, to allow myself to believe he was really there. I crouched as Davin and Maggi strode by, talking, laughing, holding the stones.

There were too many questions for Bryce and literally zero time to answer them. "Wait for me here." I butted my head against his nose and slid out of the cage, creeping along the street behind the two I needed to deal with.

"What choice do I have?" he grumbled and I smiled. There was my grumpy-as-shit brother. And to think I'd missed him.

A glance up into the sky showed me Lila flying high, way high up, watching. Waiting.

I scooted forward, knowing that I would have only one shot at this if I were lucky. And if I weren't lucky, I'd be dead in a few minutes. Maggi and Davin would hold three of Ishtar's stones and goddess only knew what that would lead to.

And why hadn't he taken the emerald? That worried me almost as much as him taking the others.

Running low with my belly to the ground, the pads of my feet were silent on the cobblestones as I closed the distance between us. Muscles bunching, I leapt into the air, shifting, pulling the flail and swinging it all in that one smooth motion.

Please, please, please, please, please, please.

The mantra whispered through me. Please let this work. The flail slammed into Maggi's back and head, the twin balls striking at the same time. She screamed and I held on tightly, dragging her backward with me, using her body for a shield as Davin spun.

"Help me!" she wailed to him, one hand outstretched.

"No." He shrugged. "I would rather have the stone, and she is hurrying that along for me."

Maggi slumped. "Fooled again. Damn you. Damn me."

The flail's handle was warm and tacky under my hand, and it pulsed as it drew her life and her magic from her in loud sucking gulps.

"I thought he loved me," she whispered. "He told me while you slept that we would be together finally if I helped him."

The looks she'd shot at him made sense now. "He fooled us both. Davin fooled us both," I said.

The flail dug in harder and her knees buckled. I held her up, keeping her in front of me. Maggi gripped my hand. "I should have died when I gave you the cuffs. I selfishly let you take me along for one last breath of life." She shoved the sapphire into my hand. I took it, tucked it under my shirt into the pouch at my waist. One down.

With a wickedly rapid pace her body shrunk, skin and muscle disappearing until she was nothing but bones and a long shank of hair. Bony fingers touched the necklace with my father's ring on it. "Lila."

"She is done." Davin flicked a hand at Maggi's shrunken body, flinging it away from me, my fingers tangling in the chain that held the ring. It snapped as she was torn away and I barely managed to catch what was left of it and the ring.

I still held the flail and it shivered in my other hand. "Not yet," I whispered.

"Talking to my weapon?" He grinned. "That flail is *mine*. I created it. And it will not fight me."

I'd heard that line before. It had been him at the Oasis, both times. Not Marsum.

The handle shivered again, and I gripped it a little harder. "Really? Maybe it knows which one of us would never throw it aside."

I tried not to think about the fact that I'd literally just traded it away, but that was different. I hoped.

He stepped toward me and I stepped back. A lion roared from one of the cages—Bryce. Damn it, I should have trusted my instincts before. I should have listened. I should have seen him for who he was.

"It's a weapon," Davin said. "That is all it is."

"No, it's not." I spun as he threw a billowing mass of magic at me. I swept the flail out and slammed it through the black cloud. It sucked down the magic so fast, there was a moment I wasn't sure it had ever been there.

"Impossible," Davin snarled, his eyes narrowing.

"What do you think it will do to you when I slam it into you?" I began to circle him, an idea forming quickly. Trickery, this was all about trickery. "Will it drain you like it did Maggi down to nothing but skin and bones?"

"That weapon will never harm me. And I doubt

you have it in you to kill the man you love." He smirked at me.

"The flail just sucked your magic down like it was starving." I smiled, feeling the predatory pulse in my veins. "The flail is *mine* now. I am Jinn, too, or did you forget that?" I let my eyes dart to look over his shoulder then back to his face.

He held out the white stone. "Perhaps I should show you what I am capable of?"

"Now!" I yelled, and he spun as if there would be someone behind him.

Only there was no one there.

Trickery it was.

I bolted forward, swinging the flail to the side. He whipped back to me, fast with Maks's muscles and training, a snarl on his face.

He grabbed me by my free arm, and kicked me in the belly, stopping me in my tracks. The wind went out of me in a whoosh.

"You think you can outmaneuver me?"

A fist connected with my face and I went down, blood filling my mouth. I clung to the flail, knowing it was my only hope. Tears leaked out of my eyes, pooling with the blood. Another fist, another and another.

My vision blurred and Davin laughed. "Tears? Tears are for children. You would be better off begging on your knees than crying in the dirt."

Another blow to my middle and then the heel of

his boot ground into my hand that held the flail. "Let it go."

He was afraid of me holding it.

"No." The word gurgled out of me. He would have to kill me to take it from me.

The handle warmed under my palm and I gripped it harder.

"Then you die."

I turned my face so I could look him in the eye, hating what I was going to do. I lurched upward and hugged him to me. Embracing him. Embracing death. "Love is strong enough. It always has been, it always will be. I trust it and the men who love me with my life."

His face twisted and he roared as his magic swirled around him. "Bitch! They can't take me!"

Distantly, I wondered where Lila was. Had he caught her, and I'd not seen? But I had no chance to look for her.

He threw me to the side and I hit the ground hard, wind knocked out of me.

I pulled myself to my hands and knees, still gripping the flail. "Maks is strong enough. He did what he did to save me. He took Marsum's head to save me and Marsum *let him* because he believed in his son. He believed love was strong enough." Blood dribbled down my chin as I lifted my head, surety flowing through me. "They are strong enough." They had to be. Just for a moment.

Long enough for me to do what I had to do even if it cracked my heart wide open.

He stumbled backward, and I struggled to stand. My vision blurred and my body ached all over from his fists and boots. Rather telling that he would beat my body hand to hand than to face off with magic.

"You can drain his magic," I whispered and the flail shivered, "and his life without me holding onto you, so I won't be his next vessel." Another shiver against the palm of my hand. Unsteady as I was, I stood as Davin flailed backward, screaming into the night.

People were stepping out of their merchant stalls, watching the drama unfold. I didn't care if there was an audience for this. If they wanted to fight me afterward, I would fight them all.

Another roar from Bryce, unintelligible other than a broad warning of danger. No shit.

Davin flailed, went down to one knee and stayed there, panting. "They are not strong enough."

With my free hand, I touched his face, tipping it up so I could look into those blue eyes one last time. The path to this moment stretched out in front of me. My need for Maks, leaving Ford behind, taking Maggi and Marsum with me, and even farther back than that to my family's crest being etched into the flail, so that I took it when I'd found it all those months ago. Maybe this had been coming far longer than even I realized.

"I wish there was another way," I said, my voice breaking with the pain in my heart. "I wish there was another way to save you."

He blinked once and a smile ghosted over his lips. "You were right. Love is strong enough, Zam. Do what you must." He held out his hands, palms up and I lowered the flail to them. The spikes dug into the flesh and he grimaced. I held the handle for a moment.

"I wish it could just take the Jinn masters and their power, not you," I whispered.

The flail flung itself out of my hand, ripping the flesh as it hadn't for a long time. A glow lit up around the spiked balls as it began to suck his life away.

Those blue eyes, those pretty blue eyes never looked away from me. "Always, Zam, I will always be near you. No matter how far you go, no matter that you think you're alone, I will be there."

My vision wobbled along with my lower lip as I struggled to keep it together. "Maks. It isn't fair. It just isn't."

"I know." He smiled and a tear slid from one eye. "But we had a little time. More than some get."

"I don't care."

He mouthed three words to me. *Use the flail.*

But I was using the flail. Marsum . . . trickery . . . Jinn magic . . . flail that absorbs magic . . . a spell to hold the Jinn masters in one body, that was magic, wasn't it? The answer was there. I'd just not seen it.

He gave me a slow wink, seeing me understand, and a sad smile. "Tell Maks I always knew he had it in him. He was always the best of us."

I reached for the flail's handle, took hold of it. A rush of power slid through me, healing my wounds, drawing from him and feeding into me. One last shot, one last chance to save Maks. "Only the Jinn masters, flail. Only them and their spell. Leave me Maks."

The weapon tried to pull itself away from me again, but I was ready for it this time. "No! I am your master now, and you will do as I say!"

The words left me in a yell that echoed through the night, and in my peripheral vision, I saw the people watching cringe away. "I brought you out of darkness," I said, "and I can leave you there again. Only the Jinn masters, only their energy and their spell!"

Goddess, would this work? Had I literally held the answer in my hands the whole time?

Those twin spiked balls dug harder into him and I tugged on the handle as if I would pull it away. There was a slow pulse . . . and then Maks threw his head back and screamed, his body shaking as the magic flew out of him in a black billowing mist that swept around us, faster and faster before it shot straight into the flail with a boom like thunder.

People screamed, echoing him, doors slammed, and I stood in the center of it, seeing the Jinn masters as they were drawn out and eaten by their own creation.

One by one, they slid into the weapon. Not as many masters as I would have thought. Only five. The first three gave me a salute as they disappeared.

The next was Davin.

He raged and fought, scrabbling against the weapon. "We are not done, you and I." His voice no longer constrained by Maks's body was harder and full of so much condescension, I was shocked I'd not heard it before.

"Yeah, we are." I softened my grip on the flail's handle. "Never again, Davin."

With a final grimace, he slid away, absorbed by the magic in the flail.

And then there was one master left.

Marsum. He stood there ghostly in form as he began his inevitable slide toward the weapon.

"I knew if he found love that we would have a chance." Marsum smiled and I realized that Maks had his smile. I'd just never seen the connection before.

"You sent him away, all those months ago? Sent him to find me, or someone like me."

"In a moment of lucidity, when Davin didn't have control, I did. I saw the Oracle many years before, and she said that love was the answer to bringing the Jinn back to what they once were. I am sorry for your losses, Zam."

My eyes welled with tears. "You threw me into the water at the Oasis."

He bowed his head toward me. "So Davin wouldn't kill you. I knew your mother." His jaw flicked. "And in another life before I was a master, I loved her fiercely, even if she did not return that love."

My jaw dropped open. Holy shit.

"But it was not to be, and I knew it." He smiled again. "I saw her in you, and something more. Something stronger than even she'd been." He reached out with a ghostly hand and brushed it against my cheek. "For the sorrow we brought you, I am sorry. For the freedom you have given the Jinn from this spell, I am not. I will watch over you two, my son and my son's mate."

Just like that, he slid away into the flail, gone forever.

I yanked the flail away from Maks's hands and went to my knees beside him. "Maks?"

Carefully, so very carefully I cupped his face, tipping it to mine so I could see his eyes. He was alive, but not saying anything as he wobbled there, his body seemingly unhinged from anything holding him steady.

I held him there. "Talk to me, Toad."

His body began to shake, and I held my breath. Goddess of the desert, what now?

Laughter spilled out of him and he slowly lifted his hands to mine. "Toad? Really?"

I yanked him to me and kissed him for all I was worth. All the hope and fear, all the worry and belief that I'd lost him were wrapped up in that one touch of mouth on mouth. Love, love was something I'd had so little of in my life, and I knew its touch like a woman dying of thirst knew the first brush of water on her tongue.

Everything, that kiss and Maks were everything.

"I'm here. I'm here." He whispered the words between touches, between kisses peppered across my mouth. Frantic, we clung to each other. How many times had we had a moment like this only to have it ripped away?

Too many to count.

Too many to not believe it might happen again.

It was my turn to shake, to tremble, with a fear of what could come next.

I shouldn't have been worrying about Maks, though. He brushed his hands over me. "Where is Lila?"

It took me a moment to realize that in the whole fight, she'd not been there. She'd not even done a flyby to buzz us and check in.

My fear for Maks shifted into instant horror. "I don't know."

25

While I would have loved for my reunion with Maks to be one consisting of stripping off clothes and rolling around in a huge bed for hours on end, it was decidedly less romantic and far more practical.

I helped him stand in the middle of the street in the Blackened Market as we both scanned the night sky for some sign of Lila.

"Can you find her?" Maks held onto my hand and I was not about to pull away.

I opened myself to the bond I had with Lila and found her to the south. "You get the horses, and your weapon. I have one more person to grab."

He let me go and turned toward the weapons merchant's stall, our fingers sliding across one another, leaving behind a tingle on my skin. Yeah, at some point we were going to have that rolling around a big bed naked scene happen. But not tonight.

And probably not tomorrow either. We were down to a single day before the golden moon rose. Two days was not enough time to make anything happen.

I ran back the way we'd come, sliding to a stop in front of Bryce's cage while I kept a bead on Lila's location. She wasn't hurt, but she was damn well terrified and her fear infected me, making me jittery and sharp in my movements.

"Out of the way!" I motioned at Bryce with one hand, waving him back.

He took a few steps back, as much as he was able in his too-small cage, and I swung the flail, smashing it through the bars that held him. The iron melted away as if the flail was hot, and the iron puddled to the ground. Bryce leapt out but didn't shift.

"Later," he said, "when we have clothes."

Like with Maks, I wanted this moment to stretch, to hold and be grateful that my brother was back with me. The two men I loved the most in this world were alive and well. And they were damn well *with* me.

But Lila was in trouble and there was zero time to be all lovey-dovey. "Let's go, trouble is coming."

"Surprise, surprise," he drawled and bounded along at my side.

I found my feet skidding to a stop in front of the

slave traders' wares. Hollowed-out cheeks, eyes full of despair. I had a moment, just a single moment, and the White Raven's voice spoke as clearly as if she were there: "You never even tried to help free me." And I made my decision. I swung the flail, catching the chains that held the slaves, shattering them like glass. "Run."

They scattered, a tiny puff of magic around several of them and then they were going for it. Their slavers came out of their homes yelling, took one look at me and Bryce and slowed. I grinned, wondering just what they were seeing in me, in us. Covered in blood, maybe with the glow of magic still on me and the flail swinging loose at my side. It was all the time I could buy the slaves.

"One more stop," I said as I ran down the street, finding the dragon egg shack easily. I kicked down the door and stepped through into a dim room. A man and woman looked up from some rather frisky behavior, the pimples on his ass all but staring me down as he thrust into her. "Where are the fucking eggs?"

He squealed like I'd stuck a pin in one of those pimples of his, then rolled so the woman was on top of him, essentially shielding him. She whacked at him repeatedly as I stared him down. "The eggs."

"All sold!" he shouted. "They're gone already, they never last long."

I should have killed him, but I had a feeling he

and I were not done. "I'll be back to have a chat with you, pimple ass. Not tomorrow, but soon."

I turned on my heel and ran out of the room. Bryce gave me a look and I grimaced. "I made a promise." I might not be able to save the dragon babies yet, but I would. I would come back, and I would pick up the trail. They were jewels of a different kind.

"Of course you did," he muttered. "Too big of a heart."

He loped along at my side until we caught up to Maks and the horses.

Maks shot a look at Bryce and his eyes widened. "Bryce?"

Bryce looked up at him. "It's a long story, man. Another time."

I hopped onto Balder and led the way because my brother was right—we were out of time. We ran past where Maggi's body was already being picked apart by the merchants, taking her bones for goddess only knew what. I shot them a look, but didn't slow Balder's feet. That was her penance for double-crossing us—I had no sympathy in me for her anymore.

Thoughts of what was coming bit at my heels like a dog herding goats. We had to be at the crossroads tomorrow night and we were a solid two or three days away for travel. The place where a curse could be broken and we had to be there. But whose curse?

SHANNON MAYER

Mine? Lila's? Or someone else's? And only there could we find the power to stop the Emperor. To dethrone him.

Something we needed even more now that I'd agreed to hand over the flail.

In person, no less. I grimaced, knowing that the cost of what I'd offered was high, but what I'd gotten in return was worth it.

"Hurry, we need to get Lila and ride like our lives depended on it," I said with a quick glance back at them. Only my eyes were drawn up by a flicker of motion across the stars, the blotting out of light by a body far too big to be a bird, or even one of the desert hunting falcons.

"Dragon." I breathed the word and knew then why Lila was afraid.

Her father had found us.

Corvalis, leader of the dragons and legendary monster, let out a bellow that shook the rafters of the shops around us. I leaned into Balder, urging him faster. We raced across the cobblestones and hit the sand at full speed. As we crossed the southern border of the market, Lila dashed out to our side as we raced away from the Blackened Market. I held out my hand to her and she shot to me and burrowed herself in my arms.

"He saw me. He knows I'm here," she cried out.

I looked at Maks, thinking that we had four stones, four powerful stones, and maybe one of them could stop Corvalis. He shook his head. "We have to run. The stones are too unpredictable and we are both exhausted."

Bryce galloped along my other side, keeping up, a grin on his face. "I agree. We run."

Another bellow came from behind us and the guttering of flames as the night lit up with dragon fire. Screams lit the air and I found myself staring over my shoulder as the market exploded with dragon fire.

Literally.

"Maybe he's here to save the eggs?" I said. Not that they were there, but maybe that was why he'd come.

Lila shivered against me. "No, he's after me. I'm sure of it." I held her a little tighter, fearing for her. Fearing for us all.

We'd survived Corvalis once, but I wasn't sure we could do it again.

We were miles away before I would let the horses slow, and even then, they rooted their heads forward, digging at the bits, wanting themselves to keep going. They danced and jigged and I struggled to shush them.

Until I realized that we were far from out of the dark, in dangerous sands.

"Oh, shit." I spun Balder to look behind us, to see the telltale spray of sand into the air caught only by the light of the moon as the ophidians raced toward us, nearly silent and far more deadly than Corvalis in that moment.

"Go, go, go!" I yelled and the horses took off with my voice, before we could cue them. Bryce kept up, running flat out, but not for long and I knew it.

"We have to do something. There is no hard ground, and no way to keep this pace up!" Maks yelled across to me.

I nodded, and my hand went for the sapphire stone. Lila stopped me, shook her head. "No, it will draw my father. He'll sense the power and he will know. He will know it's us!"

I wanted to tell her there was no other option, but that wasn't right. That wasn't right at all.

"Lila, what if we could make you big? You're strong enough to carry all of us, aren't you?"

She stared at me. "What are you talking about?"

I pulled the chain and ring out of my pouch, showing it to her. "Maggi made this to hold a curse back. It could be used for you, on your curse. You could fly us out of here."

She cringed against me as if I held a hot poker to her. "You would trust Maggi?"

"She wore the ring. She didn't die because of it," I said. "Lila, it might be our only chance to get to the crossroads, to break the curse on you for real." Because despite wanting to believe that my own curse could be broken, I knew in my heart that it would never happen.

I was what I was for a reason.

She shook her head. "I'm afraid, Zam. That other one, it almost killed me."

"I remember," I said. "But this isn't then, this is now." I tied it into Balder's mane. "Take it when you're ready, Lila. I know you can do this."

She stared at it, eyes wide. "I can't."

"I can't keep up!" Bryce hollered, out of breath and slowing rapidly. I spun Balder and hopped off, pulling my flail free.

"Then we fight," I said, even though I knew that this was the worst idea possible. There was no way I was going to leave Bryce behind.

And for once, he didn't argue. He slid to a stop and turned to face the oncoming pack of ophidians.

"What has their queen got against us?" Lila asked.

"Question of the day," I muttered.

The flail all but hummed under my hands as I held it out to my side, and a single word reverberated through me.

Stones.

I spluttered. "The stones?"

"Shit, that makes perfect sense. Everybody wants the stones and their power. Why wouldn't she?" Maks took up a position beside me, the bladed spear in both hands. He'd have good reach with that at least.

My mind, though, was reeling. The ophidian queen wanted the stones.

But how the hell had she known we'd had them in the first place? "She drove us to the Wyvern's Lair," I whispered. "We'd talked about not going. She pushed us there to get the stone for her."

But we hadn't gotten it, and so she chased us down?

The ophidians slowed as they drew closer, the sound of hissing and sliding sand the only indication that they were still there. The sand around us moved and shifted, but nothing came closer than about a twenty-foot radius.

Until an ophidian slid to the top of the desert, coiled itself and raised itself into a strike position. Mouth open, a voice came from it. Not its own . . .

Its queen's.

"The stonessssssss."

"We can't," Maks said softly, "it will be the same mess all over again. We have to see this through, Zam." I didn't know how he knew that, but I trusted him completely.

"Listen up, Queen whatever-the-hell-your-name-is. You don't get the stones, not even one of them. We'll kill your snake friends here, and then you if we have to."

"You will die," she said, the ophidian's head weaving side to side, hissing violently. Lila rose into the air, her wings shaking. "You may kill some of my pets, but more are coming, and even if you escape these, you will have to face more, and more. You cannot kill them all, not even you, Zamira."

If I didn't know better, I'd have thought there was a tone of sorrow in the words. But what reason did she have to be sad?

"Fuck off, you forked-tongue bitch!" I snapped, fear making me angry.

Anger making my brain tick.

Forked tongue.

Forked . . . I'd seen a forked tongue. But where? My memory wrapped around me and I stood with my jaw hanging open.

From where I was, the curl of a red skirt was the first of the witches that I saw. A flash of bare toes under the edge of a skirt that swirled around within the mist and on top of the water. I let my eyes drift upward, careful not to move any other part of me.

Fine-boned, dark-haired and dark-eyed, the first witch looked to be about fifteen at the oldest, though I knew that was a lie. They all looked like teenagers when I was here last too, but they were anything but. Her ruby-red lips matched her dress and she cooed softly as she walked daintily toward me, lifting her feet over the logs she encountered, her hands clutched in the material of her skirt. "Oh, there is something here, I think. Yes, Ollianna, do ye feel it?"

A second witch in a dress as black as the muddy water stepped up next to her. Auburn hair flowed around her as if held up by a thousand tiny strings. As fine-boned and beautiful as the first witch, she tipped her head to the side and ran her tongue over her lips. Check that, she ran her forked tongue out and over her lips as if she were tasting the air. I shrank into the water farther, slow and smooth, not even a single ripple giving me away.

"Ollianna?" I gasped. "*You're* the traitor?" How could I have been so stupid not to have seen this? She'd been driving us, pushing us in the direction she wanted. Forcing Marsum and me to work together. Because he had a stone. And she thought I'd take it from him. Just like she suggested I do.

The snake hissed, its mouth as wide open as it could be, flashing fangs.

"I gave you a chance to live, Zamira," Ollianna said through her pet. "And now you die. For that I am sorry."

The ophidians came at us en masse.

Lila flew above us, circling, a flash of something bright catching the light.

"My friends are not going to die. And we are not giving you the stones, you traitorous bitch."

Dangling around her neck was the chain and ring.

My father's ring, the curse breaker.

26

The ophidians took no note of Lila as she flew above us. They kept on coming.

"We just have to hold them off!" I said as I stepped into my first swing, slamming the flail through the sand and into the ophidian's skull. Maks used his hooked pike to drive through the sand and into the snakes over and over.

"What about me?" Bryce yelled.

"Saddle, shotgun, protect the horses!" I yelled back.

He'd have to shift and fight naked, but it wouldn't be the first time for him.

A second later, the boom of the gun went off and the ophidians slowed their attack. Only it wasn't the gun that slowed them.

It was the fast-moving river that raced toward them.

Screeches went up amongst the ophidians caught by the flow, the sand around them bubbling hot with the liquid acid as it raced toward us, flowing from a bigger than life Lila.

"YES!" I punched a hand into the air, then brought the flail down as an ophidian snaked toward me. The flail shivered, giddy with bloodlust that leaked through to me. I wanted to stay, I wanted to put these bastards into their graves and watch them die, but they weren't the real problem.

No, that would be Ollianna.

She'd hugged me in the dreamscape . . . hugged me, and that had to have been when she snagged the emerald stone. "You're a buggering pickpocket, Ollie!" I yelled as I smashed another ophidian. That was why the emerald hadn't done a thing, why it wouldn't work for me. She'd switched them out, stealing the real one.

That two-faced, two-tongued liar was about to get her ass handed to her. The only jewel thief here was me.

The acid rolled around us in a circle and the ophidians were gone. "Ah, Lila?"

The ophidians outside the acid fled, but we were as trapped as before, if not more so. "Lila, little help!"

Closer and closer the liquid death crept through the sand, bubbling and hissing.

"Get on the horses!" she yelled, her voice a hell of

a lot louder than before. Bigger. Everything in her was bigger.

I scrambled up with Maks onto Batman, giving Balder over to my naked brother. "Don't take this the wrong way . . ."

Bryce laughed. "Yeah, I don't want to snuggle up to you right now either."

I looked up as Lila's talons scooped us with ease, wrapping around the horses' middles.

With a whoosh of her wings, we were in the air and headed south faster than the horses could have managed on their own, even pushed as hard as we could have pushed them. I laid a hand on the closest part of Lila's talon, feeling the trembling there as she shook.

"We're going to figure this out, Lila. You will be okay."

"I just . . . it's too good to be true." She glanced down at me, her violet eyes the same as before, just bigger. Damn, I was struggling to wrap my head around her size too.

"Maybe you deserve a little too good to be true," Maks said. "Maybe we all do."

Lila snorted. "Toad, I did not take you for the dreamer."

He grinned and slid an arm around me. "Me either."

I leaned into him and just let him hold me. Maybe it wasn't rolling around on the gigantic bed with satin sheets, but he was with me. I had him back. I found myself looking back the way we'd come, searching the skies for Corvalis. Whatever was keeping him busy was fine by me, it gave us more time to get away.

But I had a feeling he would show up for the golden moon, wanting whatever power he could get from it.

"You shouldn't have bargained with the Emperor," Bryce said, breaking the cozy moment as only a brother could.

"What?" Lila and Maks yelled the question at me, in perfect tandem. I grimaced. Damn it, I was hoping we'd just pretend that part of the night hadn't happened. Like a bad dream.

"What is he talking about?" Maks asked, not yelling this time.

"There was no choice! And it saved three lives." I refused to cringe. The decision had been made, and I would live with it, even if it took me straight to the Emperor's throne. I took a deep breath. "The Emperor . . . he held Bryce captive, and he knew how to take the power I'd absorbed out of me. I made a choice."

"But what did you give him?" Lila asked.

"I told him I'd bring him the flail." I spoke quietly, but even with the whoosh of her wings and the rush of air around us, I knew they'd all heard me. Perks of hanging with shifters that had cat genetics running through them, and a dragon with the most excellent of ears. I wanted to not think about what I'd done, what I'd agreed to.

Maks tightened his hold on me. "No matter what, we are in this together. We are. We will find a way through this too."

I nodded and laid my head on his shoulder, feeling the shift in my life. Maks, Lila, and I were the triad the Oracle had spoken of. I was even more sure now that Ollianna had proven herself a traitor.

"Do we really need to go to the crossroads?" Bryce asked.

"She has the dragon's stone," I said. "We need that to deal with the Emperor. And the crossroads is where the Oracle said we have a chance to dethrone him."

"And Ollianna needs the stones to take to him?" Maks asked.

I nodded, anger flaring up in me. I hated being fooled, and I'd been fooled not only by Ollianna, but Maggi too. Fool me twice, shame on me. "I think Ollianna was playing us all along." I shook my head. "She was so good." Hells bells, I'd not seen it at all.

"No, I think in the beginning she wasn't," Lila said. "I think she is being taken by the Emperor. You said it yourself, he's been all over your dreams. Isn't it possible he was doing the same to her? Convincing her to help him?"

I frowned. "But she swapped out the stones when

I hugged her in the dreamscape over a week ago. And then she asked me where we were, right before the first ophidian attack. And like a damn moron, I told her."

"You couldn't have known she would use that information against us. She was supposed to be with us, not the Emperor," Maks said. "We have to take the stone back from her. She can't be trusted with it. Look at what she's done. Controlling the ophidians, a creature that not even the Jinn masters could manage."

I looked up at him. His blue eyes were all Maks, but there was more there now. I touched his face. "Do you have their memories?"

His smile was wry, a twist to the side. "Some of them, and all the information my father could leave with me."

One last gift from Marsum then, one that we could use.

Lila flew hard, not slowing for a minute. I dozed off and on through the night, warm in Maks's arms.

As the sun rose on the day that the golden moons would rise, Lila finally slowed. "I need to rest. I'm done."

She took us down slowly, releasing the horses and us just before she landed. We wobbled out of her way and she lowered herself to the ground. Lila in her full size was easily as big as her father, but leaner as though she carried more muscle.

With a sigh, she lowered her head. "Maybe I should take the necklace off. Then you can carry me?"

I hadn't wanted to suggest it but agreed. She lowered her neck so I could reach the clasp. The chain had expanded to reach all the way round her neck and as I unlatched it, it shrunk to a more manageable size. I dropped it into the pouch on my waist that held two stones. Two stones of power and a third held by Maks. I glanced at him, seeing no ill effects of carrying the amber stone.

"How close do you think we are?" Bryce asked as Maks tossed him a pair of pants, shirt and spare boots from the saddlebags. Ford's clothes. My heart twinged thinking about him and the others taken by Ishtar. I would get them back. I would not leave them with her.

"An hour's ride," Maks said. I arched a brow at him and he shrugged and tapped his head.

Damn, he was going to be like a walking encyclopedia and map all wrapped in one.

I turned back to Lila to find her on the ground, tiny once more, and fast asleep. I bent and picked her up, cradling her in my arms as I took Balder's reins and slid off his bridle, then did the same for Batman. Maks gave the remainder of the oatballs to the horses which they happily chewed down. We were in a green strip, by the looks of it, with trees dotting the landscape here and there, and even the sound of water nearby. I steered us in that direction first, the horses following happily, stealing bites of grass here and there.

"We need to rest before we do this," I said, plunking myself down on the bank of what had to be the smallest river I'd ever seen.

Bryce and Maks sat, one to either side of me, and Lila sound asleep against my chest. For the first time in months, I was at peace.

I was with my family, and that was home in a way nothing else ever would be.

I closed my eyes and just breathed in the air, hearing the world move quietly around me and knowing that right then, in that moment, I was where I was supposed to be. All the pain, all the hurt, the wounds of the heart, the sacrifices we'd made had brought us to right then.

"Whatever comes next," I said, "we were meant to be here."

Bryce leaned his head against mine. "Whatever comes next, I'm with you."

"Do you even have to ask?" Lila mumbled, and I laughed as I put a hand on her back.

"No, I'm not asking. But this feels . . . right . . . like we were meant to be here all along. The four of us." I tipped my head back against the trunk of the tree I leaned against. Maks wrapped his arm through mine and rested his hand on Lila too. She grunted in her sleep and curled closer. Bryce took my other hand and held it.

Sleep stole over me, and I should have been worried. I should have feared the dreamscape.

I opened my eyes, still there under the cover of the trees, Lila asleep on my chest and the horses grazing, but Bryce and Maks were not there. "Damn it all to fucktown," I muttered under my breath.

Keeping Lila tucked in my arms, I stood and did a slow turn. If I left her here, she could be hurt, which meant she was coming with me regardless of how long it took to find my way to whatever had called me here.

Only it didn't take me long, not at all.

"You have failed me, Ollianna." The Emperor's voice echoed to me from the south, from the cross-roads where Ollianna and Trick were supposed to be waiting.

"I did as you asked," she snapped. "I betrayed someone I cared about. I took one of the stones from her, and I am here. At the crossroads, where I am to get my child! And if you will not help me, I will take a child however I can."

I frowned and crept closer, the landscape shifting quickly with each step. I ended up not far from them and watched the scene play out.

"You were to bring the stones to me. Not keep any of them for yourself," the Emperor said. "Conniving witch that you are."

"I made a deal with you," she said. "You are the one who is failing that deal."

He grunted as he paced in front of her. "You want a child? From whom? I see no man to give you a child here."

Ollianna clasped her hands behind her back. "I will take any child I can get."

My mouth dropped open. She wasn't suggesting what I thought she was suggesting, was she?

He grabbed his own daughter and dragged her to him. Yup, yup, she was.

I backpedaled faster, running back the way I'd come, whispering all the way, "Wake up, wake up, wake up."

I did not need to see, hear, or think about what was happening to Ollianna. I gagged so hard, I jerked awake, still clutching Lila. "Dried shit on a camel's asshole is not as bad as what I just saw."

Maks was awake, but Bryce slept on. "What happened?" Maks asked.

"Oh, just my auntie Ollianna asking for a child from her *father!*" I shuddered and gagged again. "What is wrong with people?"

"Power," Maks said. "It's about power. She wants a child, maybe that's true, but she wants a child with power even more than that. It's why she took the stone, why she helped you. She saw you as a path to more power." He frowned. "So your aunt is sleeping right now?"

"Well, sleeping?" I raised both brows and he chuckled.

"You know what I mean."

"Yes, she's technically asleep."

"Then let's go. Maybe we can catch her off guard. The horses rested as Lila flew, and we've had a few hours here." He stood and held out his hand to me.

I took it with a groan, my body protesting. "Remember you promised me a movie night?"

"Indiana Jones, yes? I'd like to see that. I've always enjoyed history." He smiled and I laughed.

"Maybe we can get some tips from a great hero like Indiana."

Bryce yawned and stretched. "Nobody can do it like Indiana. I wish I could get the VCR to work back in the Stockyards."

We prepped the horses, and mounted up, me riding double with Maks and Bryce on Balder.

The first half hour, we talked about the Stockyards, Indiana Jones, and the things that Bryce would fix when we were back. As if we weren't walking into the fight of our lives against a powerful witch working for the Emperor.

Or maybe to remember some of the smaller things we were fighting for.

"Do you think you can sneak into the crossroads and steal the jewel back from Ollianna?" Lila asked as she woke up.

I mulled it over. "I don't know. And what about Trick? Where is he?"

Lila gave a little whimper and then hissed. "That bitch better not have hurt him."

Maks lifted his hand. The road we were on curved to the left. "The crossroads are just around that corner."

I glanced at the ground, taking note that it was still far too hard for any ophidians. That didn't mean Ollianna couldn't have another snake creature waiting with her. One bigger and uglier.

The morning was overcast, clouds rolling through the sky above. But no sign of the storm dragon, and still no sign of Corvalis. "Let me get a closer look." I slipped off Batman and shifted to four legs.

"I'm coming with you," Maks said, shifting to his caracal form as he dismounted.

"Why am I always getting left behind?" Bryce muttered.

I grinned up at him. "'Cause you're too big to hide. Hold your horses. Both of them."

He rolled his eyes but didn't argue. I wondered at his complacency, and then I saw a flash of fear in his eyes before he looked away.

Being caged had been harder on him than I'd realized. We'd talk about that, but later.

Everything could be dealt with later, if we survived the now.

I trotted forward, Maks on my left, his hip

bumping mine every other stride. "I'm not letting you out of my sight for a while," he said.

I hip-bumped him back. "Fine by me."

We slowed as we drew close to the rock formation that would give us cover. The place we'd sneak a look and the place Ollianna would be watching.

"Stop." I whispered, "She'll expect us here."

I looked up at the rock formation and leapt up to a tiny ledge, then leapt up to another and another until I was on the top of the rock. On my belly, I scooted across until I could look down at the crossroads properly.

I bit my tongue to keep from gasping.

Ollianna wasn't alone. And she wasn't surrounded by snakes.

She was surrounded by her witch sisters.

All of them.

27

I slipped and bounded back down the rock to where Maks waited. "See, I was still in sight," I whispered.

"What's wrong?" He followed me back to the horses where I shifted, mounted and turned them back the way we'd come. "Zam?"

"Hurry," was all I could manage.

There was no plan that could stop all those witches, no way we could face them, at least not head on.

We rode all the way back to the place by the river, and while they respected me enough not to ask until we were there, once we arrived the questions flew.

I held up my hands, stopping them. "Ollianna has called in reinforcements. Far as I can see, every single one of the witches from the swamp are there. Waiting for the power of the golden moons."

"And what do you think they will do?" Lila asked.

I shook my head. "I have no idea. I doubt they are there to stop the Emperor since Ollianna is working for him."

Maks cleared his throat. "I have a thought. The last time the golden moons rose and the power of the crossroads was invoked . . . that was when the wall was put up."

I pressed the heels of my hands against my eyes. "And?"

"They have the dragon stone, and presumably, they have Trick." Maks looked to Lila. "He could be used as a blood sacrifice to invoke even more power."

She gasped. "No, we have to save him!"

I held out a hand to her, slowing her down. "We have to figure this out, Lila. We can't just go running around the corner and into the crossroads without a plan or we'll all die. And we don't know for sure—"

"You mean like you did with that damn horde of gorcs?" she snapped.

"The gorcs didn't have magic," I pointed out, not upset by her words or the point she was trying to make. I knew how I'd be if it were Maks being held as a potential sacrifice. Look at me, growing up and shit.

Again, it was Maks who stepped up to help spell things out. "We have to draw them away, Lila. If we can split their forces, then maybe we have a chance at holding the crossroads. I'm not even worried about what we could do with the power that will be there, so much as blocking those who would do harm."

A tingle along my spine preceded a thought I didn't like. What if that was why the Oracle sent us here? Not for any other reason but to protect the crossroads? Not to help us, but to keep the world safe? I kept my thought to myself even as it grew clearer that the reason we'd been sent here might not have anything to do with us at all.

Bryce nodded. "Agreed, this is about protecting, not taking any of the power for ourselves."

Lila's eyes pooled with tears. Another chance at the curse on her being broken, lost. Another chance at my own curse being broken, lost. "Agreed," she said.

"Agreed." I echoed her and held my hand out, palm up. Maks put his hand on mine, then Bryce, and then Lila sat on top of our hands. It struck me how similar this moment was to when we'd made the pact with Ollianna.

And look how that had turned out.

I gripped Maks and he gave me a wink. "It will be okay."

"Last time I tangled with dragons it didn't turn out so well," Bryce said, but he was grinning.

Of course he was. A lion going into a fight was always a happy little shit. I shook my head. "Idiot. We need a plan."

We had very little time to figure this out.

"What we need is an army of our own," Bryce said. "That would be the best thing."

Another tingle along my spine turned me toward the other side of the creek. A flash of something reflective in the air; there and gone before I could even say for sure I'd seen anything at all. Calling to me, pulling at my feet.

Bryce was talking strategy, his voice a distant white noise as another flash amongst the trees beckoned me.

I waved at my companions absently, already walking away from them. "I need a minute."

They let me go as I walked down into the creek, across to the other bank, and wove my way through the sparse trees.

The witches had come here looking for trouble.

Would their natural enemies have followed them? I was hoping that was exactly what I was seeing. Or maybe that was hope making me see things that didn't exist.

"Titania?" I called out a name, that of the queen of the fairies, to be exact. "You want to go witch hunting with me? That's why you came, isn't it?"

Silence answered me. Of course, why would they want to leave their swamp now that they had it all to themselves?

But I stood there, waiting. Just in case I was wrong. In case I hadn't been seeing things.

"Zam? We need to plan," Bryce called across to me, and again I waved him off.

Out of the corner of my eye, I saw a bright flash, rainbow iridescent and moving like a little zing of lightning. I spun and dropped to one knee, my hand going to my knife at my side.

The glittering, dancing figure of the queen of the fairies floated slowly down to me. "Desert bred, desert born, with the blood of so many running through your veins." Her voice was soft and sharp at the same time. Where before she'd been nude, now she was covered in dark green armor that clung to her body from ankle to wrist. Her blue spiderweb hair was braided and woven close to her skull with a much smaller coronet rather than her larger crown from the first time I'd met her. Her gossamer green wings blurred as she approached me, a faint humming in the air like the buzzing of a large bee. "You are hunting witches again, Bright one? Funny that you share their blood."

"Not by choice. And I don't think it's dominant." I grinned. "And yeah, they are holding the crossroads —I have to stop them."

"You believe they will free the Emperor if they can?" The way she offered the question made me doubt my own words and I hesitated.

"I think that's the plan. But you don't."

She shook her head. "I have watched them, been a slave to them, and been bound in their power. They have loose tongues when they believe there is no one to listen. What they plan is far worse than releasing the Emperor. He will be but a matchstick to a raging forest fire should their plan succeed."

My stomach dropped. "What the hell could possibly be worse than—"

"The Falak," she said, and the air seemed to whoosh away from us both, the warmth of the summer heat turning to the ice of a winter's touch in a flash. "That is what could be worse. It is a serpent of great size and power. One whose magic lies hidden and asleep for now. One that thinks, and plans. One that will be reborn if it can be."

Chills rippled through me as the pieces clicked together. "They believe Ollianna can control it because of her connection to the snakes?" Like the ophidians. The ophidians that Marsum had said even the Jinn masters could not control, but Ollianna could.

"They bred her for this. They chose bloodlines and power to bring her to the light from a very old line of magic. It was all a game, giving you a few things, making you trust her, allowing her to go along with you. She needed the green stone and its connections to beasts and the earth to increase her power. They tried giving her the other stone, the one flecked with lightning, but it hurt her."

Titania watched me, her eyes shifting through the colors of the rainbow. Which was why Ollianna had been so eager to see it leave the Swamp. Titania nodded. "So yes, we will help you, if only because we came to stop them ourselves."

All around me, the sound of buzzing intensified, and I found myself looking up at an army of fairies as they flowed closer. Hundreds of them, at least as many fairies as there were witches waiting at the crossroads.

I held out my hand, palm up. "Then we fight side by side."

She landed on the tips of my fingers and bent one knee, mimicking me. From her side, she pulled a tiny dagger and cut her palm. A well of red blood beaded up, iridescent and catching the light like her wings. Then she reached out and nicked my skin. I didn't move, didn't flinch. Until my own blood welled up, red as the dawn, and flickering with lights that it shouldn't have but did.

"Blood calls to blood." She smiled up at me and pressed her tiny wound to mine.

Little bolts of energy scattered up my hand and straight into my heart. "How is that possible?"

"You carry the world with you, Bright one. We are part of this world." She pulled her hand away and shot into the air, pulling two swords from her side.

Fairy blood. I had fairy blood in me.

"Today, we fight!" she called out. "Many of us will die, but we will stop a great evil from coming into this world. We must."

The buzzing around us intensified and the air lit up with colors and shimmering lights that drew my eyes in every direction.

Before I could suggest a planning session, or a strategy, they were flying away, zipping amongst the trees and across the creek.

"Oh shit!" I turned and bolted, running as fast as I could and still losing ground on the fairy army. They were going in now, no plan, no thought as to the best way to face off against the witches. "Bryce, Maks, Lila, we're going in!" I yelled as I leapt across the creek. I landed on the other side in a crouch, scrambled against the loose soil and then was off again.

Maks stared at me. "What?"

"Titana and the fairies are here, and they are going in NOW!" I ran past him to leap onto Balder. Bryce shifted to his lion form and Maks was on Batman as I spun Balder to face them. "I love you, guys. You know, in case we all die."

Lila laughed. "We aren't dying, not today! Dream on, dream on, of bloody deeds and death!"

"Richard the third," Maks and I said in tandem. I grinned at him. Grinned at Lila and saluted my brother.

"Into battle we go."

There was no plan, no strategy, but ahead of us was the buzzing of a hundred angry fairies, and the boom of magic blasting through the air which meant this was our chance to take the crossroads.

We had an army with us now; if small, they were mighty.

Like Lila.

Like me. I let out a whoop, adrenaline coursing through me and I couldn't contain it.

Balder stretched out as I leaned over his neck, urging him faster, the call of a battle running through my veins. Batman and Maks caught up to us, his pike pole held to the side like a knight riding into battle. I pulled the flail and held it out as we took the last corner before the crossroads.

The witches were engaged already with the fairy army and didn't see us at first. Maks drove his bladed spear through three of them, right in their necks before he leapt off Batman and a bluish mist billowed up around him, tinted with a darkness that hadn't been there before.

"You left his magic in him?" I said and the flail hummed in my hand. "Thanks."

And then I let fly with my weapon, bashing it into the witches whose backs were still turned to me. We had the upper hand, and we were taking it for all it was worth. Lila shot into the fray, still small, her acid flying and her claws and teeth damaging eyes of the witches. She shrieked and roared. Maybe she could have gone big but then she would have been a target. I approved of her choice to stay small—for now.

The call of a male lion burst through the air as Bryce leapt into the fray. The witches didn't know what to do with him, or us, for that matter, and it occurred to me that they most likely had never been in a fight, never mind a full-on battle.

A good number of them scattered, chased by fairies that screamed for their bloody deaths in great detail. I jumped from Balder's back and pushed him away as I swung the flail over and over. The witches' magic slid over me, the flail absorbing it gleefully. With each gulp it took of the power, it tightened its hold on me.

The day ticked by, and the witches held us at bay far better than I'd thought they would. Darkness tinged the sky and we still weren't at the crossroads proper. I could see it ahead of us, a literal cross of stone where the four roads met. Ollianna stood on top of it, her eyes distant, not even really looking at the battle below her.

Trick lay at her feet, as if sleeping. Please, gods, let him be sleeping and not dead. "Lila, do you see him?"

"I can't get to him. They keep blocking me!" she screamed, anger and fear lacing her voice.

"To me!" I yelled at her and she dropped to my shoulder, breathing hard. "We'll get to him."

We had to.

Maks was spinning his magic, keeping both himself and Bryce safe, but they weren't making much headway.

It was then I knew we were in trouble. The witches were doing exactly what we'd planned to do.

They were holding the crossroads just long enough that no one else would take it.

"Lila, time to go big," I whispered as I swung the flail, catching another spell as it shot our way.

"What?"

"Draw their eyes. Go high, so they can't hit you, but go big. I'll go small." Already I could see how this was going to work.

Big and small, together we could get to Trick. We could save him and stop Ollianna.

I slipped the ring and chain out of my pouch and put it over her neck. She pushed off my shoulder and shot upward, her body shifting, growing in leaps and bounds. She roared as she flew, and every witch there lost their concentration. I could feel it like a buzz under my skin.

This was my chance.

28

L
ila roared above all of our heads while the crossroads beckoned within sight. Ollianna stood on the stone marking the crossroads and Trick lay wrapped around the stone. But was he alive?

I shifted to four legs and darted forward as Lila drew fire and eyes. The witches weren't looking for me as a six-pound house cat. Nope, and once more I had to admit to myself that this was a damn fine form. Not better than a big-ass jungle cat, but good in its own way.

I shot between legs, toppling witches this way and that and sending more than one onto her plump ass with an "oof."

Cat trips witches for the win!

I grinned to myself as I closed the distance between me and the stone cross. "Trick, wake up!" I yelled as I got closer to the storm dragon. His gray and white scales were duller than the last time I'd seen him, and that worried me, but finally I saw his torso rise and fall with a big breath. He was wrapped fully around the standing stone that Ollianna stood on. The stone itself was over twelve feet high, solid gray and shaped like an oversized cross. Even at a distance I could see the hand holds etched into it for climbing to the top. I just had to get there.

"TRICK!" I tried to wake him again and a blast of magic hit the ground at my front paws. Shards of rocks sprayed up, two cutting across my right cheek. I hissed and spun, finding myself face to face with the grandmammy of all the witches.

"Hey, bitch!" I puffed up my body and stood on the tips of my toes. "You sure you want some of this?"

"A mere house cat. No matter what blood runs in your veins, you will never be more than a mere house cat."

Another time that would have hurt me, wounded me deeply. I shrugged. "I'm still going to kick your ass, house cat or not."

I shifted to two legs and swung my flail, catching her off guard, and slammed the weapon into her right hip. She screeched and the sound burrowed its way into my head, reverberating over and over.

A bellow burst through it, the roar of a very angry, very large dragon. I looked up for Lila.

And saw Corvalis.

"Are you fucking kidding me?"

He and Lila were side by side, their bodies moving in tandem through the air, as if joined at the hip. Her eyes were glazed, distant, as if she weren't really there.

What was happening?

But I knew. Serpents.

They were serpentine.

I spun away from the witch, yanking the flail free as I leapt up onto Trick's back, using him as a step stool to get to the top of the rock, the handholds perfect launch points for me.

"Hurry!" Maks yelled. "Hurry!"

The fairies swarmed and reformed and the bellow of Corvalis came again, and with the roar, a burst of fire along the top of the battle, scorching fairy wings left and right.

Fuck, fuck, fuck.

I was behind Ollianna as I pulled myself to the top of the rock.

"You cannot kill me," she said, turning to face me. The emerald stone lay around her neck, throbbing with magic. "I have power over the dragons, power over the serpents. That is my gift. The Falak will keep us safe from the Emperor. *I* will keep us safe from the Emperor."

"You're fucking delusional! You want to be safe from him, but you fucked him!" I threw one hand upward, pointing at Lila and Corvalis, both ensnared by her magic. "The second you let Corvalis go, he's going to eat you, and then the Falak, what about him then? Who will control him?"

"Corvalis is not strong enough to throw my bonds." Ollianna's green eyes were so full of certainty that even I almost believed her.

Almost.

He bellowed again and I shook my head. "Don't do this, Ollianna."

The sky seemed to take that moment to dip into full darkness and the moons appeared above us, golden in their glow. All around us, the fighting stopped, fading away.

"And you'd kill Trick to do this?"

"No, of course not." She shook her head. "I only need the blood of a dragon, not the death of one." She held out a cup and poured it onto the rock at her feet, presumably Trick's blood splattering everywhere. I leapt toward her and she flicked her fingers at me. The cup flew at my face, catching me in the side of my head and sending me off the rock. I bounced across Trick and ended up on a rock spiking out of the ground. It jammed its way through the meat of my left side. I howled, the pain sharp and tearing. Before I was too weak, I pushed myself off the rock and to my knees. I stared up at her, blood trickling down the side of my face, my hand cupping the wound on the left.

"Secondary magic works well on you, I think,

while you hold that flail." She smiled down at me and the golden power of the moons above threw their light down on her.

"Lila, you have to fight her! You have to show her she's not strong enough to hold you, never mind the Falak!" I screamed at my friend and found her through the bond we had, through our pride. She was my second, and I could give her help. I pushed my energy and power the flail had gathered through the battle into Lila. Giving her strength.

Reminding her of who she was, and who her family was.

She screeched and shook her head, flew backward and then dropped toward us, jaws open wide. At the last second, Ollianna lifted her hand and Lila spun to the side and fell to the ground asleep.

"Just that easy," Ollianna said.

The power suffused her, lighting her up, green magic curling all around her, driving into the ground and cracking it open. I stumbled back, unable to keep my balance with the heaving of the earth.

"Falak, your time has come. Answer to the Serpent Queen, let your spirit find me." Ollianna's voice cut through the air.

"I thought you wanted a child!" I yelled at her. "I thought that was your desire, not this madness!"

She turned her head slowly to me. "Do you not understand?"

Even as I stared at her, her belly began to swell

until there was no doubt about what lay under her skirt. Her father's seed . . .

"A child of power, one that can be controlled," she said with a smile. "I am the Serpent Queen. I am the one spoken of in legend. The Emperor will never rule again. My child will cleanse this world."

There was a crack of lightning as Trick raised his head, his eyes glazed. I scrambled backward. "Trick."

"I'm sorry, Zam. You are too much trouble," Ollianna said. "You will have to die too. There is too much potential in you."

Trick lunged for me, jaws wide. I fell backward and my vision was filled with blue and silver scales.

"Get away from my sister!" Lila roared, body slamming Trick backward. Blood ran down her scales, that was all I could see and then her jaws clamped on his muzzle, snapping his mouth shut. They rolled over several times, and Lila jerked hard as her body hit the same pointed rock that I'd fallen on, piercing her right through her scales. She pinned him to the ground though, despite that.

Trick shook his head, as if waking from a deep dream. "Lila?" He muffled her name and she let him go.

"We have to kill her!" Lila yelled, and then, we were all moving at once. But not fast enough.

All around us chaos erupted. Corvalis swept down and caught up Ollianna and her huge belly, his wings brushing around us. His eyes blank with her power. The witches ran, disappearing into the air as if they were fucking ghosts, and the fairies were just as fast to dissipate. Leaving us there as if there had been no battle, as if we hadn't been fighting for hours, as if what we'd just seen had not happened. If not for the bodies on the ground, and even those slowly disappeared, fading into nothing but ash and dried blood.

Lila hissed and snapped at Trick. He stared at her, blinking rapidly, his eyes clearing. "Lila?"

She blinked right back at him, snapping her mouth shut. "You aren't under her power? Are you sure?"

Breathing hard, I ran around the two dragons, seeing as they weren't trying to kill each other. "Maks? Bryce?"

"We're here." Bryce's voice was beyond tired. He limped toward me. "Good thing we had the Jinn with us."

Maks limped, too, only on the opposite leg. They'd stood side by side then through the whole fight. I shouldn't have been so happy about that, not when we'd lost.

I hugged Bryce first, his mane tickling my nose, then caught Maks around the neck. His arms circled me. "We failed."

"I know."

I held onto him, and felt Bryce butt his head into

353

my hip. I dropped a hand to his head. "I don't know what to do."

"I do."

All of us turned to see Titania flying toward us. Slower than before, but still flying. "The war is coming, one the Emperor engaged in many years ago. The Falak is an elemental creature made for destruction and nothing else. Born of a witch, she will hold even more power than before. Our world is ended. Unless you gather the last of the stones and join with an enemy once more." She snapped her fingers and disappeared along with everyone else.

I turned my head to see Lila and Trick together.

"Isn't that the ring?" Maks pointed at the necklace and ring Lila had been wearing—it sat atop the stone cross, catching the last rays of the golden moonlight. I looked at Lila, squinting at her. The hard, ugly layer of magic that I'd seen on her before was gone. The curse was gone.

"It is. Should we tell her that her curse is broken?" Maks said.

"Hey, Lila!" I yelled and she snapped her head around, eyes narrowed as she searched for danger. I pointed at the stone. "You're free, my friend."

She lowered her nose to the stone, as if she couldn't believe it, blood running off her scales. "But I can feel my smaller form still."

And just like that she went from big to small and

back again. Over and over. A dragon shifter. One of a kind.

She whooped and leapt into the sky, Trick following her.

One good thing. One good thing in this place of power and death.

But I had no illusions. We were far from done in our journey to protect our desert, to protect our people.

And now, to try to protect the world.

29

The next morning found us back at the creek where we'd started the day before. Everyone was stiff and sore from the fight —with the exception of Trick, who seemed fresh as a freaking daisy and just as fucking perky.

That was until I explained what Ollianna had done, and what was coming our way.

Even as we spoke, the daylight around us darkened weirdly for first thing in the morning and a rumble of thunder cut through the sky. I looked at the storm dragon. "That you?"

"No."

"Then the child is born," Maks said. "I can see bits and pieces of prophecies and potential lines of the world's fate. A storm over the world announces the rebirth of the Falak." He rubbed his hand over his head. "This is bad, Zam. Very bad."

I thought about the Emperor, what he'd told me about the Falak. He'd lied then, saying that the creature would be reborn if he was killed. Of course he'd lied. Everyone had damn well lied to me. Everyone. The Oracle. The Emperor. Maggi. Ollianna.

I rubbed a hand over my face and sighed.

Bryce was stretched out, a piece of grass tucked between his lips. "What do we do then? We can't give up. I know that's not an option."

I nodded. "We have people to save." Kiara and Ford and the others were in the Stockyards and we had to get them out. "And I have to go to the Emperor."

"You don't really mean to give him the flail, do you?" Bryce spit out the grass.

"I don't want to." I found myself touching the handle of the weapon. "But that was the deal, and I don't think I can renege on a magical deal with the Emperor."

They couldn't argue with that, even if they wanted to—a deal was a deal, and already I could feel the pull of the agreement drawing me north and to the west. To wherever the Emperor's throne was.

But first . . . first the Wyvern.

THE NEXT DAY LILA AND TRICK SCOOPED US UP AND flew north. The flight to the edge of the Wyvern's Lair took barely a day. "This is the way to travel," Bryce said from Trick's back.

The dragon laughed. "Easy for you to say, you don't have to carry anyone."

Maybe I would have joined in their laughter and easy banter if I hadn't been scanning the sand below us for movement. But there were no ophidians waiting at the edge of the ocean that should not have been there.

And as far as I could see, there was no Wyvern waiting either.

Lila and Trick touched down, releasing the horses from their claws. I slid off Lila's back and she did a down shift to her smaller form. Funny, but she spent easily as much time small as big now that she had the option.

I smiled at her as she flew to my shoulder. "I'm glad you can still sit with me. I would have missed this."

She grinned and grabbed hold of my earlobe. "Yeah, maybe I would have too."

The water rushed around my ankles and I took a step forward. Maks put a hand on me. "Wait, what are you doing?"

My eyes were locked on the water and the waves, the movement of them. Our plan had been simple: draw the Wyvern out and use the two dragons' size and strength to pin him down and take the stone by force. None of us liked it, but on short notice, it was the best we could do.

Only I didn't think that would work.

He was serpentine too. What if Ollianna already had him under her control?

The waves grew as each crashed toward us.

"He's coming," Trick said, lightning dancing through the sky.

I held a hand up, stopping him. "Wait, just wait."

"That was not the plan," Bryce said.

"Change of plans," I shot back.

The Wyvern exploded out of the water, his head snaking toward us, teeth flashing, anger etched into every line of his body, in the narrowing of his eyes. "You dare come back?"

"Wyvern, the ophidian queen is coming for you." I spoke as calmly as I could, the waves as high as my hip and rising. "She's given birth to the Falak and has control of any serpent she sees fit. How long before she comes for you?"

I folded my arms, the water already to my shoulders, as if I were not about to get water up my nose.

I recalled something my father had said only once. *Confidence is something that can be faked. But only if you have no other choice.*

The waves slowed and he lowered his head until I could have reached out and stuck my arm up his nostril. "The Falak is reborn?"

"Yes," Maks answered behind me. "Also, my apologies for the blow before. I was not . . . myself."

The Wyvern turned his attention to Maks and my heart rate shot up. But all the big water dragon did was raise an eyebrow. "How did you get rid of the Jinn masters?"

"The flail," I said.

He grunted. "Tricky."

"Indeed." Maks smiled. "Tricky indeed."

The Wyvern shook his head. "What exactly do you think I should do? Hand you the stone? If she is as powerful as you say, then would she not kill me if I do not have something to give her?"

I smiled up at him and dug around in my pouch, producing the fake emerald stone she'd given me. "Give her this and tell her Zamira is coming for her. Nobody steals from me."

The Wyvern stared at the stone in my hand. "She might kill me anyway."

"The Falak is going to kill us all," Maks said, stepping up beside me. Lila was still on my shoulder and we stood there, the three of us, stronger than we'd ever been. His eyes rested on each of us as he spoke. "Heart, soul, magic. Perhaps you three are the answer." He shook his head. "I always hated Maggi. I'm glad she's dead. I worried she would be in your triad."

"No, there was never a chance for her," I said.

The Wyvern smiled, flashing every tooth he had.

"Not true. There were lines of fate that showed her leading your triad. Of course, those lines of fate ended horribly for the world. You three, though? I've never seen you three in any prophecy or vision. That means either you will save us all or doom us to the Falak's power."

Before I could answer him, a wave whooshed toward us, covering the Wyvern, washing him away. His voice was still there, but he was not.

"Take this stone. Its power is that of destruction untold. And may the gods of old watch over us."

A bed of kelp and seaweed floated toward us, and in the center was a pulsing red stone, perfectly round and about the size of a standard coin. I picked it up and laid down the emerald stone.

The waves sucked away from us so fast, I fell on my ass. Maks grabbed me and hauled me to my feet. "That could have gone much worse."

I wiped a chunk of seaweed off my pants. "We still have the Emperor."

Lila nodded. "And Ishtar and our pride."

Bryce shook his head. "And deal with this Ollianna and her demon spawn."

"So, yeah," I smiled at Maks and pulled him in for a kiss, "it was about time something went our way, because what's coming . . . what's coming is going to make our time together now look like a walk in the park."

Lila leapt into the air, shifting into her larger form. "The fire-eyed maid of smoky war,

all hot and bleeding will we offer them!"

I lifted a fist, the stone of destruction clutched in it. "Our battle is more full of names than yours. Our men more perfect in the use of arms. Our armour all as strong, our cause the best; then reason will our hearts should be as good."

I raised an eyebrow at Maks. He laughed. "*Henry IV*. Try again, ladies. You have yet to stump me."

Laughing, Lila scooped us up in her talons and swept us into the sky, and beside us Trick scooped up Bryce and Batman. "Which big bad ugly are we going to deal with first?" Lila asked.

The wind whipped around my face, tangling my hair. There was only one answer. "To the Stockyards. We deal with Ishtar and Steve."

Once and for all.

Well there we go, there's one more book and we'll be wrapping this series up!

www.shannonmayer.com

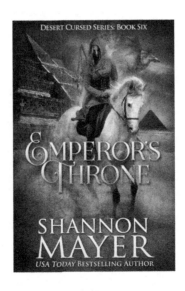